DEAD BEAT

Patricia Hall

CRÈME de la CRIME

This first world edition published 2011
in Great Britain and the USA by
Crème de la Crime, an imprint of
SEVERN HOUSE PUBLISHERS LTD of
9–15 High Street, Sutton, Surrey, England, SM1 1DF.
Trade paperback edition first published
in Great Britain and the USA 2011.

British Library Cataloguing in Publication Data

Hall, Patricia
  Dead beat.
  1. Women photographers–England–Liverpool–Fiction.
  2. Brothers and sisters–Fiction. 3. Missing persons–
  Investigation–England–London–Fiction. 4. Soho
  (London, England)–Social conditions–20th century–
  Fiction. 5. Liverpool (England)–Social conditions–20th
  century–Fiction. 6. Detective and mystery stories.
  I. Title
  823.9'14-dc22

ISBN-13: 978-1-78029-004-1 (cased)
ISBN-13: 978-1-78029-504-6 (trade paper)

All Severn House titles are printed on acid-free paper.

Typeset by Palimpsest Book Production Ltd.,
Falkirk, Stirlingshire, Scotland.
Printed and bound in Great Britain by
MPG Books Ltd., Bodmin, Cornwall.

DEAD BEAT

A Selection of Recent Titles by Patricia Hall

The Ackroyd and Thackeray Series

SINS OF THE FATHERS
DEATH IN A FAR COUNTRY
BY DEATH DIVIDED
DEVIL'S GAME

ONE

The boy scuttled like a rat through the weed-infested bomb site, half crouched, eyes flicking this way and that, careful not to make a sound except when a Circle Line train rumbled past in the steep cutting and stopped, with a hiss and a groan, at Farringdon underground station just yards away. This part of London was still a warren of derelict, bombed-out buildings and he was not the only one who had sheltered there through the recent bitter winter weather, still holding the country in an iron grip long after spring should have begun to provide a little natural warmth. Most of the men there felt safe in the knowledge that even if they lit fires to huddle round they were unlikely to be spotted either from the underground line below or the elevated streets above them. But the boy did not want to join the rest. He preferred to keep himself to himself, even more so since it happened, knowing instinctively that was best. He had not often been driven to sleeping here, wrapped in a couple of blankets which he always stowed carefully away in a rusting metal drum when he woke at dawn. Since he had arrived in London, he had usually been able to find a bed for the night, though he hated the price he paid for it.

But since he had seen what he had seen, he had been much more cautious. The shock was still there, sometimes hidden in the darkness at the back of his mind where he hid so much of his past life, but sometimes worming its way insidiously to the front, making him shudder with nausea all over again. There had been no warning that his encounter two nights ago was in any way out of the ordinary: that clean-shaven young man, nice-looking, blond, well-dressed, as good as it got, he had thought the first time he had gone home with him. He felt pleased to see him again as their eyes met over the heads of the crowd on the steps below Eros and saw the recognition in his eyes. He had nodded quickly, though almost imperceptibly, in answer to the unspoken question and followed as the young man led him up Shaftesbury Avenue and into the narrow, crowded streets of Soho, past the French pub, and towards the narrow alleyway where the boy knew his mark would unlock a door which gave on to a steep staircase which led to living accommodation above a shuttered shop below.

He had fallen behind a little in the thick crowds round Leicester Square and by the time he got to the entrance to the alley he found the young man out of sight. Suddenly cautious, he had stood for a time in a doorway on the opposite side of Greek Street, waiting for a couple of men, muffled up against the cold and clearly in a hurry to move out of the alley before he ventured down the narrow, ill-lit passage himself. He could see that the lights were on upstairs in the flat above the book-shop, as if inviting him into the warmth as he shivered in the freezing night air and eventually he had slipped through the unlocked door.

It was totally silent on the staircase and he felt slightly surprised that his mark had not put a record on. The last time he had been here the room had been filled with music. But the door was ajar, so he knew he was expected, and he pushed it open with more confidence than he had felt on the dimly lit stairway. He found himself in the small entrance hall with several doors leading off, but only the living room door was half open and even as he hesitated on the threshold he could see more than he wanted to see, then or ever. The young man he had followed was lying sprawled across a small spindle-legged coffee table which seemed to have collapsed under his weight, but it was not that which wrenched the boy's gaze and turned his stomach, so that he spun away gasping for air, afraid he would be sick. There was a chair in the tiny hallway, and he sat down on it, his knees suddenly trembling too much to keep him upright. The slashing blow which had clearly killed the man in the other room had almost severed his head, splashing blood in great gouts across the table and the orange and turquoise patterned rug it stood on. The boy knew he could do nothing for him, knew that he had to get away from the carnage quickly, for his own safety, but still he sat there for what felt like hours not minutes, unable to move, unable to think, trying to control his heaving stomach and his paralysed mind.

Eventually he forced himself to his feet, and gently shut the door on the dead man, making no sound, although nothing, he thought, would ever let him forget this. He closed the main door to the flat behind him and crept down the stairs as silently as a shadow, standing in the doorway below for a moment to make sure that the alley was still deserted, before hurrying away to the only place he knew where he could find sanctuary. It had seemed like hours, and he had lost all appetite for trade, twisting and turning through Bloomsbury, past the tall, shuttered terraces, around the squares where the trees sighed in the wind, back to the no-man's-land of derelict sites and bombed-out ruins close to the railway line where he knew he would be safe.

Kate O'Donnell walked down Frith Street with her heart thumping and her portfolio banging awkwardly against her legs as she shimmied between the crowds along the narrow pavement. She scanned the properties on each side of the street for numbers which, more often than not, did not exist. A French bistro jostled up against a bookshop with lurid stock which Kate knew would throw her mother and all her gossiping friends from Saint Teresa's into a frenzy of Hail Marys; she glanced into pubs with gloomy interiors full of men and the fumes of booze and cigarettes wafting that all-too familiar smell in her face – the smell of her father, she thought wryly, having little more than that sour memory of laughing Frankie O'Donnell who had walked out for a pint ten years ago and never come back. Her dad was just one of hundreds of merchant seamen who never came home again after a voyage from Liverpool, missing but probably not dead, just enjoying sunnier climes and new loves halfway across the world. Soho, she thought, had about it more than a whiff of Liverpool when she had been a little kid, a dark, almost threatening bass note overlaid with more exotic aromas. She stopped for a moment to take fascinated stock of the next building, where a narrow doorway boasted six or seven bells marked simply with girls' names.

'Looking for a job, dear?' a small woman, emaciated, heavily made-up and huddled into a threadbare camel coat, asked kindly as she pushed past her and disappeared up the narrow staircase inside. Kate moved on quickly. She was certainly looking for a job, she thought, but not that one. She glanced around for a moment before continuing her quest, still conscious of the thrill that London had given her as soon as she ventured from her friends' flat west of Paddington station where she had begged to sleep on the sofa until she found work. It was quite possible she would have to slink home again to the Pool in the end, defeated and deflated, if she found nothing. But that was a possibility she pushed firmly to the back of her mind, reluctant even to imagine the 'I told you so' look in her mam's eyes and the barely concealed pity of her friends and neighbours if she had to go back with nothing to show for herself. She had taken a massive gamble on this trip, a streak of her dad there, she thought, but she was determined she was going to win.

This, Kate thought as she hurried on, was where she wanted to be. The more she saw, the more she was certain of that. The crowds, the noise, the traffic, the cavernous underworld of the Tube with its rattling trains and stale, windy tunnels, nothing put her off. This was where it was all happening. This was where she could break through and become someone. Back home, unless you were a lad with a guitar and a cheeky smile, there was nothing on offer for someone with ideas and energy and ambition, especially if they happened to be female. You ended up like poor Cynthia, a mate from college, who, she had heard, was stuck at home having a baby while her man was having all the fun. That, she thought, was not for her, as she had told Dave Donovan flatly when he had suggested 'settling down' together, before he too got bored with that idea and headed south. Settling down was not her ambition yet. And the greatest incentive of all to stay was that this was where she might be able to track down her brother Tom, who had taken this road before her.

She gave an little skip of excitement, drawing a curious look from a paunchy man with long hair shuffling past in a miasma of alcohol fumes, and resumed the search for what she hoped might be her opportunity. A block further down, she found the door she was looking for standing wide open and clearly advertising the fact that it was the home of the Ken Fellows Picture Agency. Taking a deep breath, she glanced at her reflection in the window of the Italian grocery store on the ground floor and took a moment to assess her chances: dark hair, cut medium short and sweeping forward in a curve around her face, blue eyes, careful make-up but not too heavy round the eyes like some girls were wearing it now, on-the-knee tweed skirt, artfully pulled up at the waist so as not to show beneath the hem of her fitted coat: not bad, she thought, though she had to admit that she had little idea what criteria Ken Fellows might use to assess a likely young photographer.

She stepped through the open door and climbed the narrow wooden staircase, uncarpeted and dusty, to find herself in a cramped reception area which offered a couple of hard chairs and a cluttered desk with a typewriter and telephone but no sign of a human presence. Behind the desk was a display board covered with black and white photographs beneath the agency banner. A few of the subjects she recognized as she cast a critical eye over them: an actor she could not put a name to though she knew the face, decked out in cloak and sword for what looked like a Shakespeare play, a series of moody views of the Thames, a parade of exotic-looking floats, some sort of a road accident and some rainy street scenes. But her eye was drawn quickly to two or three groups of young musicians she also did not recognize and one she instantly did. She smiled faintly at the sight of the John Lennon she had known in black leather and tight jeans at art college now resplendent in a sharp, mod-looking suit, and a new haircut, and wondered if he would remember her now the band looked as if it might be really going places.

Her reminiscences were interrupted by the appearance of a young woman who poked her head round the single door leading off the lobby with an interrogatory: 'Yeah?'

'I've got an appointment to see Ken Fellows,' Kate said.

'Oh, yeah. You're the girl who wants to take pictures.' The sharp eyes, heavily lined in black, looked her up and down critically. 'That'd be a first,' she said, scepticism oozing from every pore. 'He's waiting for you.'

Kate followed her through the door and found herself in a large, cluttered space where every flat surface seemed to be covered with cameras and equipment and all the paraphernalia of a photographer's life, mixed up with overflowing ashtrays, piles of newspapers and magazines and coffee cups in various stages of mouldy senescence. There were tables and chairs, but no one was sitting at them. In fact, the room was empty, although there was a red light showing over one of several doors at the far end, and the sharp smell of photographic chemicals filled the air. The receptionist waved Kate over to another exit without the tell-tale light over it and the boss's name inscribed on the half-glazed door. She opened it and waved her inside.

Ken Fellows did no more than glance up briefly at Kate and wave her into the single rickety chair which faced his desk. He then returned to his study of sheets of contact prints which he held up to a bright desk light, grunting now and again with a sound that Kate found hard to interpret as either satisfaction or dissatisfaction, though occasionally he marked a print with what she assumed was his sign of approval. His inattention gave her the chance to look around his spartan office, a much tidier space than the photographers' room outside, and with a single board displaying some fashion shots which she guessed had been taken for a glossy magazine.

Fellows was a rangy figure, his white shirt open at the neck and the sleeves rolled up. His hair was grey and untidily long and curled, touching his collar at the back, and the lines around the eyes, she thought, could have been caused by looking too long and hard through a lens, or into the sun. When he finally looked up and his eyes met her own, she was startled by how blue they were, and how chilly.

'So you're the girl who wants to be a photographer?' he said, his voice as unfriendly as his expression. 'It's not a job for a woman.'

'So people keep telling me,' Kate said, her mouth dry. 'I brought my portfolio, any road. I came top of my class at college.'

'Liverpool School of Art?' Fellows said without enthusiasm. 'So who've they trained that I'd know about? Wedding and passport snappers? Bar mitzvah and Rotary Club lunches a speciality? This is London, girl, and I intend this to be the best agency in the business. I need speed and flair and a bit of aggression. You don't get first class pics in high heels and a tight skirt.' He glanced contemptuously at the outfit she had spent ages agonizing over that morning.

'For one of my projects at college I went down a coal mine in Wigan,' Kate snapped back, stung by his contempt. 'I know what the job takes. If you look at my work . . .' She pushed the portfolio across the desk towards him.

'What did you use? What cameras?'

'Whatever was appropriate. It was a good department. But more and more thirty-five millimetre. I've got my own Voigtlander. I sold some pics to the *Liverpool Echo* and bought it out of the proceeds. I was trying to get a job there but they didn't want to know. No vacancies, they said.'

Fellows raised an eyebrow. 'Not a bad little machine,' he said. 'The thirty-five millimetre's the future for news. No doubt about that. The old plate cameras are out-of-date.'

'I notice you're doing a lot of show business pictures, bands and groups and that. There was a group in every street back home. Liverpool's going mad for rock bands. I took a lot of pics of them – just for practice. If you look here . . .'

She flicked through her collection and paused at a couple of black and white glossy publicity shots. 'This is Dave Donovan – he reckons his band is going to do well – and this is John Lennon. You've got one of him up outside. Both lads are down here in London now trying to get a break. I was at art college with John and his girlfriend, but he didn't stick at it. Spent much more time on his music than his art. Though he's not bad, his drawing's very good in black and white . . .'

'Are they really going to be a big thing, these groups? They're not going to fizzle out like skiffle did?' Fellows asked, suddenly interested. 'More than a flash in the pan?'

'The kids in Liverpool certainly think so. The girls were going hysterical about the Beatles at the Cavern Club. They're quite dishy, especially Paul. He's my favourite . . .' She stopped, realizing she was being too enthusiastic about people Fellows did not seem to know much about.

'Yeah, I was told they were getting noticed a bit down here, too. We did a few publicity shots for one or two bands. But there's been almost no interest from the papers and magazines really.'

'I saw your pix of the Beatles on the way in,' Kate said. 'Mine are better.'

Fellows looked at her sharply, with a ghost of a smile creasing his thin face. 'Are they now?' he said. He glanced at the pictures she indicated and then leaned back in his chair and folded his hands behind his head, watching her speculatively for a moment.

'OK,' he said, at length. 'I'm short-handed as it happens. I've just sent one of my best lads to France on a commission for a magazine. I'll give you a two month trial. What you make of it's up to you. Get rid of the high heels for a start. You'll fall over in the scrum if you don't. Use your own camera. See how you get on. Start on Monday.'

'How much will you pay me?' Kate asked. Fellows sighed and looked at the ceiling in mock despair.

'She wants money, too,' he sighed. 'OK, twelve quid a week, for two months. No more. If I keep you on, we'll see. And a bonus if you come up with something really special.'

'Done,' Kate said, trying to hide her glee.

'And don't come running to me if the boys give you a hard time. I told you, it's not a suitable job for a woman.'

'We'll see about that,' Kate said.

'We surely will,' Fellows said, turning back to his contact prints dismissively.

Detective Sergeant Harry Barnard scowled across his desk at the DCI from the murder squad, once his boss but no longer.

'He's got no form that I know of, guv,' he said, glancing down again at the glossy photographs of the almost decapitated body of a young man sprawled across a patterned rug which DCI Ted Venables had just dropped in front of him. 'Nothing I've picked up, on or off the record.'

'Ask around, will you, Harry,' Venables said. 'You know

the scene. Post-mortem says he's a Mary-Ellen, a nancy-boy, called himself an actor and we know what they get up to. But he's got no form as far as I can see either. I know you're not officially on the case but I need your contacts. Your guv'nor is going to get aerated about it anyway. You know what he's like with queers.'

Barnard smiled faintly. Venables had been replaced as head of Vice by DCI Keith Jackson, a lugubrious man who took most of the activities of Soho's square mile in his stride, but tended to slip into crusader mode with the area's homosexuals.

'It'll cost you,' Barnard said.

'I know the score. You don't have to tell me about Vice. I bloody well invented it,' Venables said. 'But I'm out of touch now, since they moved me bloody onward and upward, and all the poorer for it.'

Barnard grinned but said nothing. He liked to hear Venables beg, just as much as Venables hated it, but they both knew that there was no way the older man could escape until he completed his thirty years and took himself off to the house he coveted on the coast where he could indulge his passion for sea fishing, fresh crab sandwiches, the best malt whisky money could buy and perhaps even a little boat to indulge his hobby. He would be able to afford it after his lucrative years in Vice, with no need to hunt out a second career as some sort of private investigator. Barnard knew that. The ties which bound CID officers in and around central London were strong and indissoluble, a brotherhood that most joined and few escaped, or ever wanted to. And Venables gave no real sign of being strapped for cash, in spite of his ritual complaints.

'Living right in the middle of Soho like that, off Greek Street, the locals must have known him,' the DCI went on. 'See what you can pick up for me, will you? Background's what I need. Who he knew, where he went, who he picked up, who he brought back to the flat. There's signs someone else had been living there but moved out sharpish. No one's turned up yet, that's for sure, and there's not much in the way of personal details, so I reckon the bird's flown. Quite likely the other bugger's our lad, lover's tiff maybe – it's early days. Try the queer pubs.'

'I'll ask around, guv,' Barnard said. 'It's over the top of ABC Books, isn't it, the flat?'

'Right,' Venables said. 'You have to ask who'd want to live over the top of all that muck, haven't you?'

'I know the place. Nice little earner Pete Marelli's got there. I'll have a word. I don't think he owns the building but he'll know what's been going on up above.'

'He called us apparently. Someone had left the street door open and it was blowing about so he went upstairs and found the body. He might have stayed there for weeks otherwise. But apparently Marelli clammed right up with the bloke I sent round. Not a squeak out of him, in spite of a bit of arm-twisting.'

Barnard nodded. He knew that the arm-twisting might have been real but was unlikely to have brought the murder detectives any information which Marelli, one of the clannish Maltese, regarded as private. 'Yeah, well, you have to know how to handle these boys,' he said. 'The Maltese, they're very good at keeping their mouths shut when it suits them. And you know as well as I do that it suits them most of the time.'

Barnard stubbed out his cigarette, stood up and stretched lazily. He was tall and slim and fashionably dressed in an Italian suit, button-down collar and a narrow tie, a sharp contrast to Venables' own crumpled grey suit and conservative, much-washed neckwear. Venables, he thought, was noticeably missing the wife, Vera, who had apparently gone walkabout with someone who worked more regular hours and spent less leisure time in CID's favourite watering holes. He glanced around the room with sharp, shrewd eyes before pulling on his trench-coat and pushing his floppy dark hair – an inch or so longer than totally acceptable to his superiors – out of his eyes and putting his trilby on at exactly the right angle.

'I'll let you know, guv,' he said to Venables, as he headed for the door. 'I know exactly how to squeeze his nuts if I have to.'

The DCI watched him go and ground his teeth. Another pair of new shoes, he thought. Must have cost a bomb. Barnard seemed a sight smarter than he had been back when he worked as a young DC on his team some years before. Smarter and more successful, obviously, in one way and another, and the owner, he'd heard, of a brand new flat in poncey Highgate. How the hell did he manage that on a detective sergeant's pay? As if he didn't know. Still, he thought, his own prospects were looking up, and might well be enough to tempt Vera back to cook his meals and wash his clothes. She'd soon find out which side her bread was buttered.

Harry Barnard strolled out of the nick and made his way east into the maze of narrow streets at the heart of Soho, luxuriating in the spring sunshine, though it was still cold and there were traces of rock-hard snow and ice lingering in the shade. It had been a long and bitter winter and most of the country was still shivering even as spring officially arrived. Barnard dodged through the bustling crowds, shaking a hand here and there, nodding at the girls he knew and some he didn't, feeling that he was a prince of all he surveyed. It was, and always had been, an area in flux: immigrants came and moved on, restaurants and cafes of every nationality opened and closed, bright neon coffee bars full of sharp young things had recently sprung up alongside the pubs with their smoky, dark wood interiors and clientele where hopeful artists rubbed shoulders with hopeless drunks. And in between it all, the sex trade's tentacles wove and interwove, just as fluid but even more enduring than the rest.

Barnard picked up an apple from one of the stalls packed along the pavement in Berwick Street, with its mounds of fruit and veg and wind-blown litter, giving the stallholder a wave of acknowledgement, getting a smile, or perhaps a grimace, in return. He poked his head into one or two of the gloomy little Italian and Greek shops packed to the ceiling with merchandise, to which people flocked from all over London looking for delicacies they could not get in the suburbs. Impassive faces and dark eyes watched him from behind the counters, unblinking and unsmiling.

Barnard enjoyed working in Soho, and knew its glittering, anarchic, neon-lit night life as well, if not better than its cosmopolitan daylight bustle. That was where he had truly embedded himself as a force to be reckoned with, amongst the porn shops behind their semi-respectable street-front windows, the strip clubs where girls writhed on the edge of what was legal, the clip joints which lured unwary tourists into spending far more than they planned on promises which were never fulfilled, and the tall, dilapidated houses with numerous bells at the side of doors with peeling paint and a peephole to vet visitors. 'Vice Squad,' he would almost whisper as he opened those doors and got a kick from the fear the words sparked amongst some of his targets and the grudging respect amongst others.

At one point, he was surprised to see a face he recognized, though only just, as the tousled blonde was bundled up in a heavy winter coat and a headscarf effectively concealing the curves and charms he knew very well. The lack of her usual heavy make-up revealed dark circles under the blue eyes and a few wrinkles he had not guessed existed.

'Evie,' he murmured, giving her a cursory kiss on the cheek. 'You're up early, sweetie.'

'Had to go to the quack,' the woman said in little more than a whisper. 'Had a bit of a scare. Thought I was up the bloody spout.'

'Not mine, I hope,' Barnard said quickly.

'Shouldn't think so,' Evie said. 'You're one of the careful ones. Anyway, it was a false alarm.'

'That's good,' he said, although he knew she was likely being economical with the truth and that, like most of the women on the game, she would have sought out one of the doctors who was quietly and illegally willing to help out if the fee was generous enough.

'Are you coming up?' Evie asked, gesturing to one of the doors with the multiple bells close by. Barnard made the effort to pull a regretful face, although he did not feel very interested in her hospitality in her present state.

'Not today, sweetie,' he said. 'We've got a nasty murder round the corner. Nancy-boy got his throat cut. Anyway, you look as if you should go back to bed.'

'Yeah, maybe,' she agreed and gave him a peck on the cheek. 'See you soon then?'

'Yeah,' he echoed, though the 'maybe' was held under his breath. Suddenly Evie did not appear quite so attractive any more.

Barnard was not bothering with any of his regular calls this morning. He glanced at the plate-glass windows of the Wardour Street film companies, with their glossy photographs of stars and exotic locations, without much interest. He was not a man much given to imagination. Real life provided him with all the excitement he needed, he thought, and epic battles between good and evil, black and white, justice and its opposite, struck him as essentially unrealistic. The big picture was much murkier than that, a question of mucky white and inky black at the edges and a sludgy ocean of greys in the middle. He cut through into Soho Square, a green oasis amongst the narrow, crowded streets, much used by lunching workers from the shops and offices of Oxford Street by day and vagrants by night, and finally into Greek Street where ABC Books – the object of DCI Venables' interest – lurked in a narrow side-alley, only yards long, and ending in a blank brick wall.

There was still a uniformed constable standing in the doorway which led to the flat above, and Barnard saluted him cheerily, getting only a surly nod in return. CID and the uniformed branch were seldom on speaking terms.

'Nancy-boys?'

'Looks like it,' the constable muttered.

'I'll see what my old mate Pete Marelli's got to say about it,' Barnard said, pushing against the shop door and finding it unexpectedly locked. 'Is he in there?' he asked his colleague.

The constable shrugged. 'He was there earlier, when one of Mr Venables' lads dropped in. Not that he was very welcome, I heard.'

'We'll see about that,' Barnard said, banging on the door with his fist, and then calling Marelli's name through the letterbox at the base of the blacked-out glass. Somewhere inside, a dog began to bark hysterically.

'Come on, Pete, you old bugger,' Barnard shouted. 'I know you're in there. It's Harry Barnard. Let me in.' Eventually the two officers heard bolts being withdrawn, and Pete Marelli peered out of a two-inch crack between the door and the jamb, above a heavy security chain.

'What do you want now?' The voice had a whine in it. 'I don't know nothing about the flat upstairs. I just went to take a look because the door was open. I shouldn't have bothered if it cause me all this trouble. Ask the landlord about it. I've told you lot where to find him.'

Harry Barnard wedged his foot in the opening, narrow as it was, and put his face close to Marelli's. 'Let me in, Pedro, or there will be trouble, believe me. And keep that blasted animal of yours out of my way. I hate dogs, and especially that dog.' Eventually the man on the other side of the door complied, and Barnard slipped into the shop while Marelli locked and barred the door again behind him. Barnard gave barely a glance at the lurid books crammed on to open shelves. He knew that there was nothing illegal here on open display and Marelli's boss paid him enough not to investigate any further.

'Where's that blasted hound?' Barnard asked, glancing round, and identifying a furious snuffling from the back door.

'The door closed. Hector can't get in,' Marelli said.

'He'd better not, or I'll have the RSPCA on you. You shouldn't be keeping a big brute like that in this tiny place. So – tell me what's been going on upstairs, Pedro. And don't muck me about or I'll have your place searched every day for a bloody month. That'll keep the punters away.'

'I know nothing,' Marelli said. 'I don't know even who live up there.'

'And I don't bloody believe you,' Barnard said, giving Marelli a shove which knocked him back against one of his display shelves overloaded with books and magazines which teetered alarmingly above Marelli's head. 'And you know just how interested I might get in your back room if you don't help me out when I need helping out, don't you?'

Marelli was a small, overweight man dressed in a crumpled suit and white shirt which looked as if it had long missed out on laundry. His paunch overhung his thick leather belt, and several chins overlapped his greasy collar. He wheezed slightly in response to Barnard's shove and seemed to have difficulty in regaining his balance. His eyes shifted uneasily around the dimly lit shop as if looking for an escape route but eventually he shrugged.

'You have to ask the landlord for names,' he said. 'I never spoke to them. They never spoke to me. Two young men is all I know.'

'Descriptions?' Barnard snapped.

'One light hair, blond, long, very English, you know?'

'He's the one who's dead,' Barnard said, turning the photographs he had seen over in his mind quickly. 'So the other one? What did he look like?'

'More dark,' Marelli said. 'Also, hair not cut short. Not tall. In dark trousers and a suede jacket, brown, light brown, most times I saw him. I thought they were musicians, actors maybe. I saw them just through the window sometimes, coming and going. The way people do. They were nothing to do with me, Mr Barnard. Nothing. They are going straight to hell.' *And not the only ones*, Barnard thought with a slight smile.

'Did you see them yesterday?' he asked.

'The blond one, yes, I saw him go out as I was closing up. About seven o'clock. It was dark already, and the light out there's not good, but I recognized him. But I haven't seen the other one. Not for a few days.'

'Did they make any noise up there? Did they have visitors? Did they go in and out to work? You must have known what they got up to.'

Marelli screwed up his face in distaste. 'I know nothing about what they got up to,' he said. 'They were queer boys, you know? I told you, they were like that. Mother of God, I want nothing to do with that sort. I know nothing about what they got up to. I'm a good Catholic.'

'And the Pope's a good Protestant,' Barnard said with a grin. 'You don't do books for queer boys then?'

'No,' Marelli said flatly. 'Never. Other shops do that.'

Barnard cast his mind back to the last time he had searched Marelli's back room, before he'd been persuaded not to bother again, and realized that the Maltese was probably telling the truth. The explicit pornography he stocked, most of it imported from abroad, broke the law in almost every respect but that.

He laughed. 'You should have told us about your neighbours then,' he said. 'We could have paid them a visit. My boss would have liked that. He thinks they should all be locked up.'

Marelli shrugged. 'Not my business,' he muttered.

'OK, but they must have had visitors, these queer boys,' Barnard said. 'Did they have parties, people going up there for fun and games? A couple of beefy guardsmen, maybe? Anyone else you can tell me about?'

'No, no one else,' Marelli said. 'There were just the two. They were quiet upstairs. Some music on the gramophone sometimes, but not too loud. Quiet boys. No trouble. Ask landlord about them, not me. Here, I give you name. I gave it already to other officer, but have it again, please.'

He took a piece of paper and wrote down a name and address and phone number.

'That is landlord,' he said. 'Talk to him. I just work here.'

Barnard glanced at the scrawled name and smiled faintly. It was one he recognized. Someone else who owed him a favour.

TWO

Kate O'Donnell's elation at landing a job did not last long. As she lugged her portfolio back up Frith Street towards Tottenham Court Road tube station, her other major preoccupation took the shine from her eyes. She glanced round and realized that at least there was someone she knew to talk to within walking distance. Her friend, Marie Best, schoolmate, aspiring actress and owner of the sofa that Kate was temporarily sleeping on, had given her a rough map of Soho and Kate could see that the coffee bar she worked at was just round the corner.

The atmosphere in The Blue Grotto was steamy when Kate opened the door but the clientele sparse at this time of day, apart from a couple of teenaged lads in Mod suits and narrow ties, their parkas flung over the chairs behind them, which explained the two Lambrettas parked on the pavement outside. Marie was behind the counter looking bored and served her a frothy coffee in a glass cup and saucer without complaint before joining her at a bright blue Formica-topped table close to the bar.

'You got it?' she said, when Kate told her about the job. 'That's fantastic. I'm really pleased for you.'

'Only a two month trial,' Kate said, playing nervously with the sugar shaker. 'But it's a start.'

'I wish I could get a part for two days, never mind two months,' Marie said, running a hand through her red hair distractedly. 'There's been no call back from the last three auditions I went to. They're all very sweet and encouraging, "darling this" and "darling that". But then nothing. And this job's only temporary while someone's on holiday. You'll have to pay me rent for the sofa if this carries on. I'll have to sign on the dole when this job finishes. I've pretty well used up all my savings.'

'Of course I'll pay rent,' Kate said, guilty that her friend's depression could not totally deflate her. But as she sipped her coffee she fell silent, flinching slightly from the bright blue walls painted with crude representations of Capri which would have got you flung out of her art college in a week. She listened idly to the music the two boys sitting behind them had put on the massive chrome and red jukebox.

'Hey, that's the Beatles' song,' she said suddenly, turning round in her chair to catch the eye of the Mods behind. '*Love Me Do*. That was their first record, you know? Do you like them? I knew them in Liverpool.'

'They're OK,' one of the boys conceded grudgingly. 'I reckon their new one's better though, going up the hit parade that is. But I like Gerry and the Pacemakers better.'

Kate smiled and shrugged. Maybe Dave Donovan, her former boyfriend, was right when he called John Lennon's rival band, which had managed to get a record released before he did, just a flash in the pan. And she had put that down to wishful thinking.

'Do you remember them at the Cavern?' she asked Marie, recalling sweaty, deafening evenings crammed into a small space with hundreds of other overexcited teenagers. Down here, she thought, hardly anyone seemed to have heard of the Liverpool bands.

Marie nodded. 'My brother had a skiffle group but it all fizzled out.'

'Everybody's brother had a skiffle group,' Kate said, laughing. 'Even Tom played one of those washboard things for a bit.' But her face fell again as the thought plunged her back into the anxiety which dogged her now day and night.

'What are we going to do about Tom, then,' Marie asked, sensing her friend's mood. 'You said you'd give me a picture of him so I can ask around.'

'I will do,' Kate said. 'Two months will give me a bit of breathing space to try to find him.' Kate knew she was trying to convince herself as much as her friend, and aware she had absolutely no idea where one single individual, who clearly did not want to be found, might be discovered in this teeming city.

'Why do you think he might be in Soho?' Marie asked. 'London's a huge place, la.'

Kate shrugged. 'Just a hunch,' she said. 'When we used to talk about what we wanted to do, I'd go on about coming down here to take pictures and he always said he wanted to run a clothes shop on Oxford Street. It was just one of those dreams people have. I never thought either of us would make it, to be honest. And if I'd got the job on the *Echo,* I wouldn't have done. I'd have stayed at home and married some nice Catholic boy to please my mam. I don't know where Tom is, but just up there is Oxford Street and here I am, so it's worth a look. He sent us a couple of postcards. No address of course, but a W1 postmark, so that's central, too. It's as good a place to start as any.'

'If he's that interested in fashion, there's lots of garment places up by Oxford Circus. And some small shops, in the side streets behind the big department stores. You're right, it's not such a bad place to start,' Marie said, getting up and moving behind the bar again as two young women came in for coffee and peered at the cakes under glass domes at the end of the counter.

Kate watched the sugar she'd put in her coffee slowly deflate the bubbles. She adored Tom, her older brother by two years. He had been the one who had encouraged her to stay on at school and go to college, as they had grown up in the crowded house where their mother struggled to keep four children in a neighbourhood which still regarded mothers on their own with disdain if not outright contempt. But as they all grew up, she had watched as the relationship between Tom and her mother had disintegrated until the tension in the house became unbearable and she had never been able to put her finger on what exactly came between them.

Tom had left school at fifteen and gone straight to work, ostentatiously giving his mother half his wage with a flourish every Friday night, and Kate was only too aware of how valuable that was to the family finances as she struggled through college on a grant while her younger sisters were still at school. But Tom did not seem to keep any single job long, working his way through the large stores and smaller clothing shops in the city centre, always smartly dressed and meticulously turned out in the latest fashion, but always, it seemed, looking for or being forced into something different. And every time he changed his job their mother's attitude towards him seemed to harden and Tom's switches of mood, from bravado to anxiety and back again, became more marked. He was unhappy and Kate struggled to understand why.

In the end he vanished. Their mother went to wake him one morning and found his bed empty and his cupboards bare. A scribbled note left behind the kettle said simply that he had decided to try his luck in London. And after that, silence. After six months a postcard arrived, addressed to Kate, saying that he was well and happy and had a job. A card came at Christmas. But there was no address or phone number attached to either and the presents which his sisters had bought remained forlornly under the tree until finally Kate put them away in her room at the end of the holiday, where they still lay in a dusty heap. Tom's absence tore a hole in her life but at the same time gave her hope for her own future. She was coming to the end of her course at college and already knew that her choice of career would face obstacles in Liverpool. She might make a living taking endless photographs of schoolchildren, or weddings but her chances of doing anything much more demanding with her beloved camera were minimal. She too, she had decided, would have to move on and she knew that London was the obvious place to go.

Marie came back from serving her customers and flopped down into the seat beside Kate again. 'So does your mam know you're looking for Tom?' she asked.

Kate shrugged. 'She must know, though she never said.' Her mother, she thought, had taken her own decision to move away stoically enough, although she knew that Tom's defection had hurt her deeply. Perhaps the suddenness of Tom's departure had reminded her too forcibly of their father's similar exit years before. Or perhaps her mother had her favourite and Kate was not that child. She shrugged, drained her coffee and pulled her coat on.

'I'll see you tonight,' she said. 'And I'll give you a

photograph of Tom. You never know. In a place like this, so central, someone might know him or have seen him around.'

'You never know,' Marie said, though she could not conceal the doubt in her eyes.

The fire had burnt down to embers when the boy stirred deep inside his huddle of blankets and cardboard. Everyone who lived on the bombed sites knew, and had known all that long and bitter winter, that if they were to survive they needed warmth, even though the fires they lit made them more visible to the forces of law and order. Occasionally the police came in mob-handed, as they had done the previous night, smashing up the fragile encampments, stamping out the fires and bundling all those who hadn't been quick or agile enough to run away into vans, taking them down to the nick in Snow Hill. The older men didn't mind too much, didn't try to run too hard, if they could run at all. Ever since the emaciated body of a tramp known simply as Old Ben had been found frozen stiff close to the underground line they had known the dangers of the relentless ice and snow and did not object to a week or so at Her Majesty's pleasure and the luxuries of a bed and three meals a day.

But the boy did not want that. What he did to earn enough to keep body and soul hanging together by the slenderest thread he knew would lead to more violence in custody than out of it, and eventually a return to the children's home where he had been dumped as a small child, or to somewhere just as bad. That, he had decided as soon as he ran away, was never going to happen to him again. And now, ever since he had been sickened by the sight of the young man's blood-drenched body sprawled on the floor, he was even more certain that he had to keep himself out of sight. He was haunted by the thought that if he had been a few minutes faster following his mark up the stairs to the flat, he might have been dispatched just as swiftly. The killers would never have left a witness if he had walked into the flat while they were there. The thought filled him with a sick sense of dread, and he was sure that if the men he had seen realized he might be a threat they would come looking for him.

By the time he had scrambled down through the broken fence from Farringdon Road that night, after running all the way from Soho, most of the vagrants were back, as they were after every police raid, and the boy, who was so adept at melting into the shadows when trouble loomed, was among them again, the fires were lit and the half-life of the homeless continued in the wilderness Hitler's bombers had created and London had still not yet rebuilt. He had a protector of sorts, a tall, emaciated Scot with grizzled hair to his shoulders and an equally unkempt grey beard. He spoke little and drank copiously but in the short time they had been together the boy gathered that he had been in the army during the war and had come home to find his wife and family vanished without trace, no reason to be found as to why the letters had dried up, their house abandoned and taken over by squatters desperate for a roof in the bombed-out streets of Glasgow. For some reason the boy did not understand, Hamish had become his champion if any of the other men tried to bully him, a champion with a fierce temper if crossed, and ready fists and boots. That a man might befriend him without an ulterior motive was almost beyond his comprehension and he was still wary of the Scot.

He was there now as he opened bleary eyes and squinted against the grey daylight.

'I've a bite of breakfast if ye're hungry, lad,' Hamish said, pulling a newspaper-wrapped bundle from deep inside his layers of clothes.

'Not hungry,' the boy muttered.

'But ye're freezing cold,' the older man said, reaching out a gnarled finger to touch the boy's cheek. The boy flinched and Hamish withdrew.

'What happened to ye, laddie?' he asked. 'Ye came back as if all the hounds of hell were on your tail. Ye didn't find a night's lodgings, then?'

The boy shook his head and rolled away to a position closer to the remnants of the night's fire, where a little warmth could penetrate his wrappings.

Hamish opened his bundle and pulled out half a loaf of bread which he cut into chunks with the knife he kept inside his shirt. 'Ach, ye'll do yoursel' no good by not eating.'

Slowly the boy's shivering subsided and eventually he slipped a hand out of his blankets and accepted a piece of the dry bread Hamish was chewing on slowly. When he had eaten it, Hamish handed him a bottle.

'A wee dram'll warm ye,' he said, and the boy took a swig of the fiery liquid, choking as it scorched his throat. 'I'm off to the Sally Ann in a bit for a wash and a hot meal,' Hamish went on. 'Will ye no' come with me?'

But the boy shook his head fiercely. The only thing he wanted now was to keep out of sight and, if possible, get out of London. But how he might achieve that he had no idea.

As evening closed in on her first day in her new job, Kate O'Donnell could not help feeling deflated. She had taken the Central Line into the West End, as she had done the previous week for her interview, but this time during the rush hour, strap-hanging breathlessly in a crowded carriage, and feeling infinitely relieved to breathe something approaching fresh air as the long escalator delivered her back to daylight at Tottenham Court Road. Everything here seemed like a strange and frantic dream, and her nervousness only increased as she hurried down the narrow streets of Soho, hyper-conscious of the aromas of foods she could not recognize and languages she could not understand in the foreign shops and cafes as she dodged her way to the Ken Fellows Agency.

What followed was mere anticlimax. Fellows was not there, out on a shoot apparently, and the laconic receptionist, with the dark-lined eyes and unnaturally pale face, who this time volunteered that her name was Brenda, had evidently been briefed to greet her, although the word implied more warmth than seemed to be on offer.

'That's your desk,' Brenda said, pointing to a small, cluttered space in a corner of the room. 'And this is Bob Johnson. He's minding the shop while Ken's out.' A small, middle-aged man with a greying, short back and sides and what looked like a permanently sour expression, cast an eye over Kate coldly, as if sizing up a joint of meat, from her dark curls to the slacks and flat shoes she had chosen to meet Ken Fellows' requirements. It was obvious to Kate that she fell some distance short of whatever Bob Johnson's requirements might be.

'Boss wants you to do some filing,' he said. 'All this lot need sorting.' He waved a hand vaguely at a heap of glossy prints which had been dumped in the centre of her small desk. 'Need cross-referencing. Photographer and subject. Brenda'll show you the system.'

Brenda showed her the system, and Kate stowed her bag, which contained her precious Voigtlander, under her desk and got to work. Various men came and went during the morning, with cameras and equipment, closeting themselves in the darkrooms, and chatting amongst themselves, but apart from speculative looks when they arrived, they took no notice of Kate at all.

At lunchtime, when Kate's stomach began to rumble, Johnson and the two other men who were in the office at the time, took themselves off together without glancing in her direction. Furious, Kate put on her coat, picked up her bag and followed them out. They went into the nearest pub, and she walked slowly up to Oxford Street where she bought an *Evening Standard*, and ordered poached eggs on toast and a coffee at an ABC cafe, where she ate slowly and read the paper for what she thought amounted to a reasonable lunch hour.

Back at the agency, she found only Brenda in residence, chatting on the phone as Kate made her way back to her desk, broke open a Fry's chocolate cream bar and gazed gloomily at the only slightly diminished pile of prints. Two months of this might be Ken Fellows' way of curing her of what he obviously thought was her inappropriate ambition, she thought wryly, hoping against hope that the boss would turn up soon and find her something more stimulating to do, but Fellows did not come back that afternoon and it was her friend Marie who eventually lifted her spirits. At about four o'clock, when Bob Johnson, the only other person in the office again, looked as if he was deciding to pack up for the day, Brenda put her head round the door.

'There's a phone call for you, Kate. Take it on that one on the shelf over there.' Kate located the receiver and picked up as Brenda transferred the call, to find a breathless Marie at the other end.

'Someone recognized that snap of Tom you left here,' she said.

'You're kidding,' Kate said, her heart thumping, hardly able to believe it could have been that easy to trace her brother. 'Do they know where he lives, or where he works?'

'Hold on, keep calm,' Marie said. 'He couldn't hang around, but he's given me an address. If you come up here when you finish work, I'll give it to you. It's only round the corner. What a coincidence, hey? I finish at five. We can go together.'

'That's amazing,' Kate said. 'Absolutely amazing. See you later.'

'Alligator,' Marie said, and Kate could sense her excitement down the line.

The two young women stood in the alley and gazed up at the blank windows of the building on the opposite side, but they could see no sign of life. They had found the address easily enough, only a short walk from The Blue Grotto. But when they rang the doorbell, and then banged on the door, there was no response.

'Whoever lives there, they're not in,' Marie said. 'We'll have to come back another time.'

Kate stared around the gloomy alley, where litter from the main road seemed to accumulate in heaps against the blank end wall, and felt desperation swamp the elation that she had felt when they reached the flat. The alley was narrow and the building where Tom allegedly lived looked dilapidated, the windows grimy and the narrow doorway, with no name-cards, in need of a coat of paint. This was a grim place to end up, she thought, and began to hope that it was not, in fact, where Tom was living. The only other place which showed any sign of being inhabited was the small shop immediately beneath the flat, where the lights were on. But having glanced at the sleazy-looking books in the cluttered display window, she felt very reluctant to step inside.

'Come on,' Marie said eventually. 'There's someone in there. He must know who lives upstairs.'

Kate shrugged uneasily. The very idea of Tom living here upset her more than she would admit, even to herself. Trying to find him through a dubious bookshop filled her with despair. But Marie was already heading to the door and she followed behind, not knowing quite what to expect.

The doorbell clanged as they went inside, to find themselves in a very small space crammed with a very large number of books, most of them between covers showing incredibly large-bosomed women, in various states of undress, being pawed by unfeasibly muscled young men, all carefully protected behind cellophane covers. Browsing the pages was evidently discouraged.

At first they could see no one inside the shop but eventually Kate became aware of a face watching them with unblinking dark eyes through a small hatch at the back. And beyond him, a dog began to bark. After a long moment of unspoken scrutiny, the face disappeared, and the door at the back opened.

'Stay, Hector,' the man said, backing into the shop and closing the door firmly behind him as the barking intensified. He looked at the two young women with a puzzled expression.

'What can I do for you?' he asked, raising his voice, with its distinct foreign accent, against the dog's furious protestations.

'We're not buying,' Kate said, feeling her colour rise.

'I didn't think you were,' the shopkeeper said, with a sneer. 'So what is it? You're not one of them church women, cleaning up Soho, are you? You should stick to cleaning up your houses, that's what I think.'

'Do you know who lives in the flat upstairs?' Kate said firmly, annoyed by the fat, grumpy foreigner's attitude. 'We're trying to find someone we think lives at this address.'

The question stopped the man momentarily, although if anything his hostility only intensified, turning into a deep suspicion. 'You know them?' he asked.

'If you tell us who lives there, we might know if we know them,' Kate said angrily.

'So you know the dead one, or the other one?' the man asked harshly and Kate felt the colour drain from her face and her heart skip a beat.

'What do you mean?' she asked.

'You should talk to police,' the man said. 'Talk Sergeant Barnard. He tell you.'

Marie squeezed her friend's arm. 'Tell us what's happened,' she said firmly. 'This is my friend's brother we're talking about.' She dug around in her bag, pulled out Kate's photograph of Tom, and put it on the counter in front of the shopkeeper. 'This is him,' she said. 'That's Tom. Do you know him? Have you seen him? We really need to know.'

The man glanced at the dog-eared snapshot and shrugged. 'Maybe him,' he said. 'Could be him. His friend is more blond. And he dead. Since last week. Police come. Talk to police, please. I know nothing about young men. I want to know nothing about young men like that. Is nothing to do with me.'

'How did this friend die?' Kate asked, through dry lips. 'What happened?'

'Ask police,' the man repeated. 'Ask Sergeant Barnard. Now I go out. I take Hector out.' At the sound of his name the dog began his furious barking again and appeared to fling himself at the door between the shop and whatever rear accommodation lay behind, shaking it on its latch.

For a long moment Kate stood as if frozen to the ground until Marie took her arm and almost pushed her out of the door and back into the alleyway, where she put a hand out to steady herself against the grimy wall.

'Something very bad has happened,' Kate whispered. 'I really need to find out what. I can't leave it like that.'

'We won't leave it,' Marie said, as she grabbed her friend's arm again and eased her back along the alleyway and towards the bustle of Greek Street. She glanced back to where the man was locking up his shop, and keeping firm hold of the leash of an enormous German shepherd who looked as if he could pull his master for a ten mile run never mind a stroll around the crowded streets of Soho. On an impulse, Kate pulled her camera out of her bag and took a couple of quick shots of the bookshop and its keeper being hauled away by his dog. He scowled at her and waved his free hand as if instructing her to stop.

'Go to the police,' he shouted. 'Leave me alone.'

'I need something to tell my mother,' Kate whispered. 'I really need to know what's happened.'

'We'll find out,' Marie said again. 'Don't panic, please don't panic. I'm sure it's all a dreadful mistake.'

'Mother of God, I hope so,' Kate said. 'I really hope so.'

THREE

D S Harry Barnard woke with a mild feeling of dissatisfaction the next morning. He prided himself on
knowing his patch: if a pimp laid a fist on one of his
women, if a cafe failed to pay its protection money and suffered
inexplicable losses of stock or a serious trashing as a result,
if a pornographic bookshop suddenly found its illicit supplies
drying up, he reckoned he should know the where and the
what and the why and more often than not the who. But
yesterday his trails had all gone cold and he had found next
to nothing to assist DCI Venables with his inquiries. It was
not, he reckoned, that anyone was covering up at the behest
of some of the shadowy figures behind Soho crime, as they
often did, but that in this case they genuinely did not know
anything about the death of Jonathon Mason, identified by his
landlord as the tenant of the flat where he had been killed.
And that nagged at him like toothache.

Not even his sense of satisfaction in his own new flat soothed
him as he made some strong coffee in his new Italian perco-
lator and sat brooding at his beech Ercol table on his spindle-
legged beech chair. The flat was one in a new block on the
fuzzy border between Highgate and Archway, on the hill but
not quite at the top of it, literally or socially. But for an East
End boy it was a decided step up and he had spent much time
and effort getting the new Scandinavian look from the smartest
shops he could afford just right, the pale wood, the boxy sofa,
the orange revolving upholstered chair, the bright shaggy rugs
for the parquet floor and the latest in long-play radiograms.

Barnard's passion for the latest fashion in clothes as well
as furnishings was a source of much canteen mockery amongst
his sweatily scruffy, shirt-sleeved colleagues back at the nick,
who commuted in from their semis in the far suburbs every
day. But in many ways his style was only a veneer, the lichen
clinging to a chunk of rock. He knew, when he bothered to

think about the trajectory his life had taken, that it was only the fact that his sharp brain had taken him to a grammar school instead of the dilapidated secondary modern most of his eleven-year-old mates had gone to, which had saved him from going with them down the path into the murky world of East End wheeling and dealing and crime that most had followed.

Looking back, he thought himself lucky not to have become a copper as such, but to become one of the coppers living on the edge where he could supplement his meagre pay and get some of the good things in life which his criminal acquaint-ances took for granted. He felt no guilt. He made a sharp distinction between milking the petty criminals of Soho's sex industry and pursuing real villains. And the latter he took a pride in hunting down. Which was why the fact that DCI Venables was looking for a murderer on his patch and he himself had not been able to elicit a whisper from his inform-ants about either the victim or the perpetrator was causing him serious annoyance which only grew as he went through the motions of shaving, dressing – with his usual attention to detail – and downing a perfunctory breakfast of coffee and toast.

Somewhere, he thought, as he started his red Ford Capri coupé in a thoroughly bad mood and set off down to Highgate Hill towards the West End, someone knew why an apparently inoffensive queer actor, with no criminal record, either for the bleeding obvious or for anything else, had had his throat slit from ear to ear four nights ago with no one apparently seeing anything, hearing anything or picking up the slightest hint as to why he had met such a gruesome fate. In Barnard's exten-sive experience of the overcrowded, crime-ridden streets of Soho, that was impossible.

He parked at the back of the nick, and made his way up to the CID room where he hung his coat by the door and his jacket over the back of his chair, and carefully rolled up the sleeves of his white shirt with enough attention to cause his colleagues a few amused smiles, before wading into the files piled up in his in-tray.

'Morning, Flash,' his nearest neighbour greeted him. 'Where'd you get that tie? It's a bit nancy-boy, isn't it?'

Barnard glanced down at the Liberty silk adornment in

question, a floral number which he knew when he bought it would raise eyebrows amongst his severely striped and often gravy-stained colleagues. 'It's not bad, is it?' he said. 'It's the latest thing.'

'God, we'll be getting daisies on our shirts next. If they make it legal, the bummers'll take over the world,' his neighbour came back, only half joking.

'I shouldn't worry, Greg,' Barnard said dismissively. 'I don't think they'll be trolling down Shaftesbury Avenue after you.'

He turned away and picked up a scribbled note tucked under a used coffee cup, aware of his colleague taking an interest in what he was looking at.

'He called just as I was leaving last night,' Greg Davies said. 'Wouldn't give a second name, just Pete, said you'd know who he was. Sounded like another bloody foreigner.'

'Right,' Barnard said. 'I know who he is. I'll call in on him later.' He wondered whether Pete Marelli had had second thoughts about their previous conversation. As soon as he had checked the rest of his incoming phone messages, scrawled on the pad on his desk, and decided that none of the other cases he was working on merited his urgent attention, he put his jacket and coat back on and left, making his way quickly through the crowded street to ABC Books and the now unguarded entrance to Jonathon Mason's flat. He reckoned the fingerprint operatives must have long finished their dusty work by now and Venables would be waiting for whatever information science could offer him which would not, in the nature of things, be much, he thought, as he waited for Marelli to unlock the door of his shop and let him in.

'You rang?' Barnard said, glancing round to make sure that Hector was not lurking behind the counter. He heartily disliked dogs, hairy, smelly, slavering creatures in his experience, and in this particular case, potentially dangerous. To his relief, on this occasion there was no sign of the Alsatian.

'Yeah,' Marelli said. 'Did those girls come talk to you? I told them to find you. They came round here asking questions.'

'What girls?' Barnard said. 'Tarts, were they?'

'No, no, they respectable girls, smart-looking girls, but talk funny. One had a picture of the friend who vanished.'

Barnard's interest quickened. 'You mean the other poofter who was living upstairs?'

'Yeah, looked like him. She say it her brother.'

'Right,' Barnard said, his interest increasing further. 'Let's have a description of these girls, shall we? I want to know exactly what they looked like, down to the colour of their nail-varnish, the length of their skirts and the height of their heels. And exactly what they said to you. I need to find them. This is a murder inquiry and it's already dragging on. So I don't want you messing me about for half a bloody second, let's start with the sister, shall we? Colour of hair? Colour of eyes? How tall? Curves in the right places – or not? Vital statistics, if you want to take a guess. What was she wearing? I want to walk down that street and know her the moment I clap eyes on her. Understood?'

Marelli nodded, licking his lips slightly. 'OK, OK, I understand, Mr Barnard,' he said.

Marie Best's flat was at the top of a tall building in one of the decaying terraces close to the railway between Paddington station and Notting Hill. The area had been prosperous once, as the city had spread westward, but since the war it had fallen on hard times, the stucco peeling, the columns of the porticos beginning to crack and lean drunkenly, the basement areas full of wind-blown rubbish and the accommodation built for prosperous Victorian families now, more often than not, divided up into bedsits and tiny flats. Four floors up, in the small rooms which had been provided for the servants, Marie and her friend Tess Farrell, who was training to be a teacher, shared a small bedroom with two single beds and a slightly larger living room with a Baby Belling cooker and a sink in one corner. The bathroom, with its lethal-looking gas geyser, was down a flight on the landing below.

The two girls had done their best to make the place bright and cheerful, but as fast as they painted over the black mould where the water above was seeping through the roof, the damp returned. The whole building reeked of decaying wood and plaster but Marie had soon found that the heavyweight man who came round weekly to collect the rents simply stared blankly at her when she raised the question of repairs.

When Kate had seen how small the flat was, she had almost turned away, ready to refuse Marie's offer of temporary shelter. But Marie had been adamant. Until she found a job, she insisted, Kate must stay. Once she had an income, she could find something better for herself, but she would have to be quick and determined, able to get hold of the first edition of the *Evening Standard* every day, study the columns of small ads and get on the phone and on to the Tube to hunt down anything that looked feasible within hours of the paper being printed.

Decent rooms in London were like hen's teeth, Marie had said. Rents were expensive, competition fierce. And before Kate could even consider renting a place of her own she needed more than a two month trial with Ken Fellows and she must save for a deposit. Which is why at seven thirty the next morning, after an almost sleepless night on the sofa, Kate found herself watching Tess Farrell simultaneously eating a bacon sandwich and powdering her nose in the mirror over the sink before setting off to do teaching practice in a secondary modern school in Battersea.

'One of my friends got stabbed in the bum with a pair of compasses yesterday,' Tess mumbled, with her mouth full. 'Had to go for First Aid. How embarrassing. They just think it's a joke, a lot of these kids, and student teachers are fair game. Get them under control before you try to teach them anything, that's what our tutors say. But in some schools that's a joke. It might work in a grammar school but it doesn't seem to if they've failed the eleven plus. They think they're failures and school's an imposition, like being permanently in detention. They can't wait to get out. If I can't get a job in a grammar when this is all over, I'll pack it in.'

'You scousers should be used to all that,' Marie said, half-turning from the sink where she was washing up her breakfast cup and laughing. 'You've got enough schools full of scallies your side of the water.'

'Oh, just listen to Lady Muck from the feckin' Wirral,' Tess said, rising as ever to any skirmish in the ongoing class wars between Liverpool and its more select neighbours across the Mersey. 'You were keen enough to go out with that scally Rick Davies when I first knew you.'

Marie pursed her lips together to even out her lipstick and refused to respond to that barb. 'How's your new job?' she asked Kate.

'Oh, it's OK,' Kate said. 'But I wonder if they'll ever let me take any pictures. The only other girl there is a secretary and they treat her as if she's invisible as well. She's just a walking tea machine, and if she's not there I think I'll get landed with the kettle and mugs. And I've not even seen the boss yet. He's away on some job, leaving me a heap of pictures to file.'

Marie laughed. 'We should have listened to them at school,' she said. 'Nice girls become teachers, nurses or secretaries and look for a man to keep them for the rest of their lives. But a term of teacher training was enough for me. I always wanted to act, and I'd never have forgiven myself if I didn't give it a go. If Rita Tushingham can do it, I don't see why I can't. It's not as if she's even good-looking.'

Kate broke into the theme from *A Taste of Honey* and they all sang along. 'I know how you feel. I was the only girl in my photography class at college. But I really wanted to do it.'

'It's like the lads and their bands, isn't it? Tell your Dave to chuck away his guitar and become an accountant and see how far you get,' Marie said.

'He's not my Dave,' Kate said as she rolled out of her blanket and off the sofa while Tess pulled on her coat and made ready to leave. 'Not any more.'

'And you didn't come to London to catch up with him?' Marie scoffed.

'No, I didn't,' Kate said flatly. 'I came to London to please myself.' *And to find Tom*, she added under her breath, though after their encounter with the unsavoury bookshop owner she now dreaded where that quest would lead. She pulled a face at Marie's sceptical expression. It was true, she thought. No one at school, or even at the art college, had taken her ambitions seriously either. And if she didn't make a breakthrough in the next couple of months, she had no idea what she would do next. A future of dead-end jobs in coffee bars with Marie, both of them waiting for something to turn up, filled her with dread.

'Do you think the bathroom will be free?' she asked, with a sigh. 'I daren't be late.'

'Probably,' Marie said. 'The couple below go out very early. He drives a tube train and I'm not sure what she does, but she disappears early and comes in late. There's another bathroom on the first floor for the rest of the house.'

'See you later, alligator,' Tess said. 'If I survive assault by ink-sodden blotting paper balls and compasses.'

'In a while,' Kate responded despondently.

Marie wiped her hands on the tea towel and came to sit beside her friend on the rumpled sofa. 'Are you going to go to the police about Tom?' she asked, her eyes full of concern.

'I don't know,' Kate said. 'I've been tossing around thinking about it half the night. If someone's died in that flat, been murdered maybe, and Tom lived there, I might be landing him in terrible trouble, mightn't I?'

'You don't know that,' Marie said. 'We've no idea how this man died. He could have been ill. He could have committed suicide. You can't just assume it's a murder because the police are involved.'

'Will it be in the papers?' Kate asked. 'At home, it would be in the *Echo* . . .'

'You could pick up the *Evening Standard* on your way to work. It's usually out very early and it's the best one for property ads anyway. There might be something, though that man said it happened last week. I'd come with you but I'm not on duty till eleven. But come to The Blue Grotto at dinner-time. They do give you a break, I take it?'

'No one's told me much about things like that,' Kate said with a wry smile. 'In fact, no one's told me much about anything yet. But I took an hour off yesterday and no one complained. I'm hoping the boss will be there today and I can sort a few things out. I really don't want to spend two months filing pictures and taking none myself.'

'Come on, cheer up,' Marie said. 'I'll make you some coffee

while you're in the bathroom. Then you can get to work and we can decide what to do about Tom later.'

Hunger eventually drove the boy out of his hiding place where he had lain, wrapped in his blankets for most of the last four days. It had become harder and harder to resist Hamish when he suggested coming with him to the Sally Ann for a meal, but the boy reckoned that if anyone was looking for him – and he couldn't persuade himself that someone was not – then the Sally Ann, with its well-known services for the homeless, was an obvious place to start. This particular morning he woke to find that the dull ache in his stomach had turned into a sharp pain. He had eaten nothing since Hamish had offered him a couple of slices of dry bread the morning before, when he had come back from foraging around the neighbourhood for fag ends and food. He eased himself out of the warm nest he had created and stood shivering for a moment, glancing down at an underground train that had just begun to speed up after leaving Farringdon station. The white faces staring out at him became anonymous blobs as the train speeded up for its clattering run up to King's Cross and the boy waited for it to disappear round the bend before making his move.

He clambered up the slope towards the main road, and stood for a moment in a clump of desiccated fireweed almost as tall as he was as he tried to decide which way to go. Fireweed, they called it, Hamish had told him in a coherent interlude, or bombweed, because of the speed at which it had sprung up on these derelict sites after Hitler's fires had died away, replacing flames with its tall magenta flowers. It was dying away itself now, he thought, as the calender said spring was coming, although the weather was no warmer than it had been at Christmas. Soon the bomb sites would briefly be more open to prying eyes, another reason why he knew he had to move on, and quickly. He had earned nothing since he had found the bloody body in the flat in Soho, so there was no chance of buying anything. But today he must eat.

He hesitated at the top of the slope beneath the retaining wall and listened to the traffic passing by on Farringdon Road. A left turn would take him towards Clerkenwell and Smithfield

Market where he could perhaps beg something from one of the cafes frequented by the market porters who had started work before dawn unloading cargoes of meat from the farms and the docks for the wholesale stalls which sold it on to the butchers clogging the roads with their vans. Londoners liked their meat, and had been half-starved of it during the years of rationing, and the place would be heaving with activity all morning. But heading south meant exposing himself on more main roads and that might be too dangerous, he thought.

Instead he turned north, flitting from one derelict site to another, forced back on to the road at the point where Exmouth Market crossed the underground railway, overground here and snaking away to King's Cross. Here the laden stalls and crowds of shoppers would conceal him and there was food in abundance to be begged or pilfered as he slipped quickly through the crowds, keeping close to the walls and shop fronts, head down, coat collar turned up, only half-confident that no one from Soho or Oxford Street would come this far east. He was determined to take no chances.

By the time he had begged a couple of stale bread rolls from a kindly-looking assistant in a baker's shop, he realized his head was swimming, and he took refuge in an alley where he crouched down behind a row of stinking dustbins to eat his bread and rest until his mind cleared. The food eventually made him feel less groggy, and he continued his forage through the market, picking up a couple of apples while a stallholder was distracted but taking to his heels when a second red-faced stallholder noticed his hand sliding towards a banana. He was soon lost in the crowds again and began to work his way back towards his refuge on the railway embankment when he suddenly froze. A glimpse of a man with dark hair on the other side of the street, deep in conversation with a woman, made his heart thump uncontrollably. He dodged behind a crowd of burly men standing round a stall selling hot food, the smell making him salivate, and looked again. He had already convinced himself that someone must be looking for him and fear turned uncertainty to panic and he ran, soon in streets he did not know and with increasingly little idea how to get back to his base.

The people here were better dressed than those he knew around the markets, men in dark suits or overcoats and hats, carrying small leather cases, women, and there did not seem to be many of them, with faces as glossily painted as masks, in tight skirts and jackets and high heels, almost as sombre as the men. A few glanced curiously at the boy in his thick jacket and threadbare trousers, but most ignored him and each other, hurrying along with abstracted expressions, making for tall new buildings with high windows and the long names of companies and banks the boy had never heard of, buildings interspersed with the gaping holes the bombs had left and which were only gradually being filled with scaffolding. When the boy saw a uniformed policeman in the distance he spun on his heel and turned down another street much the same as the one he had left. There were no shops and few pubs, and not even an underground station to give him any sort of idea where he was or where he was heading.

Eventually he came to a major crossroads, and to his surprise a sign which told him that this was the A1, a road he knew led north, which was the one direction he was utterly convinced he never wanted to take. North lay his home, which he could only vaguely remember, and The Home, which he could recall only too clearly, with all its nightmares. The A1 was a route he did not want to contemplate now or ever, and he spun suddenly on his heel and dodged into the traffic, oblivious to the approach of a car, which hit him a glancing blow, flinging him back on to the pavement from which he had blindly stepped. His head hit the edge of the kerb, and his emaciated body fell, limp and unconscious, at the feet of the passers-by like a piece of rubbish blown there by the wind. One of the apples he had stolen rolled away to be crushed to pulp by a bus.

FOUR

The only phone in the house where Kate was staying with her friends was tucked away in a dark corner under the stairs in the musty ground floor hallway, an old push-button affair that the landlord had not bothered to update. There was no chance of anyone in the top flat hearing it if it rang, and calls were often missed if no one on the lower floors was at home, or if they did not feel like climbing the three flights of ill-lit stairs, choosing to leave the receiver dangling while a voice at the other end begged impotently for help. That evening, though, one of their neighbours had made the effort and Kate found herself to her surprise suddenly linked to a familiar voice she had not heard for months.

'How did you get this number?' was all she could think of to say to Dave Donovan, the boyfriend who had marched out of her life, all tight jeans and leather jacket and attitude, apparently without a backward glance or a trace of regret for fumbling his way to her virginity with vague promises of marriage, before taking off to seek his fortune with his band in the south.

'From your mam, of course,' Dave said, as if tracking her down was the most normal thing in the world after such a long silence. 'She told me you were still taking snaps and had moved down here. How's it going, la? Have you got a job?'

'I have actually,' Kate said, hackles rising. 'Have you got a record contract yet?'

The question was obviously one Donovan did not want to answer and there was a long pause. Kate could imagine the scowl on his round, freckled face beneath unruly carrot-coloured hair.

'Would you take some snaps of the Ants?' Donovan asked eventually. 'We need some to put around the record companies and promoters.'

Kate laughed at the sheer cheek of it. 'I'm sure you do, but can you afford me?' she asked. She had no idea how much the agency charged for publicity shots but she guessed it was more than the band could pay if they still lacked a recording contract. And in any case she remembered now just why she had been happy enough to see Dave Donovan walk away. His plans for his unexceptional group of musicians were always put ahead of her own modest ambitions. If he wanted 'snaps', she thought, he could use his own Box Brownie and whistle for anything more classy.

'Dunno,' Donovan said. 'You wouldn't charge me, would you?'

'Ha,' Kate said dismissively. 'Haven't you got a manager to organize this stuff for you? John Lennon's never looked back since he signed up with that feller from the record shop in Whitechapel. Taking pictures costs money, you know.'

'They've got another record out,' Donovan said gloomily. 'That's the second now, and going up the hit parade. Could be number one at this rate.'

'They're good, though, you know that?' Kate said. 'Different. Not just another variation on the Shadows. You know how the girls at home were wild for them. I was surprised hardly anyone had heard of them when I got down here. I used to take pictures of them at the Cavern, you know, when they used to play at lunchtimes. We used to take our dinner in from college and they'd be eating sandwiches too, up on the stage between songs. It was like some crazy musical picnic. And it was so hot. I used to go back to class soaking wet. Didn't you come a few times?'

'I can't remember,' Donovan said, and Kate could hear the sulkiness in his voice, no doubt because his group had a distinct sound and look of the Shadows, the end of the last decade's big thing.

'I had a trip up last week but I didn't have time to go to the Cavern. Your pictures'll be worth something if they really make it big, la,' Donovan said at last, grudgingly. 'I wonder if Brian Epstein would take us on. I should have thought of that while I was back home. You're right, he's done great for the Beatles.'

'All except Pete Best,' Kate said. 'You wouldn't want anyone booted out the way he was, would you? And from what I heard, Brian Epstein was up to his neck in that.'

'They're better off with Ringo,' Donovan said.

'Not many of Pete's fans would agree with that,' Kate said. 'I heard George Harrison just didn't get on with him, but he was popular with a lot of the girls I knew. Maybe that's why some of the others didn't like him.'

'Flipping hysterical, some of them girls,' Donovan said.

'You wouldn't object if it was you they were getting hysterical about,' Kate said, with no sympathy in her voice. 'What are you doing for money anyway if you're not doing so well with the band?'

'I've got a job in a bar, Stevo and Miffy are working in some warehouse near King's Cross. To be honest, I reckon we'll have to go back up north if we don't get a break soon. It's too expensive down here. We're paying three quid a week for a crummy place in Archway. Each.'

'Archway?' Kate asked.

'Somewhere on the Northern Line,' Donovan said. 'You rattle up through Camden and Kentish Town. You don't want to know about it. It's not nice.'

'I've got to find somewhere myself,' Kate said. 'I'm sleeping on Marie and Tess's settee at the moment.'

'Where's that?'

'Notting Hill,' Kate said.

'That's all right. It's quite pretty down there, trees and parks and things. A bit of life. Archway's a dump.'

'No, it's not all right,' Kate said vehemently. 'It's all right up by the underground station but not where I am. The house we're in feels as if it might fall down any time. It's like Toxteth, but with even more black people.'

'They had those riots there, Teddy boys and Jamaicans or something, didn't they?' Donovan said thoughtfully. 'But there should be some good music around down there. P'raps I'll come and see you girls some time, take you to a club maybe? Would that suit?'

'Not really, Dave,' Kate said. 'I think I've been to all the clubs I want to go to with you. But there is one thing. Have you seen Tom at all? My mum's desperate because she hasn't heard from him for months and I wondered if anyone from home had bumped into him.'

'I'll ask around,' Donovan said. 'He'll be working in the rag trade somewhere. You know Tom, always the latest gear – winkle-pickers before the winkles had washed up at New Brighton. I'll ask Miffy. He's always mooching around Oxford Street and Soho. He's got no money to spend but he hangs around with people who have.'

'If you do hear anything, give me a ring,' Kate said, grateful for extra pairs of eyes. 'You can get me at work. This phone's useless. It never gets answered half the time.' She gave him the agency's number, hoping Ken would have no objection to private calls coming into the office. 'I really need to find him,' she said quietly, reluctant to beg but knowing she would have to grow a thick skin if she was to continue her search.

'I'll put the word out,' Donovan said. 'Scousers stand out around here like Mancs at the Pier Head. They look at you as if you've dropped in from the moon. Someone may have bumped into Tom. Don't worry, la, Dave's on the case. And I'm sure you'll think that's worth a few snaps, won't you? See you later.'

'In a while,' Kate said numbly, knowing how easily she had fallen into Donovan's trap. Maybe it would be a small price to pay, if he or his friends really traced Tom on the Liverpool grapevine which she was sure must exist in this fragmented city which seemed to suck people in from all over the world, but she did not have high hopes. Knowing what she knew, she guessed Tom was lying low, quite determined not to be found. It would need more than the dubious detective skills of the Mersey mafia to track him down.

Detective Sergeant Harry Barnard sat in a corner of the lounge bar of the George on Dean Street toying with a double Scotch and a dried up ham sandwich and feeling considerably disgruntled. He had spent the morning trudging round the pubs of Soho as one by one they had opened their doors to let the chilly air clear the fug of cigarette smoke and alcohol fumes from the night before. In his breast pocket was a photograph of Jonathon Mason which the police had found in the dead man's flat, one of a number of glossy black and white publicity shots showing a good-looking young man with floppy fair hair unfashionably long, and the stamp of a theatrical agency stamped on the back.

Strictly speaking he was stepping beyond his brief, but the more he was thwarted the more he was determined to pin down some information on the dead man which DCI Venables had so far failed to elicit from anyone else after five days of trying. One of the advantages of swapping Ted Venables for Keith Jackson as a boss was that Jackson left his detectives much to their own devices. So long as a reasonable number of charges made the books, and everyone knew he was especially keen on gross indecency, he left the stew of Soho and his detectives to bubble undisturbed.

Barnard had no difficulty following up Venables' line of inquiry as well as his other cases. Mason was on the books of a theatrical agency, which had taken the photographs, and had told Venables that they had represented him for six months and had a record of auditions he had attended and one small non-speaking role he had taken in a comedy at Wyndham's which had proved so unfunny that it had folded ten days after it opened. But the only address the agency had for Mason was the flat where he had been found dead, and they knew absolutely nothing about his origins or background. He had walked in off the street one day, claiming some acting experience at school and at Cambridge, and had been put on the books as a result. The photograph had already been sent to the Cambridge police with a request to show it to the colleges to see if any firmer identification could be made that way, but Venables obviously did not have high hopes of a result from the ancient seat of learning.

'D'you know how many bloody colleges there are in Cambridge?' he had asked Barnard, stubbing out his cigarette viciously in the overflowing ashtray on his desk and lighting another after flicking through the sheaf of photographs. 'What do they all do there, for God's sake? If they send a DC round all of them it'll take him a week, at least. And that's if they can be bloody bothered.'

'That's not a face they'll forget, though, is it?' Barnard said, glancing again at the smoothly handsome features and surprisingly dark eyes and long lashes under the softly falling fair hair. 'He must have had every nancy-boy in the place panting for a bit. You know what these men's colleges are like and he's the original pretty boy. Must keep the vice squad up there busy.'

'I shouldn't think they bother,' Venables had said. 'They lock the college gates at night, don't they? That must keep it off the streets.'

'But there are no college walls to hide behind round here,' Barnard said.

'His picture's going in the *Standard* and the *News* this afternoon. Someone'll recognize him.'

Someone might, Barnard pondered as he peered thoughtfully at the shrivelled ham in his sandwich before pushing it away. But in the circumstances whoever did recognize Mason might not be someone who would want to rush to their local nick to identify themselves as a friend of the dead man. There were some kinds of friendship which could land you in gaol. He had wasted more hours than he cared to count in his early days with Vice lurking in men's public lavatories, at then mere Inspector Jackson's behest, waiting for someone to make a pass at him and sometimes making the pass himself. He ended up feeling sorry for the poor sods, he recalled, rather than wanting to haul them to the nick full of righteous indignation and with the law on his side. But he knew that was not a sentiment which was widely shared in the Job and he kept it, and his personal reasons for feeling that way, strictly to himself.

'I'll keep asking around,' Barnard had said to Venables, helping himself to one of the photographs. 'If he was known on the street, I'll suss him out.'

But on the day that had not proved so easy, he thought, as he relented and took an unenthusiastic bite of his sandwich, wondering how much longer Ray Robertson, the man he had arranged to meet at the George, would be. His first ports of call had been the known haunts of homosexual men, the pubs which would fill up later in the day with a wholly male clientele, hot, sweaty, posing and on edge. Every now and again, Keith Jackson in person, and his officers, raided them and hauled off any couples who were engaged in overt sexual activity, usually in the lavatories, but most of the time they left them alone, preferring to tolerate that kind of activity in one or two places they knew about and leave the rest of the warren of narrow streets to the heterosexual trade which flourished in the pubs and clubs, brothels and clip joints and porn shops from which most of the squad made a comfortable second income.

But neither landlords nor barmen in the 'queer' pubs had recognized the photograph Barnard had waved under their noses, and the handful of customers who glanced anxiously at each other when the DS walked in had been similarly unhelpful.

'Lovely boy, though, isn't he?' one of the more confident young men had commented enthusiastically, and had looked crestfallen only when Barnard told him in explicit detail how Mason had died.

'You want to watch yourselves,' Barnard had advised. 'We may have a psycho out there looking for your sort.'

'I don't know what you mean, officer,' the young man came back quickly, with a brave attempt at looking offended, and not for the first time Barnard wondered whether queers ended up in the theatre because they had so much early practice at dissembling, or whether they chose the profession because they wanted to hone the skills they needed to succeed in a life of permanent subterfuge and pretence.

He finished his sandwich and went to the bar for a refill, and as he made his way back to his table Ray Robertson himself walked through the door, followed closely by two burly men in dark trench-coats and a much smaller man Barnard was much less pleased to see.

'Harry, my son,' Robertson said, striding to Barnard's table and shaking his hand enthusiastically. He moved smoothly for a very big man, the buttons of his camel overcoat straining to contain the mountain of flesh within and his chins overlapping his crisp white collar and one of the many regimental ties he favoured. When mildly challenged once on his right to sport the colours of the Brigade of Guards, East End legend had it that Robertson had landed a crushing uppercut on his questioner's chin, knocking him to the ground. 'I did my bloody National Service,' he had snarled, and no one ever asked him the question again, even more wary than they already were of a man who had gained a reputation in the boxing ring as well as the criminal courts, until an eye injury put him out of the ring for good and gave him more time and energy for his other passions, eating and building up his illegal empire.

This morning he seemed in an expansive mood, although the same could not be said for his companion, smaller, darker, and with a brooding air of menace about him which Barnard had never liked and became more wary of as the years passed. Georgie Robertson, Ray's younger brother, was becoming a serious threat, Barnard thought, violent, unpredictable and given to sudden outbursts of rage which verged on the manic. He had no doubt that Georgie was heading eventually for a long jail sentence, and just hoped that he did not turn out to be the one to arrest him. Whatever reservations Ray himself had about his little brother, Barnard guessed that he would protect him to the end.

Ray eased his bulk on to the bench beside Barnard and gave the sergeant's thigh a hefty pat while his brother took the seat across the table. The two heavies made their way to the bar and brought back double Scotches for all three of the seated men.

'How's it going, my little cock sparrer?' Ray asked. 'Long time no see.'

'Fine,' Barnard said, taking no offence from the man who for a while, as a disoriented evacuee during the war, he had come to regard pretty much as an older brother. Barnard and the two Robertson boys had found themselves transported overnight from the tightly packed streets of Bethnal Green to a village in Hertfordshire where the three of them clung together in the tiny school, the only outsiders amongst country boys who regarded anyone from further away than St Albans as an alien species. These incomers, the locals decided on first sight of their dark hair and pale city skin amongst clans of weather-beaten blonds, must be gypsies, and their lives were made a misery accordingly. Ray had been handy with his fists even as an eleven year old, and he was prepared to use them

not just on his own account but to protect his brother and
Harry Barnard as well. The local lads quickly learned the hard
way to leave the evacuees alone.

Ray glanced at the remnants of Barnard's sandwich. 'Any
cop?' he asked.

'Lousy,' Barnard said.

'Yeah, well, I've got a table booked at one of my clubs,'
Robertson said. 'So what can I do for you, Harry? You know
I'm always willing to help an old mate.'

Barnard showed him the photograph of Jonathon Mason,
and explained how he had been found.

'Yeah, I heard there'd been some unpleasantness. A knife,
was it?'

Barnard nodded. 'We can't get any information on where
he came from, who he was living with, friends, contacts. He'd
been in his flat six months, went to Cambridge University
apparently, but before that it's a complete blank. No background, no family we can trace, nothing. And I've not found
anyone in Soho who seems to know him.'

Nancy-boy, was he?' Robertson asked, curling his lip.

'Bloody perverts,' his brother muttered from opposite.

'Actor,' Barnard said.

'Bloody perverts,' Georgie said again.

'That's as may be,' Barnard said mildly. 'But we don't want
throats cut on our manor, do we? Gets the place a bad name.'

'Messy way of carrying on. I don't know anything about
it, but I'll put the word out,' Ray said, draining his Scotch in
one. 'But if it's a knife man you're looking for, I'd guess the
Maltese, wouldn't you? You could do worse than ask the
Catholic priests up at St Aidans. They hear all sorts, they do.'

'But won't tell,' Barnard said.

'Don't you believe it,' Georgie said unexpectedly. 'They'll
tell if you ask them the right way.' And he offered Barnard
the teeth-baring rictus which passed for a smile with him. A
flash of irritation crossed his older brother's features before
he too smiled, patted his belly and buttoned up his camel coat.

'Nice to see you, Harry, but I'm famished,' he said. 'I'll be
in touch if I hear anything.' He got to his feet and allowed
his two bodyguards to push tables and chairs out of his way

to ease his lumbering passage. 'I'm having a little party at the Delilah on Friday night, charity do. I'll drop a couple of tickets in at the nick if you'd like to come. Formal togs, you know the score. Bring a lady friend. Should be a good night. Government minister and his latest paramour, Christine, I think she's called, and some theatre people. They might know your dead actor, a lot of them like it up the backside.' Both Robertson brothers laughed loudly and Barnard could see a couple of fellow customers looking anxiously towards the door, not sure whether to stay or attract attention to themselves by leaving. As the Robertsons moved off they decided to stay, but gulped down their pints nervously.

Barnard sat in his seat for a while longer until the disturbed air left behind by the departing quartet had calmed and the barman had stopped staring uncertainly in his direction. The Robertsons had been part of his life for so long that he had almost ceased to see the effect they had on others. But at the back of his mind he recognized Georgie's increasing instability and he reckoned Ray did too. Ray's empire was large and growing larger, spreading from the East End into Soho and even the West End, and becoming ever more profitable. But he knew that Ray's *modus operandi* was to use the threat of violence rather than actual violence to get what he wanted. The odd bar or club might get trashed, but generally no one was physically hurt as protection debts were enforced. But Georgie increasingly looked and sounded like a loose cannon becoming more unscrewed by the day. Barnard wondered how and when he might explode.

FIVE

The doctor and the ward sister, magisterial in her starched cap and white apron, gazed at the empty bed in some perplexity and not a little annoyance, every inch of the sister silently saying that things like this did not happen on her ward where grown men were treated like children and expected to behave as such. The doctor, young and uncertain, turned to the elderly man in the next bed, sitting up against his pillows with his heavily bandaged arm resting across his chest and a dazed look in his eyes.

'Did you see where the young lad went?' the doctor asked.

The patient shook his head. 'Gone for a widdle, I expect,' he muttered. 'These bottle things are a palaver and no mistake.'

The sister pursed her lips and scowled. 'He wasn't fit enough for that,' she said sharply, before turning back to the doctor. 'We'd hardly got a word out of him since he regained consciousness and came on to the ward, Doctor. If he stirred at all it was only to pull the blankets over his head. It's only today I've made him sit up and eat something. He's certainly not been out of his bed. It's all here in his notes.' She took the chart from the bottom of the bed and waved it under the doctor's nose. 'See? He was checked just after he had his midday meal. Still confused, the nurse noted. Temperature and blood pressure normal.'

'You'd better inform the porters, Sister,' the doctor said. 'If he's wandered off and collapsed somewhere in the hospital we need to find him quickly. He was severely concussed when he was brought in. You'd better get a search going.'

'Yes, Doctor, of course,' the ward sister said, smothering her anger with some difficulty. Patients didn't simply disappear off her ward. It was an outrage and she would make sure the boy understood that when she laid her hands on him again, the scruffy little urchin.

'Did you ever get a name for him?'

'No, we didn't,' she snapped. 'Whenever we asked him his name he shook his head or said he couldn't remember. I can't say I believed him but what can you do? And when we informed the police his description didn't seem to fit with anyone reported missing. A constable came in to have a word with him yesterday but he got no more joy than we did. Either he genuinely couldn't remember or he didn't want to.'

'Amnesia's not uncommon after a head injury,' the doctor said mildly. 'But I'm much more worried that he's lying in a coma somewhere. He can't have left the hospital dressed just in a hospital gown.'

'His clothes, such as they were, are in my office in a bag, just as they came up from Casualty,' the sister said. 'Pretty filthy and smelly. Nothing looked as if it had been washed for weeks. I was wondering whether to send them to the hospital laundry myself. He can't put them on again the way they are and there's no sign of a family to bring clean ones in.'

'Makes you think he must be some sort of runaway,' the doctor said. 'Poor kid.'

The sister pursed her lips again at that but did not argue. 'I'll get a search going,' she said. 'Though that won't be quick in this old place. You could conceal an army down in the basement alone, and every floor's got its nooks and crannies.'

The doctor shook his head in exasperation. 'He can't have got that far, can he?'

'Well, I wouldn't have said he could have got to the end of the ward without help, Doctor, but clearly he did. So I just don't know.'

A thought struck her and her mouth turned dry. 'Just a minute,' she said, and she walked quickly back to her office and closed the door. Just as she had suddenly suspected, her cape had gone, and when she turned round to look she realized that her fur-lined boots had gone with it and a spare cap that had been on the windowsill ready to go to the laundry the next day.

'The little beggar,' she said under her breath and wondered how she was going to explain this to Matron.

Half a mile away the slightly bizarre figure of a young nurse, her cape wrapped tightly around her against the biting north wind, clutching her white cap as it threatened to blow off, and wearing heavy boots seemingly too large for her, clomped up Farringdon Road towards the bomb sites alongside the Circle Line. The boy inside the disguise fought off the dizziness which threatened to overcome him, determined to make it back to his hiding place on the embankment in spite of the cuts and bruises he had sustained in the accident. He had lain in his hospital bed for two days, much more conscious than he allowed the ward staff to realize, watching closely what was going on around him. He had said little or nothing, especially to the red-faced young copper who had come in to talk to him, but he had soon noticed that the sister, whose small office was at the end of the ward, arrived in the morning in a thick navy cape and boots but appeared soon afterwards on the ward in her starched uniform and black flat-heeled shoes. Somewhere, he realized, the outdoor clothes were stowed away for the day. And somehow, if he wanted to get away, he would have to find them.

In the end it had proved remarkably easy. When his tray of food was taken away after the midday meal, he watched as several of the nurses, including the ward sister, went through the double doors evidently for their own meal. They would not be back, he reckoned, for some time. Glancing at his neighbours, both elderly and falling into a heavy doze after eating in the overheated ward, he had slid out of bed, slipped unnoticed into the sister's office and taken her cape down off the hook behind the door. The boots were under the desk and a spare starched cap, which neatly covered the bandage on his head, was on the windowsill. He had not been challenged on his way out of the hospital into the chilly street outside. He had, he reckoned, at least half an hour before the sister came back and noticed that her clothes had gone, and he had gone with them.

Glancing round cautiously as he came to the broken section

of fence leading down to the railway, he waited until he reckoned that most passers-by on this still largely ruined section of Farringdon Road had their backs to him before pulling back the loose boards and slipping through. He pulled off the nurse's cap and flung it away and then stumbled and slid the rest of the way to his hiding place, where he was relieved to see Hamish slumped under a pile of blankets with a bottle in his hand. The older man looked up blearily, pushing his matted grey hair out of his eyes.

'Wha' happened to ye?' he asked. 'Ye look like a lassie in that thing. An' wha' did ye do to your head?' He handed his bottle to the boy. 'Have a wee dram,' he said. 'Ye look terrible.'

The Scot scrambled to his feet and fetched the boy's blankets from their hiding place and wrapped them round the shivering teenager with surprising gentleness as he choked on the whisky.

'Will ye no' tell me what's going on?' Hamish asked. 'Ye've been as nervous as a kitten since that night ye came back late. And how did ye hurt your head? Hae ye been to the hospital? Is that where ye got that thing?' He fingered the thick navy cape in astonishment and pulled it aside to reveal the hospital gown underneath.

'I got hit by a car,' the boy mumbled, feeling the sip he had taken from Hamish's bottle firing his throat and sparking some semblance of normality in his head. 'I don't remember how it happened, but I didn't want to stay in the hospital. I need to get away. I need to get out of London. How'm I going to do that with no clothes and no money?'

Hamish heaved himself into a sitting position again and shivered. It had been a long, bitter winter and did not seem to be much better as spring supposedly approached. 'We can get ye some clothes from the Sally Ann,' he said. 'Money's more of a problem. Can ye no' earn a wee bit? I thought that's what ye'd been doing, away the nights.' He glanced away. The boy had never told him what he did 'the nights' but he clearly had a good idea.

'I can't do that any more,' the boy said. 'I need to get out of London.'

'Aye, well, we'll hae to think about that,' Hamish said. 'Stay here, and I'll go down the road and see what I can find ye to wear. That'll be a start. What do ye say?'

The boy nodded. He was trembling and his head had begun to throb. 'It'll be a start,' he said, fighting down the panic which threatened to overwhelm him as Hamish got to his feet and wrapped his own blankets around the boy's skinny shoulders. He curled into a ball, still shivering and trying to keep warm as he watched the old man scramble up the steep slope to the road and disappear through the fence. One way or another his short life had been filled with fear but the still vivid recollection of the blood-spattered flat he had stumbled into had added a new dimension. Somehow he had to escape.

'What are all these?' Ken Fellows asked when Kate dropped several sheets of contact prints on to his desk.

'I was just getting a bit bored filing prints all day,' she said airily. 'I thought I'd bring you some more of the stuff I took at home, and a few more I've been taking here, on the street. Soho's full of surprises, isn't it?'

Fellows glanced at her offerings without much interest. 'What are you doing wandering round the streets at night?' he asked. 'It's not a very safe area for a girl on her own.'

'Oh, I've not been on my own,' she said. 'I've had a friend with me. Actually, I'm looking for my brother. We've lost contact but he's supposed to be working round here and I'm sure he'll be in a pub at night.'

'There's pubs and pubs around here,' Fellows said, looking again at her prints without enthusiasm. 'You want to be careful.' He pulled out a set of prints she had taken in Liverpool of Dave Donovan's band.

'D'you really think these Mersey bands are the next big thing?' he asked sceptically. 'Aren't they just a flash in the pan?'

'I'm not sure about this band,' she said cautiously. 'Though I do know they want some proper publicity pictures taken. They've had a new bass player since I took these. But I'm sure some of the others are going to be huge – Gerry and the Pacemakers, the Beatles. I've got pictures of them I took while I was at college. Look at the crowd in these. This is the Cavern Club. It was like this wherever the Beatles went last year in the north of England. Amazing.'

'Could you get some more up-to-date ones of the bands you think will be big?' Fellows asked.

'I reckon I probably could, but it might mean going home for a few days. I knew John Lennon's girlfriend at college. I should be able to make contact again. John can be a bit tricky but Cynthia's OK.'

'Well, I'll think about it. These shots in the pubs are not bad. Someone might buy a picture feature based on those. Leave them with me, will you? And get on with the filing. Someone's got to do it.'

Kate bit back a protest and turned reluctantly back to her desk. She had been in the job nearly a week and had still not been asked to use her camera once on an official assignment. She was beginning to wonder if Ken just regarded her as a cheap office girl and the precious Voigtlander she carried every day in her bag just a bit of window-dressing. She was due to meet Marie, on her day off, at lunchtime and she determined to carry on snapping as they continued their hunt for Tom. No one took John Lennon seriously at first, she thought, and just look at him now, down here in London and with a record heading for number one in the Hit Parade. She didn't see any reason why she shouldn't make it big in her field too.

It took the two young women a few minutes to realize that the first pub they entered at lunchtime was different from many of the others where they had touted Tom's snapshot around and where Kate had taken some pictures. They barely noticed that when they went through the door almost every eye in the place turned in their direction and every eye in the place was male. Kate slipped through the crowds to the bar where a tall man dressed entirely in black seemed to be in charge. She did a double-take when she saw his single gold earring as she took out her photograph of Tom and placed it on the beer-stained bar counter.

'This is my brother,' she said. 'Have you seen him at all?'

The barman glanced at the picture and shook his head almost imperceptibly. 'Nah, I don't think so,' he said, without much sign of interest. But the man standing next to Kate also glanced at the picture, and stared at it for a long moment before giving a dramatic shrug.

'Pretty boy,' he said. 'But no, sadly, he hasn't crossed my path, darling.'

Kate became aware that if the barman's earring had seemed unusual enough to have earned him considerable baiting on the streets of Liverpool, the way this man was dressed verged on the bizarre and might have caused a riot in Anfield. He wore a green felt hat which did not entirely cover his long, golden, curly hair, earrings in both ears, a purple silk shirt, mauve tie and a suit of such garish checks in shades of brown and purple that Kate could barely restrain a laugh and, then, a faint sense of horror as she noticed a touch of artificial colour on his lips.

'Come on, Kate, let's get out of here,' Marie said suddenly, but Kate had taken a deep breath and turned to her neighbour at the bar with a brilliant smile.

'Can I take your photograph?' she asked. The barman gasped slightly but the man in the green fedora merely smiled.

'Of course you can, darling,' he said. 'Feel free.'

'Outside, if you don't mind,' the barman snapped. 'Some people like their privacy.'

'Vincent,' green hat announced, holding out his hand to Kate and then to Marie to be shaken. 'Vincent Beaufort. They all know me round here. They get upset in the pub if I rock the boat, though the truth is that deep down every one of them wishes they had the balls to be me. The only trouble is, if you don't hide what you are, some people like to give you a good thumping now and again.'

He unhitched himself from his stool and sashayed through the crowded bar and into the bustling street outside to a few ribald cheers and as they pushed through the swing doors they were greeted by strident whistles from some builders working on the other side of the road. One or two passers-by stopped in their tracks to gaze at Vincent in astonishment while a burly young man muttered 'Dirty poofter' aggressively the moment he set eyes on the girls' companion. Vincent meanwhile held his hand behind his head in an exaggerated film-star pose, with a wide smile that revealed several gold-capped teeth.

'There you are, my dears. What more do you want?'

Kate grinned and took several quick shots, with Marie watching from a distance.

'Did you mean what I think you meant when you said Tom was a pretty boy?' she asked Vincent quietly when she had finished.

'I've no idea, petal. I've never met your brother – though I wouldn't say no if I did. But he might run a mile if he saw me, like most of this lot.' He smiled beatifically and raised a regal hand in salute to the passers-by who had gathered round to watch the impromptu photo-shoot and who moved on in embarrassment in response to Beaufort's acknowledgement. 'So is that all? Can I get back to my drink now?'

'Have you any idea where I might look?' Kate asked, grabbing the violently chequered arm in panic. 'It's very important to find him.'

Kate's desperation obviously had its effect because Vincent took the photograph of Tom O'Donnell out of her hand and studied it carefully before shaking his head.

'I don't know, petal,' he said. 'Maybe he looks vaguely familiar.' He hesitated. 'There's a place called ABC Books in a little alley off Greek Street . . .'

'We've already been there,' Kate said cautiously. 'He lived near there, but he's moved out. That's the problem.'

'I'm not surprised,' Beaufort said, suddenly looking gaunt and revealing two red patches of rouge on his cheeks. 'Some boy was killed round there a few days ago. A boy called Jonathon. Him I had met, in the pub here. He caused quite a stir too. We were just talking about it. A very pretty boy. Not that the Old Bill will bust a gut looking for whoever killed him if he's one of us.' He glanced back into the pub and shrugged. 'If your brother's queer, darling, he's not been on the scene long, as far as I know. And I would know, believe me. He'd be noticed all right, looking the way he looks. I hope you find him safe and sound.' And with that he tipped his hat, spun on his heel and pushed his way back into the pub.

'Oh my,' Marie said, watching the door swing shut behind him. 'Where on earth did he spring from?'

'You know about people like that,' Kate snapped, not wanting to admit how unnerved she had been by Vincent's speculations. 'You must do. You must know about Oscar Wilde.'

'I didn't go to the art college with all the bohemians like you did,' Marie said plaintively. 'I went to a nice Catholic college with Tess where they didn't talk about things like that.'

Kate sighed. 'Well, you've seen *A Taste of Honey* at least. You remember Geoff who wasn't interested in women? If you're going to be an actress I think you'd better find out a bit more about all that. From what I hear, there's plenty of people like that in the theatre. Anyway, let's get on. I've got to be back in the office at two.'

But as they turned away, they became aware of a man watching them intently from the other side of the street and suddenly, as if on an impulse, crossing over and putting himself directly in their path.

'Hello, girls,' Detective Sergeant Harry Barnard said, giving them the benefit of his most charming smile. 'Can I have a word?'

'I don't think so,' Kate snapped, instantly irritated by the sharply dressed stranger with his confident air and calculating dark eyes. 'We're in a hurry.'

'I'm afraid I'll have to insist,' Barnard said, bringing his warrant card out of his inside jacket pocket and holding it so that Kate and Marie could read it. Kate recognized the name at once. This was the policeman Pete Marelli had told them to contact about her brother.

'I noticed you taking photographs yesterday, as it happens, with a very smart little camera,' Barnard went on smoothly. 'Thought that was unusual. Can I have a look at the photograph you just showed our flamboyant friend, Vinnie?'

Kate was tempted to refuse. She was still not sure she wanted the police involved in her hunt for Tom, but she supposed that in the end she would have to ask for their help and if it was a bit sooner than she had expected it might do no harm. She offered Barnard the enlarged snapshot which she had taken herself shortly before Tom left home.

'It's my brother. He's in London somewhere, probably working around here. He's in the fashion trade. But we've not heard from him for a while and my mam's getting anxious. I've just got a job in Soho and I'm trying to track him down.'

'I hope it's the sort of job you can tell your mother about,' Barnard said with a grin. He studied the photograph handed him of a good-looking young man, with more than a look of his sister, dark hair flopping across his forehead and a faint, enigmatic smile lighting up his face. 'And his name is?' he asked Kate.

'Tom, Tom O'Donnell,' she said, surprised at how reluctantly the words came out. 'He came down from Liverpool a year or so ago. At least we think he did. He's not kept in touch . . .'

'And in the rag trade, you said?'

'He was working in various shops back home,' Kate said. 'He really loves fashion . . .' She hesitated, catching the knowing look in Barnard's eyes, but he did not comment directly.

'Do you know where he was living?' he asked instead.

Marie and Kate exchanged an anxious glance before Kate replied. 'Someone told Marie that they thought he shared a flat off Greek Street, but when we went round there it seemed to be all locked up. So we're not sure.'

'And you wouldn't have popped into the shop downstairs and spoken to the owner?' Barnard asked, his tone suddenly changing. 'A Mr Marelli who told you to contact the police?'

Kate felt herself blush and it was Marie who jumped in to reply.

'He didn't tell us his name and anyway we didn't believe him,' she said. 'He looked at the photograph but didn't really recognize Tom. Anyway, Kate's mam didn't want Tom reported missing. She could have done that herself ages ago if she'd wanted to get involved with the bizzies at home. But she didn't.'

'Well, she doesn't have that luxury now,' Barnard said,
suddenly cold. 'We very much want to talk to your brother,
Miss O'Donnell. His flatmate has been found dead and your
brother seems to have disappeared, probably the same
evening. He has, at the very least, some explaining to do.'

'You can't think—' Kate felt her mouth dry and her heart
was thumping uncomfortably.

'We don't think anything,' Barnard said, surprised at how
sorry he felt for Kate, who had gone understandably pale,
her eyes full of tears. 'But we need to talk to your brother
urgently. It's not impossible that he himself might be in
danger. I really need to ask you some more questions at the
police station.'

Kate glanced at her watch with a sense of panic. 'Could
I come after work?' she asked. 'I'm in a new job and I'm
due back in the office. I really don't want to mess up my
chances with my new boss. He's not going to be impressed
if he knows I'm at a police station.'

Barnard's instinct was to turn her down flat but something
made him hesitate. The bloody girl had got under his skin,
he thought irritably. 'What time do you finish?' he asked.

'Five,' Kate said.

Barnard pulled out a notebook and flipped it open. 'Right,'
he said. 'Give me your details, home address, work address,
phone numbers, all that. And be here at the nick at five fifteen
on the dot. OK? And bring me that photograph of your
brother. I'll need that.'

'There's no phone in the flat where I'm staying,' she said.
'Just a payphone down in the hall but I don't know the
number.'

'Can you find it for me?'

Kate nodded and did as she was told, and took the page
on which Barnard had scribbled his own name and the address
of West End Central police station.

'Don't be late,' he said sharply, as the two young women,
both looking relieved, turned away into the crowds, heading
north.

'You're a bloody fool,' Barnard muttered to himself, though
he was pretty sure the girl would turn up. He spun on his

heel and pushed open the doors of the pub Kate and Marie had just left, shoving his way to the bar with scant regard for the crowds who stood in his way.

'Right,' he said to the barman. 'Tom O'Donnell. One of you poofs must know him and I'm going to make myself very unpopular until I find out who does.'

SIX

Detective Sergeant Harry Barnard met Kate O'Donnell in the front office of the police station and led her past the duty sergeant's desk and through a door into an interior of gloomy corridors lined with institutionally painted doors, ignoring the curious glances and a faint wolf whistle which greeted Kate's arrival.

'I've found us a nice cosy interview room,' he said, seeing the tension in her face, and hoping she would relax. He smiled slightly at the thought as he took in her slim figure and shapely legs, which had been so openly appreciated by his colleagues. A bit different from the usual women West End Central entertained, he thought, and in different circumstances he could really fancy getting Kate O'Donnell to relax very completely indeed. He knew next to nothing about Liverpool, apart from the rivalry of its two football teams, and its reputation for fierce disputes in the docks, and he wondered how far nice girls up there were prepared to go. Kate seemed very young but surprisingly self-confident for a new arrival from the sticks. Perhaps when this case was over . . . ? But perhaps not, he thought wryly, if he ended up serving up her brother to Ted Venables on a murder charge.

He held the door open and waved her into a seat on one side of the table while he took another on the opposite side. He lit a cigarette and offered Kate the packet but she shook her head.

'I don't,' she said, and watched him pull the ashtray towards himself.

'When did you last see your brother, Miss O'Donnell?' he asked.

Kate slipped off her coat before answering. The room was stuffy and airless and had a faintly unpleasant smell of sweat, cigarette smoke and disinfectant which turned her stomach.

'About two years ago,' she said quietly. 'It must have been

February, or maybe the beginning of March, when he went. I was in my second year at art college. We've had a couple of postcards from London since then, that's all, no address, nothing really at all.' She glanced away from the policeman, not wanting him to see the hurt she knew must show in her eyes.

'Tell me about him,' Barnard said. 'Is he older than you?'

'Two years older,' Kate said. 'He's twenty-five. There are four of us altogether. I'm the second and I have two younger sisters.'

'Catholics?'

'Yes,' Kate said, slightly defensively. 'Not that I bother much with religion any more. I don't think Tom did, either. He didn't go to mass, not since my father walked out on us. We've not seen my dad for about ten years.'

'Or your brother for two? Quite a family for walkouts then?'

'I suppose so,' Kate said, feeling suddenly miserable and trapped. 'I don't know much about what happened between my father and mother, but I know Tom had been unhappy at home for a while. He never talked about it, but I could tell.'

'And he worked in shops, you said?'

'Yes, he worked in various fashion shops in Liverpool – Lewis's, Bon Marché, before it joined up with John Henry Lee. He lost his job after that and went to work in a little place near St John's Market, selling cheap gear, up-to-the-minute men's stuff, Mod suits, all that. He was always into the latest thing. Loved his clothes. Spent all his pocket money on them when he was at school. Drove my mam mad.'

Barnard smiled faintly and straightened his Liberty tie. There was something in the description that he could identify with. 'So we're looking for a young man in the latest trend, then. Did you bring his picture?'

Reluctantly Kate took the snapshot of Tom out of her handbag and handed it to Barnard. 'It's the only one I've got down here,' she said.

'You can have it back,' Barnard said. 'I'll get our people to make a copy of it.'

'You won't—'

'Won't what?' Barnard snapped. 'Use it to help find him?

Of course we will. This is a murder inquiry.'

'Did he live in that flat, then? The one over the shop?'

'With Jonathan Mason, the dead man? Yes, as far as we can tell, he did. Did you know Mason? Or ever hear his name mentioned?'

Kate paled and shook her head, gripping the edge of the table tightly for a moment. 'No, never,' she said. 'If he met him in London, I wouldn't have, would I? I told you, we've barely heard a word from him since he went.' She took a deep breath. 'Tom couldn't kill anybody,' she said. 'He's a gentle person. My mam used to have to make him stand up for himself at school. He never got into fights. Not like my da – he was always coming back from the pub with black eyes and cuts and bruises. I'm more like him. My mam used to say I should have been the boy and Tom the girl.'

Barnard took a sharp breath. She really didn't know, he thought. But he was going to have to tell her. 'Did you realize that your brother was . . .' He hesitated, wondering which word would shock her least. If possible, he wanted this girl on his side in spite of the difficult position she found herself in. 'Not quite normal?'

'You mean homosexual?' Kate came back fiercely. 'It's not something we talked about at home, if that's what you mean. In fact, I never heard my parents talk about sex at all. What I knew I learned at college, when I got away from the nuns at school.' She smiled slightly at the memory and Barnard realized again just how very attractive she was. But the smile was just a flash of sunlight and the clouds descended quickly again. 'Yes, I did wonder about that, anyway,' she said quietly. 'I had an idea, but I never found the courage to ask him straight out. People explain these things to you, but I never really understood it, deep down.'

'We think he and the dead man were lovers,' Barnard said carefully. 'It's illegal, of course, but it goes on.'

'But Tom wasn't like that man Marie and I talked to this morning, Vincent, the man in the purple checked suit. Tom liked his clothes but he wasn't weird, like that.'

'They say with most of them, you can't tell,' Barnard said. 'Anyone can be queer, in any job, even a copper, though that sounds a bit unlikely to me.'

'I suppose if they think they could go to prison, they hide it,' Kate said quietly.

'You say your brother never got into fights? If that's the case, he must have hidden his tastes quite well. A lot of normal blokes would have given him a good thumping if they'd guessed.'

'He did get beaten up once. He'd been to Anfield to watch Liverpool and he said he got set on by supporters from the other team. I can't remember who it was now. Manchester United probably. There's no love lost there. But I suppose there could have been some other reason, apart from the football, I mean.'

'Do you know if Tom had friends in London when he came down here?'

'We never really knew where he'd gone. We just guessed it must be London because he used to say how much he'd like to work in one of the big shops in Oxford Street. It was his ambition, like all the boys in the bands want to come down here to make their name now. But I never heard Tom mention anyone he knew in London.'

'But he could have known someone in the music business maybe?' Barnard persisted. 'Someone else who's come down from Liverpool, just like you and your brother?'

'I suppose so,' Kate said doubtfully. 'Though I never heard him mention anyone in a band. But every other lad was playing in some group or other the last few years, so it's quite possible some of his mates did.'

'So we need to talk to his mates in Liverpool, see what they can remember? See if they might have any idea where he could have gone? Or even if he's been in touch.'

Kate nodded gloomily. 'I suppose so. We asked around when he went but no one seemed to know anything. And what about the family? Will you have to talk to my mam?'

'We already have,' Barnard said. 'We asked the Liverpool police to call round as soon as you told us who our missing flatmate was. Then they'll chase up any friends they can trace.'

Kate felt sick and numb. She should have expected that, she thought, but she still could not get her head round the idea of Tom on the run, living hand to mouth maybe, afraid of his own shadow. In spite of being the younger, she had always tended to look out for Tom, protect him, even at times from their father, whose explosive temper had frightened all his children.

She looked at the man on the other side of the table, well-dressed, good-looking but with a bleakness in his eyes which she supposed came with the job, seeking a hint of sympathy which was not there. Her mouth felt dry, the room was airless and she desperately wanted to leave, but she needed the answer to one last question.

'Do you really suspect him of killing this man in the flat? What's his name?'

'Jonathon Mason,' Barnard said.

'How . . . ? How did he die?'

'His throat was cut,' Barnard said bluntly, knowing the answer would shake her.

Kate went pale and swallowed hard. 'Tom couldn't have done that,' she whispered.

'In my experience, people involved in sex can do pretty well anything,' Barnard said flatly, leaving no space for contradiction.

Kate sighed. 'I don't see how I can help you,' she said, struggling to hold back tears.

'You can't, unless he gets in touch,' Barnard said. 'If he does, I want to know about it. No excuses, no family loyalty, no messing me about at all. I want you to phone me. And if I hear nothing from you, believe me, I'll be in touch with you myself. If he knows you're in London, you're the obvious person he'll get in contact with. Do you understand, Miss O'Donnell?'

'Yes,' Kate said. 'I understand.' But she knew with absolute certainty that if Tom got in touch, she would do no such thing.

Hamish and the boy walked slowly up Farringdon Road, turned left into Rosebery Avenue and then, just beyond the sorting office, alive with postmen and delivery vans, dodged into a warren of derelict bombed sites and the vestiges of former streets until they came out into Gray's Inn Road.

'Are ye sure ye know where ye're going?' Hamish asked

anxiously as he stood on the edge of the pavement opposite a pub, waiting for a gap in the traffic speeding towards King's Cross.

'There's flats over there.' The boy waved vaguely towards Bloomsbury.

'Big houses,' Hamish said. 'I ken them.'

'Flats,' the boy said, his face obstinate. 'I know where he lives.'

They dodged through the traffic as the boy led the way north again and then into side streets lined with nineteenth century terraces, grey and decrepit in the bright morning sunshine. They could see the gothic brick bulk of St Pancras now at the end of the grid of streets, like some dilapidated medieval castle looming over the neighbourhood. Still within sight of the station, the boy stopped at the doors of a neglected-looking six-storey mansion block, its brickwork chipped and its windows grubby.

'This is it,' he said. 'I'll be all right now.' He glanced down at himself with some satisfaction. 'Good old Sally Ann,' he said. He ran his hand down the green duffel coat he was wearing over a warm wool shirt and dark slacks which were only slightly too big – nothing that could not be disguised by turning over the waistband to stop them flapping too obviously round his ankles, and the nurse's warm boots he had insisted on keeping. His new outfit was topped off with a tweed cap which covered the dressing he still wore on his head.

'He won't know me in this clobber.' *And nor will anyone else*, he thought, with some satisfaction. In the end he had given Hamish a sketchy version of the murder scene he had stumbled into, but had not admitted that his accident had been the result of panic at the thought of being recognized in the street. His fear now was that the old Scot would abandon him if he thought he was at risk of violence. Best, he thought, to keep that to himself.

'I picked the smallest things I could find,' Hamish said. 'I told them you'd just come out of hospital, which was true enough.' He was wearing a thick duffle coat himself, which he had also acquired that morning, and he had tucked his matted grey beard and hair into the collar, but his boots were split where the soles joined the uppers, revealing a couple of filthy toenails like claws on his left foot. While the boy, in his new clothes, could pass for normal, in spite of his thin features and the fear in his eyes, Hamish had failed to disguise what he was.

The boy looked at him warily. 'You can't come up with me,' he said.

'Aye, I know that, laddie,' Hamish said, but still seemed reluctant to turn away. 'I wish . . .' He did not finish the sentence.

'It's all right,' the boy said. 'This bloke's all right. He won't hurt me.'

'And he'll give ye money?'

'He will.'

'Aye, well, if ye say so. I'll wait for ye over there.' Hamish waved at a small patch of grass with a couple of wooden benches overshadowed by the tall brick blocks all round. 'Naebody'll bother me there.'

The boy watched as his friend crossed the street, settled himself on a bench and pulled a bottle from his pocket. Then he turned and walked up the steps to the heavy doors which swung open with a push to let him in and made his way up the stairs with more confidence than he felt.

Barnard leaned back lazily in his chair and smiled at the man across the beer-stained table between them. But there was no warmth in the smile, more the anticipation of a shark circling in murky water knowing that sooner or later a swimmer's leg would conveniently appear above his head. The man opposite wriggled uncomfortably and took a sip of his half pint. Barnard's companion was small and dark-haired, with a thin, almost wizened face, calculating eyes and an ingratiating smile which he was offering Barnard now, between sips.

'I haven't heard a whisper, Mr Barnard, and that's the truth.'

But Barnard did not believe him. 'Come on, Joe. You know that's not good enough. We've known each other a long time, haven't we? You've done very well out of it, too. You could have been deported after that last little episode and you got away with six months. But I need something back. You must have heard something.'

Joseph Inglott shrugged helplessly. 'Nothing,' he said.

'What I don't understand is why?' Barnard said, barely able to contain his frustration. 'Here's a couple of queer boys, an actor and some sort of a minor player in the rag trade, both apparently working, quite legit, no police records, low profile, and some beggar cuts one boy's throat and the other's disappeared. Maybe he did it, or maybe he's lying dead somewhere too, with his throat cut, for all I know. And no one, and I mean no one, not a soul, has heard a whisper.'

'The boy who ran away cut his friend's throat,' Inglott said. 'Is obvious. It happens all the time with these queer boys.'

'Sure, it happens,' Barnard said. 'After a quarrel, a lover's tiff, jealousy, all that, but there was no sign of that. The place was neat and tidy, no sign of a fight, no jealous frenzy, just a dead body and a lot of blood. Nothing smashed, nothing broken, except the table he fell against. It doesn't look right. There's more to it. Must be.'

'The Man has nothing to do with queer boys,' Inglott said. 'You know that.'

Barnard nodded. It was true that the man Inglott was referring to, another Maltese, Frankie Falzon, who controlled much of the prostitution and pornography in Soho, had apparently steered well clear of the homosexual scene, perhaps from religious scruple, as hangers-on like Joe Inglott piously claimed. Barnard thought it more likely it was simply because Falzon had not yet succeeded in ousting someone else who was controlling that segment of the business in Soho.

Whoever ran the trade, homosexual pornography was increasingly getting on to the streets and Barnard was sure that not all of it was any longer being smuggled in from abroad. Some of what he had seen recently had a distinctly home-grown look. And while his bosses tolerated, and in many cases connived with, most of what went on in Soho, the head of the Vice Squad, Keith Jackson, disliked queer porn with a particularly visceral hatred. Jackson wanted to stamp out the trade in what he called 'queer filth'. It was a vain hope, Barnard thought, but he was wise enough not to share that view at the nick.

He sighed regretfully in the face of Joseph Inglott's ingratiating look. 'It's a pity, Joe,' he said. 'And you're the poorer for it. I'm not going to shell out when you've got nothing to offer.'

Inglott nodded enthusiastically. 'Of course not, Mr Barnard,' he said. 'I wouldn't expect—'

'And I may not be able to hold my bosses off on that other matter for much longer. You and I both know you were involved in smashing up the coffee bar on Wardour Street. The manager's still in hospital.'

Inglott's face paled and he licked his dry lips but he did not deny the charge. 'I'll keep my ears open, Mr Barnard,' he said. 'I'll ask around. I promise I'll do my best for you.'

Barnard got to his feet lazily and put a hand on Inglott's bony shoulder as he squeezed past him, with a lot more pressure than was strictly necessary. Inglott winced.

'I'm sure you will, Joseph, I'm sure you will. So let's not be strangers, eh? I'll hear from you soon?'

'You can bank on it,' Inglott said in a whisper, missing entirely Barnard's satisfied smile as he made his way out of the bar. Inglott remained slumped over his half-finished half pint, until the tremor in his hands subsided sufficiently to let him pick it up again. He was a very small fish in a very large and dirty pool and he was beginning to think, in the light of events he had heard whispered and that the police had not even come across yet, that he might be better off in jail.

Barnard continued his slow perambulation around his manor, feeling frustrated by his lack of progress. It was a matter of pride that if Venables asked for his help, he could come up with something more than his former boss could uncover for himself. Inglott was just one of a stable of informants whose palms he greased regularly for information, or whose own misdemeanours he downplayed or ignored in the interests of keeping the facts flowing. He wondered if it was his imagination or whether his contacts were really thin on the ground this morning.

Coming full circle he found himself back in Greek Street outside the queer pub where he found Vincent Beaufort staggering out of the door, looking very much the worse for wear in spite of the relatively early hour. Barnard took Beaufort's elbow and drew him into a doorway with six separate doorbells, each labelled with a separate woman's first name.

'Vinnie, you old poofter,' Barnard said, leaning heavily against him to thwart his feeble arm-flapping attempts to move away. 'I don't think you lot are being entirely open and honest about this boy who got his throat cut. What do you think?'

'I don't know what you mean,' Beaufort said, subsiding slightly and leaning against the door, which creaked under his weight.

'Oh, I think you do,' Barnard insisted. 'Are you telling me those two lads never came down here to the pub? That can't be right, can it?'

'Not when I was in here,' Beaufort said. 'Believe me, dear, I'd have noticed those two through the wrong end of a telescope.'

'You're a dirty old queen, Vincent. But I'll let you off if you do me a favour. There's no point me or those two girls asking questions in there. You know as well as I do that all we'll hit on is a bloody brick wall and a cascade of that bloody secret lingo you talk. So I want you to ask the questions for me. All right? I'll give you a couple of days and then you call me at the nick. That's fair enough, isn't it? A good deal for a twisted old pervert like you?'

Beaufort slumped against the door. 'And if I don't, or can't?' he whispered, although he knew the answer from long experience.

'Then you'll all be getting a visit from DCI Jackson's heavy brigade, and I can't guarantee what'll happen to any of you girls after that, can I?' Barnard gave Beaufort a grimace which might pass for a smile in a poor light, and took his weight off the other man's shoulder. 'See what you can do,' he said and spun away to make his way towards Soho Square and fresher air. He fancied a pint himself but he made a point of not drinking in the crowded pubs of Soho itself. He reckoned you never knew what undesirables you might bump into.

*   *   *

'What do you think of the new clobber, la?' Dave Donovan asked Kate O'Donnell, spinning on his axis, with his guitar at arm's length. 'Dig this? Cool or what?'

The last time Kate had seen the band they had been wearing tight black jeans and leather jackets so the shiny new suits in a slightly electric blue came as something of a shock.

'OK, I suppose,' she said non-committally. 'But won't they say you're copying the Beatles?'

'Nah,' Donovan said. 'They don't make the fashion, do they, la? This is the latest gear, a bit Mod, you know? Not so rock and roll? But we really need some good pictures. Everything we've got is so Fifties now, antwacky, really out-of-date. It's all happening down here, you know. Up-to-the-minute stuff.'

'Did you try to get a better manager?' Kate asked. 'You said you would.'

'Brian Epstein didn't want to know us. I sent him a demo tape. Didn't even bother to reply.' Donovan scowled, looking slightly ill at ease in his new suit which looked a bit tight around the shoulders. 'And you know? He took on that Judy, what's her name, Cilla something. And she's just a flipping typist who reckons she can sing. So will you do us some glossies? It's really important to have something good to take to booking agents, all that stuff. We'll never get anywhere without.'

'All right,' Kate agreed reluctantly, looking round the bleak and very chilly rehearsal room near Tufnell Park which she had found with some difficulty after rattling up the over-crowded Northern Line from King's Cross at the end of the working day with her precious Voigtlander in her bag clutched tightly to her chest. She slipped off her coat and hung it on the row of wall hooks by the door and glanced around to try to find some angle from which to shoot which would not expose the grubby walls and stained wooden floor in all their glaring inadequacy.

'We need a better background,' she said uncertainly. 'What's outside there?' She waved at an emergency exit on the opposite side of the room.

'Nowt much,' Donovan said. 'Just a yard and a fire escape coming down from upstairs.'

Kate pushed past Dave and his three fellow musicians and through the fire door, searching around for some sort of background against which the band could maybe look just a bit original. Donovan watched her anxiously until she finally nodded her head.

'Set up the drum kit in the corner there and then the rest of you fellers get one above the other on the fire escape with your guitars. I think I can make that look quite good.'

Donovan looked at her doubtfully for a moment and the boy she knew as Miffy sniggered slightly, but the drummer, Stevo, nodded and Mike, the quiet one with the bass guitar, looked interested.

'That's clever,' he said. 'It'll look like New York. Know worra mean?'

'Exactly,' Kate said. 'Now let's get on with it.' She spent almost an hour coaxing the four of them into various poses on the fire escape, until the light had faded and she had run out of fittings for the flash. She pushed her hair out of her eyes wearily and turned back into the gloomy rehearsal room again.

'I'll do you some contact prints and we can choose the best,' she said.

'Ta, Kate,' Donovan said. 'I'm really grateful, you know.'

'And what about your side of the bargain?' she asked anxiously. 'Did you ask around about our Tommy?'

'I did, babe, and I had a stroke of luck,' Donovan said, putting a proprietorial hand around Kate's waist which she firmly pushed away. 'I told you Miffy would scout out the fashion scene for you. He was the one who found these suits. Dead cheap, they were. He says he saw Tom a couple of weeks back, bumped into him outside the tube station at Oxford Circus, and he told him he was working in a little men's shop in a back street behind a big shop called Liberty's.' He turned to Miffy, who was the only one who looked at home in his smart new suit. 'Where was it Kate's brother was working, kidder?'

'Can't remember the name of the shop but it was in Carnaby Street,' Miffy said as he zipped his guitar into its case. 'Never been there meself, but Tom rated it, said it was the coming place.'

'I've never heard of it,' Kate said. 'But I'll go and have a look anyway. It sounds just the sort of place he would be, doesn't it?'

'We're going for a bevvy now, babe. D'you fancy coming down the boozer?' Donovan said, when the band had packed their instruments into a battered van parked just behind the rehearsal rooms.

Kate hesitated for a second and then shook her head. She and Donovan had been together for almost a year back home, a relationship which had been more on-and-off than the Liverpool docks, and she did not want to give him even the slightest impression that she might be ready to resume where they had finally and acrimoniously left off. 'It's a long way back, and I told Marie and Tess that I'd be in for something to eat. I'll phone you when I've developed the pics. So I'll see you soon.'

'Tarra for now, then,' Donovan said, as she turned to head back to the tube station and slipped her camera into her bag and zipped it up, feeling a sense of relief that he had not insisted.

SEVEN

The boy stood with Hamish at the top of the embankment, looking down and breathing more freely behind the fence which concealed them from the road.

'D'ye ken there used to be a river down there?' the old man asked the boy, as they gazed down at the Circle Line below. 'The Fleet it was called, like Fleet Street, ran right down to the Thames at Blackfriars till they filled it all in because of the stink and the rubbish, and put it in a drain. Terrible thing that, putting a river in a drain. Like putting it in jail.' For once Hamish was relatively sober and pulled a dog-eared book, with only one frayed hard cover, out of his pocket.

'It's all in this wee book I found,' he said. 'Did ye ken London was once a Roman city?'

But the boy was not listening. He was worried about the promise he had given his client to go with him to a party the next day. The lure was the promise of more money, enough, he reckoned, to pay his train fare far away from this terrifying place in whose history he had not the faintest interest. 'Is Scotland a nice place to live?' he asked.

Hamish looked at him sharply. 'How much did that pervert gi'ye, laddie?'

'Not enough for the train,' the boy said. 'But he said if I go with him tomorrow he'll give me more.'

'Go where?'

'Just to a party,' the boy said. 'No harm.'

'Nae harm?' the old man said, raking his fingernails through his matted hair. 'Nae harm? Ye must be kidding me, laddie, ye really must. Where's this party?'

'I dunno,' the boy said. 'He wants me to go round to the flat at teatime. Says he'll take me in his car. I've not been in a car since . . .' He stopped and Hamish glanced at him, his rheumy eyes blurring his vision too much to see the skinny boy, still a child in all but experience, clearly. The boy did not talk about his past or the reasons he found himself on the streets but Hamish guessed from the nervous tics he showed when he was tired that wherever he had come from had been grim and probably brutal. When he was not drunk the old man was frequently angry and the boy's life made him angriest of all.

Detective Sergeant Harry Barnard sat at his desk in the cramped quarters which were allocated to Vice at West End Central, and turned back again to the page which had originally caught his attention in the magazine and grinned. So that's what you were up to, you naughty boy, he thought. There was nothing there that particularly shocked him. Very little did these days. He was inured to the wilder shores of human sexuality by now, and there was far more hard core pornography in the back rooms of Soho, of both the normal and the more unusual variety, than the slightly grainy photographs he was looking at now. What he had been seeking was another glimpse of a face he thought he recognized, amongst the writhing limbs and buttocks of this particular offering, but so far he had failed. Picking out individual faces was not always easy, especially as the activity these models were engaged in was strictly illegal simply on the basis of their gender. There was not a woman to be seen and for that reason faces tended to be blurred or half-hidden, turned away from the cameras rather than towards them. But on just one page, Barnard was sure that he had found a recognizable image of Jonathon Mason, the dead actor from the flat off Greek Street.

He got up and went upstairs to DCI Ted Venables' office and tapped on the door. 'Think I might have something here, guv,' he said, when summoned in. He dropped the magazine on to the cluttered desk, avoiding a couple of empty whisky glasses and the overfilled ashtray. 'Isn't that our pansy thespian who got his throat cut? Seems to have been doing a bit of modelling on the side.'

Venables glanced at the picture with more weariness than apparent interest, though he looked rather more cheerful than Barnard had seen him recently. Perhaps Vera had come back to cook his dinner, he thought.

'Not much of a surprise, is it?' Venables said. 'You know what these actors are like. I don't know why we have to waste our time chasing these buggers when they fall out and get carved up. It's like the toms, isn't it? They all put themselves in harm's way and then run whingeing to us when it turns nasty.'

Barnard looked at the older man for a moment, his face impassive, but he said nothing. If he had learned one thing during the course of his career it was that it did not do to question the wisdom of those even one step above you on the ladder. Since the first time in Soho, still a wet-behind-the-ears recruit in CID, when he had been slyly offered a fiver to turn a blind eye by someone he and his puppy-walker had stopped in the street, and he had waved it away, he had learned that you conformed to the culture or you got nowhere as a detective in the Met. The DC who had been with him that day had turned on him furiously after the encounter and told him in no uncertain terms which side his bread was buttered in Soho if he wanted to progress. The bread had been well buttered ever since and Flash Harry Barnard had progressed to detective sergeant accordingly.

'Do you want me to follow it up?' Barnard asked eventually. 'We've got an ongoing inquiry into the publishers of these things. It's not all coming from Holland any more, though no one wants to advertise the fact that the photo sessions are probably being held in a semi-detached in Pinner or Ilford or wherever they can find an empty house in a quiet road. We've got a lorry driver on board who's been delivering this stuff all unawares, and was pretty peeved when he found out what he was dropping off at various outlets around town. If we could track back to where they're taking the pictures we'd likely find out a lot more about our man.'

But Venables handed the magazine back to Barnard with a shrug, making no attempt to hide his evident boredom. 'I've got my own lads on some very promising leads, Harry,' he said. 'These two were well known for smoking dope, apparently. I reckon this may have more to do with that than what they got up to in bed, or for porn mags, come to that. Maybe a bust-up over the proceeds, if they were supplying the stuff.

Anyway, the Liverpool police are following up O'Donnell and
Mason's mates up there. Leave it for now. Don't bust a gut.
I'll let you know if I want any more help, but at the moment
we're doing OK, thanks. We'll find O'Donnell eventually.'

Barnard hid his surprise and shrugged. 'Fine,' he said.
'Whatever you say, guv. I'm not short of something to do.'

'There is one thing, though,' Venables said. 'Something a
bit odd. We had a call from one of the emergency doctors at
Barts, a medic I happen to know. Keeps us informed from time
to time. He'd had a young boy brought in after a road accident
in the City, about thirteen or fourteen, he reckoned. He was
unconscious when he came in and as soon as he came round,
he nicked a nurse's outdoor clothes and scarpered almost as
soon as he could get out of bed. Very odd, the doctor thought.
There wasn't much wrong with him, apart from a bang on the
head, apparently, but when they examined him in Casualty, he
said it was obvious he was into queer sex, willingly or not,
who knows? And when he was coming round one of the nurses
heard him rambling on about someone who'd had his throat
cut, covered in blood, pretty graphic, apparently. She didn't
think he was dreaming, but he didn't remember what he'd said
when he came to properly. When he was awake the doc asked
him about it. He couldn't remember being hit by the car and
when he asked him about what sounded like a murder, he went
very quiet and wouldn't say a word, clammed up completely.
Bit odd. I reckon we need to talk to him if we can find him.'

Venables rummaged through the jumble of papers and files
on his desk and handed Barnard a sheet torn from a notebook.
'The doc gave us a pretty detailed description,' he said.
'Though he ran off in a hospital gown, so we don't know what
he's likely to be wearing now. But when he left his head was
bandaged. He was quite badly cut and bruised on the left side,
and that's not going to disappear in a hurry, the doc said.
Worth keeping an eye open. He might have strayed on to our
manor from the City. Makes you wonder, doesn't it, the
mentality of some of these poofs, interfering with kids? That
I don't like. I'd castrate the lot of them if I had my way. But
if he saw someone with his throat cut – if it wasn't just a
delirious nightmare – it could be our nancy-boy in Greek

Street, in which case we'd better have a word. Could even be he wanted to do things the young lad didn't like and he took a knife to him. No more than he deserved maybe, but we'd best go through the motions.'

Barnard raised an eyebrow at that but said nothing. His own DCI turned a blind eye to a lot of things but he was a hardliner on queers and there was deep hostility in the upper reaches of the police force to any change in the law, in spite of pressure for reform. He himself couldn't see the point of chasing grown men for a victimless crime, but he jumped heavily on anyone he caught using young boys.

'I'll keep an eye open,' he said. 'I'll ask around. He might have got himself to St Peter's. They reckon to take anyone in who wants to get off the streets, and they'd certainly give him some new clothes.'

'Good, do that,' Venables said. 'We don't want him appearing in the *News of the Screws* at Holy Joe's behest with some sob story about nobody bothering about him, do we?'

Barnard walked back downstairs to his own desk with a thoughtful expression on his face. He had been surprised at Venables' sudden conviction that Jonathon Mason was using cannabis. Nothing he had picked up on the ground had given a hint of that and he had seen no indication in the reports he had seen on Mason and O'Donnell's flat that they were even occasional users of pot. But there had been no doubt about the DCI's main message. He had been told to back off the case, and not for a moment did he accept the reason offered. There had to be more to it than that and he wondered if someone was buying Venables off, and why. If he was accepting backhanders in a murder case, he reckoned he was heading for disaster. And no way was Harry Barnard going to be caught up in that catastrophe.

Kate had developed the pictures of the Ants she had taken the previous evening and showed the contact prints to Ken Fellows, who looked at them sceptically.

'I took them in my own time,' she said defensively. 'They can pay for the cost of materials, but not a professional's time. But they're hoping to get a record out soon.'

'Get Brenda to do an invoice,' Fellows said. 'They can have half a dozen prints, but no more. If they make it big we'll be ahead of the game, but as far as I can see most of these bands are going to sink without trace.'

'Do you still want me to go to Liverpool to get some background on the Beatles?'

'Take a long weekend,' Fellows said. 'It's not worth more than a day off work. But not this Friday. There's something I may want you to do Friday evening. I can't get there myself and I don't think anyone else is free. That's not a bad little camera you've got there and you seem to know how to use it. Have you got a party frock?'

'A party frock?' Kate asked, slightly bemused by the backhanded praise. 'Yes, I've got a party frock.'

'A smart one, I hope. You may need it,' Fellows said enigmatically. 'I'll let you know.'

That lunchtime Kate left the office and wove her way through the narrow streets towards Regent Street, the western boundary of the bohemian quarter. She was alone because Marie was working and she had to borrow an *A to Z* from Brenda so that she could find her way through the bustling maze that was Soho on a working day. Carnaby Street turned out to be a narrow lane lined with small shops, many of them selling clothes which only young people would buy, skirts shorter than parents would like, shirts and ties in fancy prints that would raise eyebrows in the suburbs, the rockers' leather gear and the Mod suits that the two antagonistic tribes of young men yearned for.

The pavements were crowded with young people on their lunch break and Kate wondered where on earth she should start. If Tom worked here it could be in pretty well any one of the shops. He must have found, she thought, his natural element right here. She pulled her photograph of her brother out of her bag and went into the first of the menswear shops, pushing through the browsing shoppers and the packed rails of clothing to the casually dressed assistant at the back, but, distracted by clamouring purchasers, he only glanced at the picture and shook his head. It was the same in most of the crowded boutiques. No one, it seemed, had employed her brother or even seen him in what must have been a place he had at least visited to browse himself. Fashion-mad Tom just had to know this street, she thought desperately as she worked her way down one side and up the other. He couldn't have been in London for long without discovering its delights.

Only when she was beginning to despair, did she finally strike gold. Just as she was glancing at her watch anxiously, knowing time was running out, she noticed a small shop front almost entirely hidden by pavement racks of shirts and ties in bright flowery designs. Her mother wouldn't have minded some of the fabrics to make up as dresses for her younger sisters, Kate thought wryly, but not in a month of Sundays on a boy. She pushed her way through the open door and found herself face-to-face with a tall, willowy young man with blond hair down to his collar and a fringe flopping into his eyes.

'I'm looking for someone,' she said, pulling out her photograph, now slightly dog-eared and dirty, yet again. 'This is my brother Tom. You don't happen to know him, do you?'

The young man took the picture out of her hand and to her surprise scowled at it slightly. 'Of course I know him', he said. 'And I'd like to bloody know where the kidder is an'all.' The voice, for all the southern sophistication of the young man's exterior, was pure Liverpool, and Kate felt her heart quicken.

'Where are you from then, la? My lot are in Anfield, used to be in Scottie Road. We can hear the cheers on match days now.'

'Croxteth, me,' the young man said, smiling shyly now, and holding out his hand for Kate to shake. 'Derek Stephenson. Tom told me all about you. And your sisters. He works here. At least he did, but I've not seen or heard from him for days.'

'We haven't heard from him since he left,' Kate said, the burden of that knowledge suddenly weighing her down again. 'I've come down to work as well, and I thought I'd tracked him down, but the kidder he shared a flat with is dead and Tom's disappeared and the whole thing is a nightmare.'

'Dead?' Stephenson said, looking suddenly pale and ill at ease. 'Here, sit down a mo' and I'll make some coffee. That's a stunner.'

Kate sat on the single chair at the back of the shop while
Stephenson disappeared into a back room and came back with
a mug of instant coffee which she clutched like a lifeline as
he moved to serve a couple of customers clutching trendy ties.
She took a deep breath when he came back and told him
quietly all she knew about Tom's disappearance. Stephenson
took it in without comment, flinching slightly as she skated
over Jonathon Mason's gory end.

'You do know what you need to know about Tom, don't
you?' he asked when she had finished. 'He and Jonathon
weren't just sharing a flat.'

Kate nodded, and wondered whether Stephenson shared her
brother's tastes. Was there a triangle here? If so, she had no
doubt the police would be interested in Derek Stephenson as
well as Tom, but at the moment Derek showed no inclination
to confide.

'I don't suppose your mam would be very keen on all that
stuff,' was all he said, as Kate nodded numbly again.

'The bizzies are looking for him,' she said. 'I've had a
detective sergeant asking me questions.'

'You're bound to have,' Stephenson said. 'But Tom wouldn't
do something like that. He wouldn't have it in him.'

'I know that,' Kate agreed. 'But it's difficult to convince
anyone who doesn't know him.'

'Tom seemed to be made up with this Jonathon when I first
met him, soon after they came down from the Pool,' Stephenson
said.

'They both came down from Liverpool?' Kate said,
surprised. 'I didn't know that. I thought he must have met
him in London.'

'No, no, he met him at home. Jonathon went away to school
and university somewhere, but he was around on the scene,
like. I'd met him once or twice. I think he persuaded your
Tommy to come away with him. He was older than Tom, but
like I say, they seemed really made up with each other. But
just lately I thought it was cooling off a bit. Your Tom told
me Jonathon was into things he didn't like, didn't want to get
involved in. There's some nasty stuff goes on behind closed
doors in London, you've no idea.' He glanced somewhat

distractedly at the customer trying to attract his attention. 'What time do you finish work?' he asked. 'I close the shop at five thirty. Come back then, and I'll tell you everything I know about Tom. He's a great kidder, I really like him. Perhaps we can find him before the bizzies get to him. Or even worse, the scallies who murdered his friend.' He put an arm round Kate's shoulder as she got up to go. 'Cheer up,' he said. 'We'll get the scousers on the case. There's a few of us around. You're not on your own, you know.'

Kate smiled wanly. 'It's nice to know,' she said, meaning it, and she headed back to work feeling slightly happier than before. But before she had even turned out of Carnaby Street she felt a hand on her arm and spun round in surprise to find herself facing DS Harry Barnard, who had a less than friendly look in his eyes.

'So,' he said. 'Did you find him then?'

'Who?' Kate said, although she knew in the pit of her stomach that playing dumb would get her nowhere. Barnard, she thought, could put on the charm, but there was steel behind the smiles. 'Are you following me?' she asked, her anger only partly feigned.

Barnard laughed. 'You were unlucky,' he said. 'I happened to see you coming out of your office. I've been watching you hawk your little snap around. So – did you find him? Was he in that last place you went to? You were in there much longer than you were anywhere else.'

Kate shook her head. 'You're wasting your time,' she said flatly. 'He's been working there but he's not been in for days. It's a dead end. You can check it out yourself.'

'Oh, don't worry, I will,' Barnard said. 'But not until you tell me what made you come to Carnaby Street in the first place. I'm sure you didn't just stick pins in the map, did you? Who told you this was a likely spot to look for him?'

Kate thought about that carefully. 'I talked to some friends from Liverpool,' she said. 'They told me they'd seen Tom and thought he was working somewhere round Oxford Circus. This seemed like an obvious place to look. It's just the sort of thing he likes, all this stuff . . .' She waved a hand at the pavement racks of clothes but trailed off slightly miserably, looking for a sympathy which, judging by the look in Barnard's eye, she was not going to get.

'Didn't it cross your mind that you should have contacted me before you came down here making your own inquiries?' he asked. 'If you'd actually found him, what would you have done, Miss O'Donnell? Bought him a ticket to France?'

Kate managed a wan smile. 'Don't be silly,' she said. 'I'd have persuaded him to talk to the police, of course. What else can he do?' But she knew Barnard did not believe her.

'By rights I should take you back to the nick and hand you over to the officer in charge of this case,' he said. 'But as you haven't found him I'll let it go for now. But only for now, mind. I don't want you doing your own detective work on this case. Not only will it not help your brother, it'll land you in court yourself, if you're not careful. Do you understand that? Helping a suspect evade the police is a criminal offence, Miss O'Donnell, make no mistake about that. And it has serious consequences, believe me.'

'But I haven't helped him,' Kate said quietly. 'I haven't even found him, any more than you have.' She glanced at her watch. 'I need to get back to work,' she said.

'And I need to talk to this man you say knows him,' Barnard countered quickly. 'Keep in touch, from now on, Miss O'Donnell, won't you?'

'Of course, Sergeant,' Kate said, offering her sweetest smile, while she wondered just what good all those years of confessing her sins had done when it came to the crunch. To keep Tom safe she knew she would lie for as long as it took. What she also knew was that she would take more care to keep out of Sergeant Barnard's way in future.

EIGHT

Kate O'Donnell stood as if mesmerized on the edge of the crowd. She was not normally a reticent person and she knew she looked good in her strappy green silk dress, tight at the waist and full in the skirt, and the only item of clothing she had ever bought at Liverpool's top department store, Bon Marché, and spent more than ten pounds on. Teemed with high-heeled court shoes and a bag just big enough to contain her camera and a few other necessities, she knew the effect she was having, not least because Ken Fellows had cast a critical eye over her outfit and told her so before sending her off to the charity boxing match and reception organized by Ray and Georgie Robertson at the fashionable Delilah Club just off Regent Street.

'Not bad,' he had conceded, evidently in spite of himself. 'Not bad at all. You'll do. Now you're quite clear what you're at, aren't you? Get a list of the guests from Ray Robertson's fixer, feller called Tony Statham, big bloke with not much hair. Think you can manage that?'

'I'll try,' Kate said, biting back her irritation.

'Then call me and we'll go through the list, see who's worth a picture. He generally pulls in some big names: sportsmen, theatre people, politicians. What I want is people like that letting their hair down. Some of the rags'll be there themselves, but not all of them, so we've a good chance of flogging a few snaps to the rest if they're good enough. So I'm relying on you, Kate. And make sure that if you get a shot of an interesting bloke with a pretty girl you find out who the girl is. There's a rumour going around that a government minister is up to no good with some tart called Christine. Ask Tony if she's there and then keep an eye on her. Could be a really good story, that.'

'Fine,' Kate said.

'And you'd better take a taxi home. You don't want to be

getting the last tube back in that outfit.' Fellows had made the offer slightly reluctantly and took the edge off it by insisting that he wanted her contact prints on his desk by nine the next morning. 'If you've got anything good I want it on the evening picture desks by ten,' he said. 'The do's too late for the morning papers to get pics in, except perhaps for the last edition, so the *Evening Standard* and the *News*'ll be right in the market. The diaries will love it.' Ken had looked at her doubtfully for a moment.

'Are you sure you can handle this?' he asked. 'I'd planned for Bob Johnson to go but he's off sick.'

'Of course I can,' Kate had answered, but now, feeling small and nervous in the throng of large dinner-jacketed men, and a few elegantly dressed women, with jewels which she guessed must be real and heady perfume she guessed must be Chanel, not to mention the fur coats they'd been handing into the cloakroom to hang beside her modest tweed, she wondered if she had bitten off more than she could chew. 'Come on, girl,' she told herself, intending to seek out Tony Statham and taking a deep breath before pushing off into the melee, which was drifting towards the seats around the boxing ring set up in a farther room.

Statham turned out to be a huge man who looked as if he had been shoehorned into his starched shirt and dinner jacket, putting the buttons under considerable strain. The room was getting hot when Kate at last found herself being pointed towards Statham who was standing in the doorway to the boxing arena tightly packed with gilt and red velvet chairs, directing people to their seats while mopping his brow with a large handkerchief and holding a slightly crumpled list in the other.

'Name, darling?' he inquired as Kate approached, an anxious frown creasing his brow.

'I'm from the Ken Fellows Agency,' she said. 'Ken said you'd help me with the guest list if I asked you.'

'Ken recruiting pretty birds now, is he, the old lech?' Statham asked, casting a lingering but jaundiced eye over Kate from head to foot. 'Hope you don't faint at the sight of blood.'

'It's the party I'm more interested in than the boxing,' Kate said. 'Ken says Mr Robertson's parties are quite something.'

'He raises a lot of money for charity, petal,' Statham said. 'Sporting charities mainly. He's got a name for it. People come to support the charities, don't they?'

Kate dodged out of the way of a tall man waving a glass of champagne in the direction of his companion, who was wearing a strapless dress which exposed more of her breasts than Kate thought was possible without getting arrested. She raised her eyebrows and Statham gave her a sardonic look.

'You'd better come and meet Ray and Georgie, or they'll wonder what you're doing here,' he said. 'Georgie'll have your knickers off as soon as look at you if he doesn't know who you are. You want to watch out for him.'

Statham grabbed hold of another thickset man who seemed just as seriously ill at ease in his dinner jacket. 'Make sure all these people get to their seats before the bell goes,' he said. He took Kate's elbow in a massive grip and steered her back into the main reception room, where a thinning crowd was still enjoying the champagne and canapés, and took her towards an area close to the bar cordoned off with gold tasselled rope. The two men she took to be Ray and Georgie Robertson were evidently in expansive hospitable mood, surrounded by a cluster of guests, all drinking champagne and several of them smoking mammoth cigars and exhaling clouds of blue smoke.

Statham edged his way towards Ray, with Kate in tow. 'A minute, boss, before you go in?' he said. 'This young lady's from the Ken Fellows. He usually sends Bob Johnson, but I thought you'd want to know that it's a doll this time.'

Kate saw both Robertsons' eyes swivel in her direction, Ray's coldly neutral and Georgie's hotly appraising. By the time the night was over, Kate thought, she looked likely to have been mentally undressed by almost every man in the room. Someone in the crowd behind her gave a faint wolf whistle of appreciation, which earned him a filthy look from Statham.

'Have a word, Tony,' Ray Robertson said angrily. 'I'm not having that nonsense here. Lowers the tone.' Statham moved back into the crowd of guests looking for the importunate whistler, while Robertson turned his attention back to Kate and his expression back to as benign as she guessed it ever got.

'Got your camera in good nick, then, have you, sweetheart?' he asked. 'This is my brother Georgie, if you haven't met before.' Kate gave Georgie a faint smile as his appraising look grew more intense but turned away thankfully as Ray waved his hand around the circle of his guests. 'Lord Francome, just joined the government, you know, Sir David Seal MP and Lady Seal, Winston Jones, hot from Her Majesty's Theatre, John O'Reilly, won the Derby last year.' He waved towards a couple slightly apart from the other guests. 'And that's Fred Bettany, my accountant, most important man in a business, you know.'

Kate was about to ask about the tall, blonde woman in what must certainly be a designer dress, figure-hugging to emphasize her abundant assets, to whom Georgie Robertson was paying close attention, but Ray had not finished.

'Anything else I can help you with, just ask. Tony knows everyone and anyone. He'll look after you.'

Summarily dismissed, Kate felt everyone's eyes flicker again briefly in her direction and then swivel back to their conversations. She was, she thought, one step above the hired help and just as invisible to these VIPs. The only person whose attention she had really captured, she thought, was Georgie Robertson's, and that could turn out to be a distinct disadvantage. He was still watching her with unsmiling dark eyes and a slight smile which she did not like. She pulled her camera out of her bag and took a couple of token shots as Ray Robertson began to shepherd the group towards the exhibition boxing match which seemed to be about to begin. She would do better later, she thought, when the exhibition was over and people were more relaxed as the drink continued to flow and the food on the buffet tables at the far end of the room was unveiled.

In the event, the boxing match turned out to be a short, sharp affair between two young men who looked to Kate's untutored eyes far too skinny to go anywhere near a boxing ring. She stood beside Tony Statham at the back of the room watching while they pounded each other ineffectually for several rounds before one of the boxers began to bleed freely from a cut above the eye and, to groans of disappointment from the crowd, the referee stopped the fight and the young men put on their dressing gowns again and danced back the way they had so recently come to their dressing rooms.

'Pity, that,' Statham said, turning away, disgruntled. 'Ray had hopes of that lad, but it looks as if he's a bleeder. That's the second time he's not got past round three.'

'I thought you had to be beefy to be a fighter?' Kate said.

'Not to be a flyweight,' Statham said dismissively. 'Don't you know anyfink? Right, it's buffet time. Can you get on by yourself now? I've got stuff to do. Here.' He waved a sheet of paper at her. 'Mr Ray said to give you the guest list.'

'I'll be fine,' Kate said, turning to join the general exodus from the auditorium, feeling slightly more confident that she could now do her job. But as she was jostled by the crowd she realized that someone had an exploratory hand on her hip. She pulled away sharply and spun round to find herself face-to-face with Georgie Robertson, this time with more of a leer than a smile on his face.

'Please don't do that,' she said so loudly that a handful of people in the crush turned towards her and she flushed before catching the amused eyes of the last person she expected to see at the Robertsons' party.

'What on earth are you doing here?' she asked, realizing that Robertson had quickly melted away behind her.

'I might ask you the same question,' Harry Barnard came back quickly. 'I thought you were slumming it in Notting Hill with your girlfriends. Who brought you to this do, then?'

'Nobody brought me, I'm working,' Kate snapped, pulling her camera from her bag and waving it in Barnard's face.

'Still a little one?' Barnard said, with an unapologetic grin. 'Those hefty beggars the men use too heavy for you, are they?'

'This is the latest thing, thirty-five millimetre, and a good one too,' Kate said defensively. 'Ken Fellows reckons it's the future for news. What about you? What are you doing here?'

'The Robertsons like to keep well in with the Met. There's usually a few coppers here – one of my bosses tonight, as it goes. But I was really invited because I do a bit of sparring

at the boxing club Ray and Georgie run in the East End for
these lads. The Robertsons and I go way back. We all lived
in Bethnal Green and were evacuated together during the war.'
He glanced back at the area sectioned off for important visitors, catching sight of an angry exchange between the
Robertson brothers which he would dearly love to have been
closer to, before taking Kate's arm and steering her to a quiet
corner of the room. 'Has anyone told you you look stunning
tonight, even if you are working?' he asked. 'I hope Ken
Fellows appreciates you.'

'I hope he'll appreciate me even more when he sees my
pictures in the morning,' Kate said, disentangling herself from
Barnard's grip. 'I really need to get on.'

'Ah, but do you know whose pictures to take?' Barnard
asked. 'You see that tall bloke with Ray?'

'Lord Francome?' Kate countered, recognizing the man
whose name she had been told earlier. She had a good memory
for faces.

'Well done,' Barnard said. 'Just been given a junior job at
the Ministry of Defence. Well, if you keep an eye on who he's
chatting to you might get a really good story. There's a girl
here called Christine Jones – tall, blonde, in a red dress, low
cut, lipstick to match – rumour has it Francome's got the hots
for her and she's no better than she should be, a high class
tart, in fact. Get a picture of those two together and you could
make your fortune. Or Ken Fellows', I suppose, more likely.'

'You're joking?' Kate said, slightly bemused.

'Certainly not,' Barnard said. 'Anyway, you can take it or
leave it.'

'And who's the woman in the gold dress, looks like a film
star, talking to Georgie Robertson? Is she a high class tart,
too?'

To Kate's surprise, Barnard looked startled by her question
and took a moment or two to answer. 'No way,' he said very
quietly. 'She's Mrs Shirley Bettany. That's her husband talking
to Ray Robertson. Fred Bettany is his accountant.'

Kate looked again at the tall, greying accountant with the
unexpectedly glamorous wife and raised an eyebrow.

'Doing very nicely for himself, is Fred, big house in

Hampstead . . .' Barnard drew her further away from the VIPs' enclosure. 'But if we ever pin anything on Ray, I'd put money on Fred going down with him. Now, are you going to let me get you a drink?'

'I'm working,' Kate said again.

'So you are,' Barnard said with a shrug. 'You'd better get on with it, then. I won't get in your way.' And he turned away and disappeared into the crowd, leaving Kate with a slight sense of disappointment.

Later that evening, Harry Barnard stood in a doorway across the road from the Delilah Club watching the swing doors disgorge the Robertsons' guests. He saw DCI Venables and Assistant Commissioner Arthur Wright stumble into a taxi together, spotted Lord Francome pull up outside in his Jag and lean over to open the passenger door for the blonde in the red dress and a fur stole, and Georgie Robertson storm out, his pale face knotted in fury as he hailed a taxi which turned into Piccadilly and headed east at a rate of knots. Barnard was still wondering what Georgie Robertson and DCI Venables had been discussing so animatedly when he had happened to stumble on them together in the Gents. They had cut their conversation short when he arrived, Venables ducking into a cubicle with a muttered greeting to Barnard, and Georgie turning on his heel and letting the door slam heavily behind him. Barnard guessed that the only topic of conversation between the pair would have to be financial but the nature of the favours conferred to whom by whom, and why, he could not even begin to guess.

Next out were the Bettanys, Shirley also clutching a fur stole around her shoulders, concealing her revealing neckline, Fred with a hand raised imperiously for the next cab in the line waiting outside the club doors. Barnard wondered if he imagined that Shirley had seen him across the busy road, and smiled faintly to himself. He would ask her next time he saw her more privately, he thought, confident that it would not be too long before that happened.

Finally the person he was waiting for appeared and he dodged through the traffic to greet Kate O'Donnell for the second time that night, to her evident surprise.

'It'll cost you to get a cab as late as this,' he said. 'My car's just round the corner. I'll give you a lift. It's not out of my way.'

Kate shivered slightly, her coat too thin to keep out the evening chill. She wondered if spring would ever come this year. She was tired, she had to get up early next day and her defences crumbled, although she was sure that she would live to regret it. 'All right,' she said, wearily. 'If you're sure it's on your way.'

'Of course it is,' Barnard lied easily. He took her arm and steered her into the narrow streets behind the club where he had parked, and opened the passenger door of the red Capri.

'This is nice,' Kate said, more out of politeness than because she knew anything at all about cars. Where she had lived in Liverpool for most of her life you took the bus or you walked. Private cars were as rare as hens' teeth. 'I like the colour.'

Barnard got into the driver's seat and started up, wondering what on earth attracted him to this girl who was so utterly out of her depth in London. So far he had had no more luck tracking down her brother than she had had herself, but maybe, he thought, if he played his cards carefully, she would lead him to the wanted man in the end. But he knew there was more to it than that. Neither of them said much during the short drive down Oxford Street and Bayswater Road to the tall, crumbling house close to Notting Hill where Kate was staying. But when he pulled into the kerb, careful not to switch the engine off, he put a hand lightly on her knee, and felt her tremble under the silky fabric of her dress.

'There you are,' he said. 'Safe and sound.'

'Thank you,' Kate said, fumbling for the door handle. Barnard leaned across and opened it for her.

'I shouldn't really tell you this, but I think the DCI in charge seems to be cooling on the idea that your brother had a row with his flatmate and killed him,' he said. 'He's working on other leads which may involve other people. So maybe in a day or so, when it's all a bit clearer, you'd like to come out for a drink with me. I could show you some of the sights.'

Kate slid out of the car and shivered slightly again in the

night air. 'Perhaps,' she said. She glanced at her watch. 'I have to get to bed. I've got a load of work to do in the morning.'

'Do you have the phone number for your house now?' Barnard asked.

Kate hesitated for a moment and then gave it to him. She didn't doubt that he could find it for himself if he really wanted to. 'It's on the ground floor and I'm at the very top, so we don't always hear it,' she said.

Barnard gave her a flashing smile. 'I'll keep trying,' he promised, closed the car door and watched her make her way up the steps to the front door and close it behind her. As he eased the car away from the kerb he grinned to himself and began to whistle Cliff Richard's latest hit. 'Softly, softly, Harry,' he said to himself but he was confident that all sorts of things were looking promising. Even so, when he got back to his own flat, gazed at the gleaming parquet and the smart Scandinavian furnishing, and dropped into the bright orange revolving chair where he sat to watch TV or listen to his collection of records on the teak radiogram, he felt a slight niggle of dissatisfaction.

He had married early while still a uniformed copper on the beat and he and his wife had shared a rented two-room flat in Kentish Town for as long as the marriage lasted. Joan had slipped out of his life without much regret on either side, and like most officers in Vice he was not short of sex when he wanted it. But now he had what he considered a proper home, and one which from its vantage point close to Hornsey Lane looked down, literally and metaphorically, on the smoky, teeming expanse of the East End where he had grown up, still pock-marked with derelict bomb sites, he was increasingly aware that there was something missing in his life. He spun round and got to his feet again, tossed his sheepskin jacket on to the tweed sofa, poured himself a large Scotch from the small cocktail cabinet, and put a record of the Shadows on the turntable, more to avoid the question than to seek an answer. He glanced round his carefully furnished living room as the spirit warmed him, every last cushion and glass ornament paid for by the sex trade he was paid to police, and knew that this was not enough.

*   *   *

The boy sat in an armchair in a corner of the room, swamped in a sweater that the man who called himself Les had loaned him. When he had gone round to the flat again, Les had stripped him, in spite of his protests, and thrust him into the bath, washing him all over, shampooing his hair and re-dressing him in fresh clothes. He had stood for a moment looking at the stitches in his head wound and the shaved patch in the blond hair before covering it with a plaster.

'There,' he had said. 'You see? You scrub up quite nicely. You're a pretty boy, aren't you? You'll do fine.'

'I need twenty quid,' the boy said, his voice breathless and small, his heart thumping uncomfortably.

'Of course you do, and you shall have it, I promise,' Les said. 'More, maybe. You'll be able to go wherever you like then.'

The boy nodded doubtfully, trying not to think about what would come before, but knowing he had even more to fear from other men at the party Les would take him to than he did from this particular man, even with his soft, probing hands.

Outside the flat, Hamish hovered in the shadows, huddled in his new duffle coat, one hand buried in his pocket and the other clutching a bottle of cider. He swayed slightly on his feet, and propped himself up against the wall, determined, in spite of the grey mist which seemed to clog his brain, to find out exactly where the boy was being taken. He knew the boy was not doing anything he had not done before but he had seen a new fear in his eyes since he had run away from the hospital and felt a new urgency in his determination to get out of the city and go somewhere new. Somewhere deep in his fuddled head he knew that something dangerous was happening which he had not encountered before. The boy had been spooked for a week and his panic was growing. Tonight, he had determined he would keep an eye out for him. Tonight, for once in the chaos that was now his life, he would try to do the right thing.

It was not long before he saw the boy come out of the flat with his companion and head in the direction of the Euston Road with its busy traffic, and the tube and railway stations. If they went far, Hamish realized, he would not be able to keep up. He had no money for fares and his pace was considerably slower than the two fitter, younger people he was following. But just before the main road they turned again into a side street and he watched as they stood for a moment on the doorstep of a tall terraced house, with all its windows lit up, before the door opened and they disappeared inside.

Hamish grunted in frustration and then settled down with his bottle at the top of the area steps of a house several houses down the street. In spite of being so close to the main road and the stations, the street was quiet, and no one disturbed him as he sank into a doze, huddled in his new coat. He eventually woke with a start, with no idea how long he had been asleep or what had broken into his dreams. But when he worked out where he was, and why he was there, he became aware of movement close by and the sound of the boy's voice. He stood up cautiously and noticed a car parked outside the house where the boy had gone. He was there, with two men who opened the car doors, put the boy in the back seat and got into the front themselves. Before Hamish could react in any way the car had pulled away from the kerb and headed east.

'Where've ye gone now, ye stupid wee fecker?' Hamish asked himself, trying to dull the pain he could scarcely bear to acknowledge with another gulp of cider, draining the bottle as he went. Slowly he trudged his way back to his hidey-hole on the railway embankment, only to find as he turned into Farringdon Road that the street was lined with police cars and vans, blue lights flashing, into which the inhabitants of the encampment were being herded. Hamish hesitated for a moment too long as a couple of uniformed officers spotted him and came running.

'Here's another of 'em,' one shouted. 'Come on, grandad, there's nothing for you here. This place is being bloody fumigated. Get in the van.'

Hamish shrugged and did as he was told. Even in his new duffle coat he was cold and stiff. A night in a cell would not be too bad an option, he thought. It was only as he was being bundled into the van he noticed that one of the officers was clutching a crumpled piece of white fabric which looked like a nurse's cap.

Hamish slept only fitfully in the cell he had been put in after arriving with the rest of the vagrants at Sun Hill nick, and he was awake immediately when the duty sergeant opened the door the next morning.

'Did ye bring a young laddie in last night, a boy about fourteen?' he asked, taking the mug of tea he was offered greedily.

'A boy?' the sergeant came back, surprised. 'Not that I know of. He'd have been taken to a juvenile home, anyway, wouldn't he? We'd not have kept him here.'

'A home?' Hamish whispered, thinking of the homes the boy had mentioned during the brief time he had known him. 'He'll nae stay in one o'them.'

The sergeant looked at him strangely again, several stray items of information coming together in his head. 'I heard something about a boy running off from Bart's in a nurse's uniform. Is that why one of our lads found a nurse's cap down by your camp last night – lacy thing, white, would that belong to your boy?'

Hamish gulped his tea and handed the mug back without saying any more, flinging himself back on to the bunk and turning his face to the wall. 'Gae tae hell,' he muttered.

The sergeant shrugged and left him there, banging the cell door behind him. 'You'll be in court at ten,' he said through the cell peephole. 'Vagrancy and drunk and disorderly.'

Hamish did not move, cursing himself bitterly under his breath. He knew he should not have mentioned the boy, and he was not surprised when the door to his cell was opened again and a tall, dark-haired man in civilian clothes came in, pulling a face in distaste at the sour smell in the tiny room.

'I think you and I need a little chat, Hamish,' DS Harry Barnard said.

NINE

Kate O'Donnell stood for a moment outside a steamy Lime Street station and took a deep breath of salty air as she looked across at the familiar scene. The Adelphi Hotel with a cluster of taxis outside, St George's Hall and the art gallery away to the right, and a glimpse of the huge hole in the ground, which still shocked her, where St John's market had recently stood. Then, as she slowly crossed the road, there were all the familiar shops, Lewis's, Owen Owens, and the rest. She only had a light weekend bag with her and she did not feel like going home yet, so she made her way down through the shopping crowds in Dale Street and followed Water Street to the Pier Head, where she stood gazing across the choppy grey Mersey, as she had done so often as a restless teenager. Sometimes Tom had been with her, as ambitious as she was, but never so explicit in his dreams, both wondering then how they could get away and now whether she could succeed in staying away and whether her brother would ever come back.

There was a cold wind off the water, and the ferry coming into the landing stage was pushing a bow wave and rolling slightly. She used to be seasick on the ferry, she recalled with a faint smile. Her sisters, scampering around unaffected, had laughed at her as she had curled up in a tight ball in a corner, miserable at the start and end of a rare day out over the river. Away to the right she could see the towering shapes of a couple of liners in the docks and across the water the cranes of the Birkenhead shipyards, all so familiar and yet slightly foreign now, even though her stay in London had been so short. She did not feel that she belonged here any more.

With a sigh she walked across to the bus terminal and jumped on to a bus to Anfield where her mother had been given a corporation house when the old Scotland Road terraces had begun to be pulled down. They had called Scottie Road

a slum and condemned it, but she had been sorry to leave,
more aware than her sisters of friends left behind, new schools
to adjust to, a strange neighbourhood, in spite of the attractions
of an indoor lavvie and a patch of garden for the younger ones
to play in. It was then that she had decided to get out and
begun to work hard at school, determined to go to college.
She had already worked out for herself that the door marked
Exit was there.

Her mother opened the front door to her knock, looking
pale and tired, and gave her a peck on the cheek. 'You got a
job down there then?'

'I wrote and told you,' Kate said, dropping her bag in the
hall and making her way to the kitchen where she put the
kettle on.

'I thought the letter was from our Tom,' Bridie O'Donnell
said. 'Your writing looks the same. Have you heard anything
from him at all?'

Kate could imagine the excitement her mother must have
felt before she realized her mistake. Kate knew she had always
played second fiddle to Tom.

'London's a big place, Mam,' she said non-committally. She
had already decided not to elaborate on what she knew of
Tom's predicament, although she knew the police had been
round seeking information.

'The bizzies were here,' Bridie said, as if reading her mind,
and it was obvious that this was what had knocked the stuffing
out of her usually combative mother. 'I couldn't believe what
they were saying, as if our Tommy would kill anyone. I told
them to feck off.'

'I don't think that'll do any good. They're not going to stop
looking for him,' Kate said, pouring boiling water into the
teapot which was standing ready. 'He may have run away
because he was scared, but they're going to want an explanation. They won't give up.'

Bridie took her cup of tea and sank into a chair at the kitchen
table. 'You know what else they were saying about him?'
Bridie would not meet Kate's eyes.

'I do,' Kate said.

'Is it true?' Bridie asked.

Kate nodded bleakly. 'It is,' she said.

'Holy mother of God,' Bridie whispered. 'And I brought him up a good Catholic boy.'

'He probably still is,' Kate said, knowing that Tom had pretended to take his religion more seriously than she had, one reason he had remained the apple of his mother's eye.

'Not if he's doing that sort of thing,' Bridie said. 'It's a mortal sin, so it is. And they'll put him in jail for it.'

'I think it's something people can't help,' Kate said. 'Did you really not know?'

'Of course I didn't know,' Bridie said angrily. 'I'd have had him round to Father Reilly before his feet touched the ground. Do you think he was like that before he went away then? This isn't something he's learned in London?'

'No,' Kate said slowly, thinking back to the brother she had known as a teenager and realizing how little he had been like most of the other boys she knew. 'No, I think he's been that way inclined for a long time. He met the friend he was living with up here, any road. He just never told us, never talked about it.' *Never trusted us enough*, she thought to herself, though the fearful wrath of Father Reilly hanging over all their heads probably made that inevitable.

'Anyway, I think that's the least of Tom's problems just now,' Kate said, feeling a wave of depression sweep over her and tears prick her eyes. 'He needs to talk to the police about his dead friend. They'll catch up with him in the end and the longer he leaves it the worse it'll be for him. Could he have come back up here, do you think? Have you heard anything from him at all, or from his other mates?'

'His friend in London was killed with a knife, so the bizzies said,' her mother said dully, clearly not listening to much that Kate was saying. 'Surely to God they don't think our Tom did that, do they?' Bridie had gone even paler than she'd looked before. 'They didn't exactly say that, but—'

'They don't exactly say anything much,' Kate said bitterly, thinking of her encounters with the importunate DS Harry Barnard. 'But yes, I think he's a suspect.'

'But they could hang him . . .' Bridie looked sick and the cup in her hands began to shake. She put it down carefully.

'I don't think so,' Kate said, her mouth dry. 'They changed the law. Don't you remember? I think it's only robbers and people with guns who get hanged now.' She put her hand over Bridie's. Her mother had never been a very demonstrative person, seldom given to hugs and kisses, even when they were all small, and Kate felt awkward offering even that level of comfort, but to her surprise Bridie clutched her hand tightly.

'Your brother's friend, Declan, came round yesterday, asking after him,' Bridie said. 'The bizzies had been asking about Tom round his place an' all. I couldn't tell him anything, could I, because I didn't know anything?'

'I'll go round and see Dec later,' Kate said. 'And any others I can think of. But I've got some work to do, too. I want to get some pictures of the Cavern Club and see if I can track down John Lennon's girlfriend. You know? Cynthia Powell? She was at art college when me and John were there. The Beatles look like making a name for themselves in London now and people are interested in where they came from.'

'I heard that,' Bridie said. 'Up here it's still Gerry and the Pacemakers the kids seem to like best.'

'Them and the Beatles are in the Hit Parade,' Kate said. 'It's all beginning to take off for them. Who'd have thought the Mersey Beat would go national, Mam? It's quite something.'

'I heard Cynthia Powell's pregnant. John's baby, they say. Did you know that?'

'Is she?' Kate said, surprised. 'It's incredible, you know, that those two are still together. John was such a scruffy Teddy boy when we started at college, and she was a real stuck-up little Hoylake miss. Even when they got together they seemed to fight all the time. I can't imagine John being a dad, I really can't. Are they married? You hear different tales.'

'I think so, though the *Echo* says they're not. There seems to be some sort of mystery about it. But someone told our Annie Cynthia'd moved in with John Lennon's auntie to wait for the baby. I dare say her parents aren't best pleased.'

'The place is still a gossip mill, then?' Kate said with a grin. She could guess why John Lennon, darling of thousands of hysterical teenage fans who packed out every local venue the band played at, wanted to keep his marriage quiet. She had never much liked him and she did not envy Cynthia her lot. But she hoped that she was married. The life of an unmarried mother would not be easy for the nicely brought up girl from the Wirral she remembered turning up at college in her twinset and pearls. She was not the only one who had been astonished when Cynthia had latched on to the anarchic Lennon with his talent for drawing, his sometimes cruel wit and his apparently vain musical ambitions.

'I'll take my stuff upstairs,' Kate said. 'I need a bath after tea. I'm hot and sticky after the train.'

'I'll put the immersion heater on, pet,' her mother said.

DS Harry Barnard parked his car outside a gym in Whitechapel and locked it carefully, checking every door out of habit as much as any real fear that it would be nicked in this street where Ray and Georgie Robertson's writ ran more or less unchallenged. He went inside and was hit by the familiar smell of sweat and the sounds of gasping breath and monotonous thud of leather on punchbag and, softer but even more deadly, splat against unprotected flesh. Ray himself was standing by the ring watching intently as two well-muscled young men, one black and one white, wearing helmets for protection, sparred energetically with each other until one put up an arm to deflect a blow and sat down heavily in his corner, gasping for air. Robertson had noticed Barnard come in.

'Leave it at that now, lads,' he told the sparring partners as he turned away to greet his visitor. 'Harry, my boy, nice to see you. Good of you to come down. Come into the office, it's a bit quieter in there.' The two young boxers scrambled out of the ring clutching towels, the black boy still dancing on his toes on the way to the dressing rooms while the white boy, who had obviously come off worst, and was still panting heavily, took a detour to put a glove on Ray Robertson's arm.

'He hits low, that nigger,' he said, his face pinched with rage.

Robertson pushed the boy off. 'He's better than you,' he said. 'Don't come moaning to me. Bloody work at it.' He led Barnard away, glancing back only briefly. 'Funny thing,'

Robertson said. 'I thought that lad had the makings but he's fading already. You can never tell, can you?' Barnard shrugged. Robertson had thought Barnard had the makings himself when he was about sixteen but he had not lived up to his older friend's expectations in the ring and now only came to the gym occasionally to work out and do a bit of training with the younger boys. Robertson took over the tiny office, dismissing the burly man in grubby vest and shorts who was occupying it, and shut the door.

'Ta for coming over, Harry,' he said. 'I've got a bit of a problem you might be able to help me with.'

Barnard took the only remaining chair in the narrow space and accepted the cigar that Robertson waved in his direction. As he went through the ritual of lighting it and making sure that it was burning satisfactorily, and Robertson did the same, the silence only broken by their furious puffing, he felt a slight sense of unease. He had done Ray and Georgie countless favours over the years, but he had felt recently that the need for his back-up had begun to fade away with the brothers' success in courting friends in high places. He was becoming surplus to requirements.

'So what can I do to help?' he asked, hoping that he was keeping any buried reservations out of his voice.

'It's Georgie-boy,' Ray said. 'I think he's going a bit mental.'

Barnard had a sudden vivid recollection of Georgie Robertson hurtling out of the Delilah Club evidently in a rage and being driven off fast. 'What makes you think that?' he asked carefully.

Robertson did not reply directly. 'Do you remember that time, when we was out in bloody Hertfordshire, when Georgie took against that old witch who lived next to the Post Office, the one with half a dozen cats?'

Barnard nodded. The village where the three boys had been evacuated to a farm had consisted of a modest cluster of houses on a narrow lane with a pub, a church and a post office cum village store as its only amenities. The boys, ranging in age from Ray, moving into his teens when they were delivered to the care of Farmer and Mrs Green, to eight-year-old Georgie, with Harry in the middle, had suffered a massive culture shock

on their sudden translation from the crowded streets of East
London to a landscape of woods and fields and not much else.
They had, Harry thought, been knocked sideways for a while
and Georgie perhaps the most seriously affected. He gazed at
Ray who seemed to be as lost in thought as he was himself.

'The old witch with the cats? Yes, I remember her. What
about it?'

'Georgie hated her with a bloody passion. She had a go at
him one time when she caught him nicking apples from her
back garden. Falling off the tree, they were. I saw them meself,
lying on the grass. But she didn't want him helping himself
to those rotten old apples.'

Barnard nodded and waited, knowing that there was more
to come. As incomers from the big city the village had treated
all of them with unrelenting suspicion. Worse, Georgie had
been a wild child, given to unpredictable screaming fits when
he couldn't get his own way, and he seldom got his own way
with old man Green, the farmer, who expected children to be
seen and not heard, and to get on with the chores they had
been allocated without complaint, and who gave them a sharp
clip round the ear when they failed to meet expectations.

'Georgie went a bit doolally down there, I reckon,' Ray
said. 'Especially over those cats. He fucking detested them.'

Barnard nodded. 'So he did something to the cats?'

'It was after your ma came to collect you. After you'd gone
home.' Robertson's tone still gave the impression that he had
regarded it as a personal affront that Barnard's family had
whisked him away as soon as he reached the age of eleven to
take up a place in the local grammar school which had itself
been evacuated to Norfolk. 'The cats started disappearing,
didn't they? One at a time. I don't reckon he could manage
more than one moggie at once. I saw the scratches he got. It
went on for months. We had the police round asking questions
because I reckon the old bat must have known who it was.
But there was no evidence. She put 'em out at night and every
now and again one of 'em didn't come back. Old man Green
reckoned the foxes was getting them. But I knew it was
Georgie.'

'What did he do with them?' Barnard asked, his mouth dry.

'You know there was an incinerator thing at the back of the barn?'

'Jesus,' Barnard said. 'They went in there? Dead or alive?'

'Oh, alive,' Robertson said. 'He brought them back in a box, one at a time, and tipped them in. I caught him at it eventually and told him to stop. He usually did what I told him.' Most people did, Barnard recalled. He had watched the older boy evolve from juvenile bully to gangster from an increasing distance as he had decided that was not a path he wanted to follow, but there had been enough times when he too had done what Ray Robertson had told him, and he feared that this might potentially be another.

'He's a nutter,' Barnard said. 'He always was.'

'Yeah, that's right,' Robertson agreed, exhaling cigar smoke like a steam train. The room was thick with it. He waved a hand to clear the air and fixed Barnard with a glare of such intensity that the younger man shifted uneasily in his chair. 'He's becoming a liability, Harry,' he said. 'I want him off the streets. He's out of control. You know me. Some of what I get up to may be illegal and all that, but I don't do violence unless it's absolutely necessary. Georgie's gone over the top. He's gone too far. And he's threatening to mess up some delicate deals I'm in the middle of. I can't have that. If it was anyone else, I'd get rid of him, though it's not really my bag. But he's my brother, isn't he? Family?'

Barnard's mind was racing as he took in the implications of what Robertson was saying. Georgie was not the only one whose sanity might be in doubt in this particular family, he thought. He had never heard Ray talk so openly about how far he might be prepared to go if pushed hard enough, but he did not doubt for a moment that he was speaking the truth. The look in his eyes said it all. 'So what are you thinking of?' he asked.

'I want Georgie locked up for a long time,' Ray said. 'No messing. Out of my hair for good.'

Barnard took a deep breath. 'That's a tall order,' he said. 'What's he supposed to have done, for God's sake? Unless you can give me chapter and verse . . .'

'Oh, I think we can do that,' Robertson said. 'You know

that lad who was killed in Greek Street, nancy-boy, actor or something? Don't tell me it wouldn't do you a bit of good to clear that up.'

Barnard nodded reluctantly. 'But Georgie's not a queer,' he objected. 'Is he?'

'Gawd no, my ma would go bananas if she thought that. But what if the lad had propositioned Georgie? What if Georgie was so furious that he followed him home? What if I can give you witnesses who saw all that? You don't have anyone else lined up for it, do you? Not that I hear, anyway. Clear up a nasty murder, get a feather in your cap, get Georgie out of my road so I can get on with things my way. Everybody happy.'

'Except Georgie,' Barnard muttered.

'I keep telling you, he's a nutter,' Ray snapped. 'He will kill someone one day if someone doesn't stop him. And they've stopped hanging them now, haven't they? More's the pity, but there you go. Safe as houses in Broadmoor, he'll be, when they've done all their tests and that. Our ma can live with that. "Poor Georgie's a little bit mad. Poor Georgie was provoked by one of them perverts." All that garbage. What do you say, Harry? Isn't that something you can live with too?'

'It's a bloody big thing you're asking, Ray,' Barnard objected.

'Not something you can't handle, Harry boy,' Ray assured him, with a fatherly arm on his shoulder. 'No trouble. No trouble at all.'

TEN

Kate O'Donnell met Declan Riley at the Cracke, spelt Ye Cracke for no very adequate reason Kate had ever fathomed. It was a down-at-heel and certainly not very ancient pub off Hope Street which was much frequented by students, including, she recalled, John Lennon and Cynthia, when they had all been at the art college a few years before. Declan followed her in and waved her from the bench she had chosen in the crowded main bar into the quieter back room, equally mysteriously known as the War Room, and went off to buy her a half of shandy and himself a pint of Guinness.

She had been surprised at the nostalgia she had felt as she had walked past the Institute, with crowds of uniformed boys behind the railings, and Blackburne House, its sister girls' school, in its stately old merchant's house nearby. The sense of familiarity reminded her forcibly of what she had left behind. She had not been away long, and the changes were subtle but enough to put another barrier between her future and her past. Another concrete support or two had been swung into place on 'Paddy's wigwam', the modernist Catholic cathedral being built at one end of Hope Street, a much-mocked challenge to the slow emergence of the traditional Anglican pile closer to the Mersey. The boys' school looked a bit tattier than it had when she used to pass it every day, an elite school evidently losing its gloss in changing times. The students in the bar suddenly seemed much younger to her, as if a month in London had added years to her age, though she guessed that was more to do with the constant drag of anxiety than any suddenly acquired southern sophistication.

Declan reappeared and put the drinks down on the table. He looked pale and anxious, Kate thought, and knew that it must have been as much of a shock to Tom's old school-friends as it had been to her to be told by the police the unbelievable news that Tom was wanted in connection with a murder.

'What's going on, Kate?' the young man asked after he had taken a long draught from his glass and wiped the froth off his top lip. 'What the hell are the bizzies on about, for God's sake?'

Kate shrugged. She spelt out everything she knew.

'I remember Jon Mason,' Declan said, looking angry. 'I met him a few times but I never liked him. And when Tom palled up with him I got really worried. There were a lot of whispers about Jonathon, even when he was a lad. He went to some posh private school in Cheshire and then away to university somewhere, so he wasn't around a lot. I never got to know him well but there was a group of queer lads used to meet in a pub out in West Derby and he turned up there every now and then, Tom said. Tom took me there once though I think he realized it was a mistake straight away. They said they were a fishing club or something daft but everyone knew they got up to a lot more than fishing. Especially Jonno. He'd got a really weird reputation even before we left school. I told Tom to keep clear but even then he seemed to be fascinated by him. I wasn't really surprised when he said he was going to London with him, and not to tell his mam or anyone. Not surprised, but pretty worried. But what do you do? If you start making a fuss about lads like that they'll get the bizzies after them anyway. And I didn't want that for Tom. Most of us just steered clear in the end. Left him to it, and now I really wish I hadn't.'

Looking embarrassed, he reached to a pocket inside his coat and pulled out a tattered-looking magazine, which he opened at an inside page before pushing it across the table towards Kate, shielding it with his arm to prevent anyone else getting a glimpse of it. 'This has been doing the rounds,' he said. 'I don't know who first spotted it, but that's Jonathon.' He put a finger on a slightly blurred face, half turned away from the camera amongst a group of naked men. 'If that's what his mate's got into I'm not surprised there was trouble.'

'I don't think I ever met Jonathon,' Kate said, her face flushed in embarrassment. She'd had no idea such magazines existed. 'After he left school Tom never brought friends home much. Only you and Sean, who he'd known since we were all little kids at St Jimmy's.'

'So you really didn't know what he was like? Why he didn't have a girlfriend?'

'No, of course not,' Kate said. 'We just thought he was a bit shy with girls. Even now, I've only got the vaguest idea what men get up to together. You know what our school was like. It's a wonder good Catholics like us ever manage to reproduce at all given the sex education we got. Or didn't get.'

'They seem to manage all right once they get the hang of it,' Declan, who had six brothers and sisters, said with a grin.

'Anyway, never mind all that,' Kate said sharply. 'Tom's still my brother and he's in trouble. Has he come back up north, do you think? Have you any idea where he might be?' Declan took a gulp of his Guinness and glanced away for a moment as if in thought.

'Do the bizzies in London know you're up here?' he asked eventually.

'No, of course not,' Kate said.

'Unless they're following you,' Declan said gloomily.

Kate had a sudden vivid recollection of Sergeant Harry Barnard's charming but crooked smile and shivered slightly. 'Only my boss knows I'm here',' she said. 'I'm supposed to be getting some pictures of John Lennon's girlfriend, Cynthia. And he didn't know what train I was getting or anything like that. They couldn't have followed me.'

'I hope you're right,' Declan said. 'You're chasing the elusive Cynthia, are you? She's supposed to have married him, you know? Silly cow.'

'And up the duff, apparently,' Kate said. 'I never thought it would take long for those two to find out how to do it.'

Declan laughed. 'Must be better sex education at Quarry Bank than with the monks and nuns,' he said, and then buried his head in his drink, avoiding her eyes. Kate looked at him. Her glass of shandy sat untouched on the table between them and she felt the faintest flicker of hope since she had arrived at Lime Street Station.

'You know where he is, don't you?' she said quietly.

'I think I know someone who does,' Declan admitted.

Kate felt tears prickle her eyes as she gave a sigh of intense relief. 'He's safe?' she breathed.

'Safe enough, I reckon, la,' Declan said. 'They keep themselves to themselves, these queer boys. I don't mind. I wouldn't
want the bizzies breathing down me neck. But I've always
liked Tom, ever since we were at St Jimmy's together. I used
to look out for him right through school but I hadn't seen him
for a long time after we left. He seemed to steer clear, especially after he took me to the so-called fishing club. Then I
bumped into him in town a couple of years ago with this
kidder, Jon. I remembered him from the first time we met and
I still didn't like him. He was all over Tom, in a really nasty
way. Trying to control him. Making snide remarks to him
about his school friends, as if we weren't good enough in
some way. I think what he really meant was we weren't queer
enough. I told you, I really wasn't happy when I heard they'd
gone off together. At least everyone I talked to seemed to
assume they were together.'

'Everyone knew then? Except his family,' Kate said bitterly.

'Well, it wasn't something we were going to come round
and tell your mam about, was it? We knew that Tom wouldn't
want that,' Declan snapped back. He glanced round the room,
where the only other drinkers were two men deep in reminiscences of El Alamein and the war which had been the high
point of their lives. 'Stay here for a mo and I'll make a phone
call and find out what's what for you. I'll see if I can track
him down. I won't be long, la. I promise.'

Less than an hour later, Kate found herself following Declan
Riley down a suburban road which seemed to end at an inde-
terminate off-white horizon. She could taste the salt in the air
and she knew, if nothing else, that they were near the sea.
After he had made his phone call, they had walked back into
the city centre and picked up a local train at James Street
which followed the Mersey as it widened out to meet the Irish
sea. They had got off at a station which seemed to have lost
its name board, leaving Kate no idea of exactly where she
was. These seaside suburbs were new to her, dormitories
feeding the city and further out than she had ever ventured as
a child. And as the bungalows and houses grew more isolated
but the road continued, getting sandier underfoot, she realized
that their destination must be the estuary itself. Eventually the

road petered out into a track and then that too ended and only
a line of sand dunes and marram grass stood between them
and the beach. Declan strode ahead confidently.

'You've been here before?' Kate asked tentatively.

Having agreed to take her to meet Tom, his friend had been
infuriatingly sparing with information. Tom was with another
friend, he had said, and would meet them in an hour. The less
she knew the less she would have to hide if the bizzies came
knocking again, he had said, and she could not disagree. Her
good-looking detective sergeant might well wheedle things
out of her that she did not want him to know, so she had
resolutely kept her questions to a minimum on the journey
out of the city. If she saw Tom and reassured herself that he
was all right, that would have to be enough for now. Clearing
him of suspicion was something else entirely.

Trudging through the deep, soft sand of the dunes, which
sucked at their feet like treacle, they eventually found themselves standing above the shore line, where a slight chop on
the grey water lapped and swirled relentlessly on to the flat
expanse of beach as the tide came in. Across the estuary, the
Wirral shore was a dark line on the horizon and beyond that
the faint smudge of the Welsh hills were hardly distinguishable
from the cloudy sky to the south. There was no sign of life
on the strand which stretched unbroken in both directions, and
only a single Irish ferry on the vast expanse of water in front
of them, ploughing towards the open sea. Maybe Tom was
hoping to be on one of those, she thought, heading for Dublin
or Belfast or even the Isle of Man. She took a deep breath of
the tangy air and turned to face Declan, her heart thumping.

'Now what?' she asked in little more than a breathy whisper,
as if raising her voice would bring retribution in its wake.

Declan glanced at his watch. 'We wait,' he said. 'We're a
bit earlier than they said. We were lucky with the train. I
wasn't sure how often they ran.' They sat down on the edge
of the dunes in an uneasy silence, huddling into their coats
against the cold, blustery wind, and invisible to anyone
approaching from the landward side. Eventually they spotted
two figures walking along the edge of the water towards them
as if out for an innocent afternoon stroll.

'Is that them?' Kate asked, unsure of herself suddenly as she realized that she had not seen Tom for almost two years and that in that time he might have changed beyond recognition. Declan stood up, brushing the sand off his clothes, but did not move until the two figures slowly turned towards them and eventually gave a slight wave of greeting.

'It's them,' he said. 'Thank Christ for that.'

Kate felt relief surge through her and bring tears to her eyes. Both young men were wearing duffle coats with the hoods up and it was not until Tom held out his arms to her that she could distinguish him from his friend.

'I am so glad to see you, Katie,' her brother said, as he grabbed hold of her and hugged her close. She could feel his tears on her cheek. Declan and his friend, who did not offer a name, strolled off together, leaving Kate and Tom to sink down again into the shelter of the dunes with their arms around each other.

'We've been so worried,' Kate whispered. 'I didn't know what to say to Mam, but the police had been round there so she was beside herself anyway.'

'I know,' Tom said. 'I'm so sorry, but as soon as I heard what had happened at the flat I thought I'd better stay out of the way for a bit. I knew the police would think the worst. You've no idea what it's like living like we do, doing something illegal all the time, never knowing when the police might come storming in like they do at the pubs and clubs we go to. You can't even use a public lavvie for fear of being arrested.'

Kate took a moment to digest exactly what her brother was saying. 'Do you mean that you didn't know your friend was dead when you came up here?'

'Of course I didn't,' Tom said. 'Jon and I had been having a lot of rows. He was getting into things I didn't want to be involved in. I began to think weeks ago I should leave.'

'Like what?' Kate whispered.

'Nothing too heavy but I could see the way he was heading. We'd been doing a bit of modelling, and it was getting more and more near the knuckle. And then he got interested in boys.

I found him in the flat with a young lad one night, so I decided I had to get out. I needed some time to sort myself out.'

Kate looked at her brother for a long moment, not daring to admit she had seen a 'not too heavy' photograph of Jonathon in the magazine Declan had let her keep. To her, it felt as heavy as a guilty conscience concealed in her handbag. 'How did you get here then?' she whispered.

'I hitched a lift with Dave Donovan's band last Monday. They were playing at a club in Wallasey. They dropped me off and I went to stay with . . .' He hesitated. 'Just a friend. You don't need to know. Let's just say I'm with a kidder I knew before I went down south, I don't want the bizzies knocking on his door. Anyway, Declan gave us a ring a couple of days later. He was ringing round everyone he could think of trying to find me. He told us what was going on. He'd had a visit from a couple of detectives and he'd heard our mam had too. I just couldn't believe it. I still can't.'

Kate took a minute to absorb what Tom had just said. 'You haven't been to see our mam, have you?' she persisted.

Tom glanced away, not meeting her eyes, and shrugged helplessly. 'Course not,' he said.

'But you weren't in London when your friend was killed?'

'No, that's what I'm telling you. Jon had gone off to work as usual on the day I left. He was working lunchtimes in a bar in the West End – "resting" is what actors call it. He seemed to spend most of his time resting, which is why he got into the modelling and stuff. I left after he'd gone, met up with Dave and the lads and came north.'

'So you don't have anything to worry about,' Kate said. 'You don't have to hide from the police.'

'That's what Declan said, but I'm scared, Kate. Really scared. I didn't tell anyone I was coming away, obviously not Jon, but not even the kidder I was working for in Carnaby Street. I'd just had a blazing row with Jon about what he was up to and as soon as he went out I packed my stuff and planned to go and catch a train. Then I remembered Dave was in London and I wondered if he or any of his mates was going north. I was walking out on my job as well, remember, and I knew I was going to be broke. Anyway, it turned out he was driving up home that night for a gig the next day so I hitched a lift. I don't think I really realized what I'd done till we got up near Warrington and stopped for a drink. Then I sat there with a pint and couldn't work out what to do for the best, go on or go back. I didn't want to go home to mam. I even thought of bailing out and getting the next train back to London to try to make it up with Jon. But in the end I called my mate and fixed to stay with him for a few days to try and sort myself out. Then Dec phoned a few days later, because the bizzies had been round, and I found out what had happened to Jon. It's all a bit of a blur, that day I came away, and knowing Dave he'll be pretty vague about dates and times. My mate up here knows when I arrived but you can bet your life the bizzies won't believe him if they don't want to. We're all queers to them and deserve anything they chuck at us. And it's true Jon and me hadn't been getting on for a while. Some people down there know that. They know we'd been at each others' throats. It'll all sounds really bad, bad enough for them to be sure I did it.'

'You couldn't cut someone's throat,' Kate said angrily.

Tom went pale and buried his head in his hands. 'Is that how it happened?' he whispered.

Kate hugged him hard. 'You didn't know?'

'No, I didn't know. Dec didn't tell me that.'

Kate left Tom with his friend, failing in every effort to persuade him to talk to the police who, she was sure, would track him down eventually. The most she achieved was a tentative promise to think about what to do next and to ring her in London when she got back. Disappointed and depressed, she said little on the journey back into the city with Declan, and they parted at the station without making any plans to meet again. Kate had extracted a phone number from Tom so she knew she could contact him but it was a measure of his paranoia that she had to work hard to get even that and swear not to give it to anyone else.

Back in the city, Kate knew that she would have to do something to justify to Ken Fellows the day off she had taken for her trip to the north. She did not know where John Lennon – with or without a wife – was living and knew she had almost no chance of finding out. The Beatles were so famous in Liverpool that hysterical teenaged girls were in constant hot pursuit of all four of them and they kept their whereabouts as secret as they possibly could. But Kate knew there was one place where she might just possibly find out.

She walked across the city from the station and made her way to the lane just off the shopping centre which was Matthew Street. A gaggle of teenaged girls was, as usual, hanging around amongst the litter and detritus from the fruit warehouses around the entrance of the Cavern Club, hoping to see one of their heroes go in or come out. Kate could remember going to the Cavern as a young teenager with a boyfriend who was a jazz fanatic, but since those purist days when jazz fans regarded themselves as a distinct cut above the burgeoning rock groups, with their Teddy boy reputation, the Cavern had effectively caved in to fashion. For the last few years it had given a home to the Mersey Beat and was regularly filled beyond capacity at lunchtime and in the evenings with near hysterical fans.

Kate pushed past the teenagers and stepped through the open door and down into the familiar, fetid, almost airless hole that was the club. There had obviously been a lunchtime performance and the floor was still littered with sandwich wrappers and smelt of sweat and faintly of the gas which provided the only lighting under the brick cellar arches. If a fireman had seen the place when it was heaving, Kate thought, he'd have closed it down on the spot. A couple of women were making a desultory attempt to clean up and on the stage, where the amps regularly shorted and failed during perform-ances as moisture ran down the walls, she spotted a man she knew was something to do with running the place.

'You won't remember me,' she said by way of greeting. 'But I used to be at art college with John Lennon and Cynthia. I work in London now as a photographer, and I'm trying to track them down. You don't have a phone number, do you?'

The man looked at her with deep suspicion on what she could see of his face in the gloomy light. 'Who's Cynthia?'

'Ah,' Kate said carefully. 'His girlfriend? Or she was when we were at college.'

The man shrugged. 'I wouldn't know about that, petal,' he

said. 'And I can't go handing out the musicians' phone numbers, can I? There's a couple of thousand girls like you who want John Lennon's phone number.'

Kate thought for a moment before she tried again. 'Do you know his Auntie Mimi?' she asked eventually.

The man snorted. 'Do I know Mimi Smith? I should say so. She used to come down here laying the law down, trying to get John to do this and that, anything but play in a band. I know Mimi all right. Why she can't just go along for the ride and enjoy it like George's mam I can't understand.'

'Well, do you know where she lives? I could ask her if she could put me in touch with John and Cyn,' Kate pleaded. 'I think I can help the Beatles out with some publicity pictures in London. I work for a big agency. Honestly, I'm not trying it on. I've known them for years.'

The man sighed heavily. 'Might have her address in the files. John was still living with her when I first met him. He's got his own place now and I'm not telling you where that is. Come on, let's have a look. But I wish you luck with Mimi. She's a real tartar, she is. No messing.'

And five minutes later, hot and sweaty, but with an address on a piece of paper in her bag, Kate climbed back up to street level and wearily went looking for a bus to Woolton.

Number 251 Menlove Avenue was an unassuming suburban house in a tree-lined road, another ride out of town, and when Kate knocked she thought at first no one was at home. But eventually the front door opened and to her surprise Kate found herself face-to-face with a heavily pregnant Cynthia Powell, or was it now Cynthia Lennon? she wondered.

'Cyn,' she said, with as cheerful a smile as she could muster. 'I bet you don't remember me. Kate O'Donnell from the college of art'

Cynthia stared at Kate for a long time before she shrugged, offered a faint smile and motioned her through the door, looking carefully up and down the street before closing it again. Kate was no expert but looking at Cynthia's bump she thought it could not be long before the baby was born.

'I'm here by myself,' Cynthia said. 'Mimi's gone shopping.

I come up here sometimes just to get out of the flat. It's so poky I think I might come here permanently after the baby's born. John's away so much now . . .' She trailed off and Kate felt sorry for her.

'You got married then?' she asked as she followed Cynthia into the front room and took a seat.

'Of course we did, once we knew the baby was coming. Nothing big. Just the registry office. My parents didn't come.' She shrugged and flopped down heavily beside Kate. 'If you want a cup of tea you'll have to make it yourself. The kitchen's at the back.' Kate shook her head and wondered just how much Cynthia had craved the big white wedding her parents must have expected one day.

'No tea thanks, I'm fine,' she said. 'I was hoping I'd find you and John together to take some pictures of you. I work for a photographic agency in London now and they're really interested in the Liverpool bands. They think the Beatles are going to be really great.'

'Well, it's not for want of trying,' Cynthia said. 'John's away more than he's at home these days. They're down in London this week talking about the next recording. You know they've had a couple of records out?'

'Yes, I heard one just last week,' Kate said.

'I don't know if they're going to be a success,' Cynthia said doubtfully. 'They seem to have been at it so long now. All that time they spent in Hamburg.'

'I can't imagine John as a dad,' Kate said lightly, thinking that the future of this little family would be pretty grim if John Lennon's fortunes did not improve. Cynthia would find it hard to launch a career of her own with a baby at home. 'Their new record seems to be doing all right, anyway.'

Cynthia nodded and gazed out of the window with a hand on her extended belly. 'If they get as much support down south as they do up here we'll be fine,' she said. But her bleak expression told Kate that perhaps she thought that unlikely. 'Though I get pretty sick of the girls running after him all the time. That's why we kept the wedding quiet. I think some of them would try to kill me if they knew I was married to John.'

'Well, you won't be able to keep it secret if they really do make it,' Kate said. 'You'll have all the London papers and magazines running after you. Will you let me take a picture, ready for when you're famous? That would be really good. And my boss would be pleased. I've only got my job on trial so the more I can do to keep him happy the better for me.'

Cynthia looked uncertain. 'What would you do with it?' she asked.

'Well, if the bands begin to look as though they're going to make it, not just the Beatles but Gerry and the Pacemakers and the rest, my boss wants to be able to offer some picture features to the papers. The Liverpool Beat, they could call it.'

'The Mersey Beat they're calling it up here. There's a magazine now, you know. I ought to ask John, or Brian,' Cynthia said, still doubtful. 'Brian Epstein, their manager. He runs that record shop in Whitechapel, Nems. You must know it. Some of the lads were always hanging about in there when we were at college. He looks after all the Beatles' publicity and stuff now.'

Including their pictures, most likely, Kate thought ruefully. But she was not quite ready to give up. 'But this will be *your* publicity,' she said. 'There's no reason why you should be left out if they get to be famous,' Kate persisted. 'I wouldn't want to be kept in the shadows like a guilty secret by my baby's dad.' She glanced again at Cynthia's left hand but could not see a wedding ring.

'Yeah, you're right. Just let me go and powder my nose and you can take a couple of snaps. What's the harm in that? You can let me have one as well. It'll be funny to see what I looked like in this state when it's all over, won't it?' She lumbered to her feet and went into the hall and came back with her hair combed and her lipstick renewed. 'Go on then,' she said more cheerfully. 'Let's have a picture of Mrs Lennon and baby. Why not?'

ELEVEN

D
S Harry Barnard had made it his business to be at the magistrate's court that morning when the vagrant Hamish Macdonald came before their worships. After the hearing, when most of the derelicts who had been picked up the previous night had been handed down fines that they had no possibility of paying, and had resigned themselves to a week or two in jail instead, he went down to the cells and located Hamish sitting on a bench with the rest, waiting for prison transport to arrive.

'How much was it, Hamish?' Barnard asked, making sure that the Scot could see the ten pound note he had folded in his hand.

'Ten quid or ten days,' Hamish muttered, his mouth dry as his thirst grew.

'It's worth that to me to have a chat with your young friend you were telling me about last night,' Barnard said quietly. 'Are you on?' He was sure that this must be the boy DCI Venables was interested in, his suspicions confirmed by the duty sergeant's report that they had found a nurse's cap lying in the mud on the railway embankment where the vagrants had been rounded up.

'I'm bloody not on if ye arrest him instead of me, ye devious bastard,' Hamish muttered.

'How about if I find him somewhere safe to stay? He sounds too young to be on the streets.'

'Aye, he's that all right,' Hamish said. 'He's naething but a wee lad, whatever he gets up tae. Says he's sixteen but I don't believe him. And he'll come back to the gaff looking for me. Bound to. He's got nowhere else to go and I keep an eye out for him.' He gave Barnard a pleading glance and got a brief nod in return.

'So let's clear your fine and go and see if we can find him,' he said.

Barnard ducked the issue of giving the less than savoury-smelling Macdonald a ride in his own car by hitching a lift in a police van which was heading towards Bloomsbury, and getting the driver to drop them off at the corner of Clerkenwell and Farringdon Roads. From there they could walk.

'Do you think he'll hang about if he finds that your place has been cleared?' Barnard asked as they went slowly past the boarded-up bomb sites beyond the underground station, Hamish looking longingly into the open doors of the corner pub which had somehow survived the Blitz, and which, Barnard thought, would be very unlikely to serve him anyway. Eventually, beyond a ruined warehouse, they came to the fencing where the police had broken through on to the railway embankment the previous night. The encampment appeared deserted from the road, the rough shelters some of the men had made demolished and scattered, bedding in a smelly heap ready to be taken away by the refuse collectors, and the ashes of fires no longer even smouldering. Hamish stood at the top of the steep slope, beneath which a Circle Line train was trundling, evidently seeking out any sign of life, but eventually it was Barnard himself who thought he spotted a movement in a shady corner beneath a few frost-blasted remnants of fireweed and a couple of ragged shrubs which were clinging to life in spite of the fire-ravaged soil and the still bitter weather.

'There,' he said quietly to his companion. 'There's someone there. You go over and persuade him to talk to me. I don't want to risk him running so close to the railway line.'

Hamish glanced down the slope and nodded. 'He'd nae be the first to get electrocuted down there,' he said. 'I'll fetch him for ye.'

Barnard leaned against the wooden fencing as the old man picked his way through the remnants of the encampment and disappeared into the undergrowth. A few minutes later he came back, helping a young boy along by his arm. Barnard took a deep breath when he saw the state of the boy, who seemed to find walking difficult and was bruised around the face and neck, and with a still livid scar just above his forehead where the hair had been shaved away.

'You and me need a chat,' Barnard said, taking hold of both

the boy's arms in a firm grip as he saw the panic in his eyes. He nodded to Hamish. 'I'll do what I said,' he promised. 'Don't worry about that.'

Hamish did no more than grunt in acknowledgement and turned away quickly, to avoid the suspicion in the boy's eyes and to hide the guilt in his own.

'Bastard,' the boy snarled in little more than a croaking whisper. 'I thought he was my mate. You a copper?'

'Detective,' Barnard said. 'It's all right, he is your friend, as it goes. He's doing his best for you. I only want to ask you a few questions, and then we'll find you somewhere safe to stay. I promised the old man I'd do that. You look as if you need it.' He pulled his unwilling companion back through the fence and turned him up the hill towards Rosebery Avenue where he shepherded him into a cafe and sat him at a table close to the counter while he ordered two teas and bacon sandwiches which the boy fell on wolfishly.

'How long is it since you had a proper meal?' Barnard asked. The boy gazed at him blankly, shivering inside his over-large sweater. The sergeant took one of his arms and pushed the sleeve up carefully, wincing at the bruises round his wrist where he had obviously been manacled in some way. The boy looked at him with blank eyes, offering no explanation.

'Don't remember many meals,' he muttered, his mouth full. 'They gave me a lot of booze last night. I don't remember eating much.'

'You're not a Londoner,' Barnard said, unable to place the slight northern accent he detected.

'You're reet,' the boy conceded, and it was obvious he was not going to admit any more than that about where he had come from. He was, Barnard thought, one of the hundreds of runaways who got this far every year and more often than not were never heard from again back in their home towns.

'Where were you last night?' Barnard asked, guessing he might be more willing to talk about recent events.

'Dunno. They took me in a car from Les's place. A big car. All leather seats an' that. Right posh.'

'And then what? You look as if you had a rough time somewhere.'

'It was a party, wasn't it? Les took me to a party. He promised me twenty quid if I'd go.'

'And did he pay you?' Barnard asked, his eyes angry.

'Nay, he didn't, he said he'd give it me next time, didn't he?' The boy's eyes suddenly filled with tears and he dashed them away angrily. 'Bastard. I really, really need that money.' And he would be really, really unlikely to get it, Barnard thought wearily, while the men who were using him found the promise an easy way of keeping him compliant.

'And what went on at this party? You don't look as if you enjoyed it.'

'They took pictures, didn't they? Lots of pictures. With me yelling like a banshee for them to stop.'

'They hurt you?' Barnard asked although he knew the question was redundant. One look at the boy's bruises was enough to tell him that. 'So you don't want to go back for your money?' he asked.

The boy glanced away before replying. 'I need twenty quid,' he said.

'If you help me find the men who were at this so-called party, I reckon I can find you twenty quid, no trouble.'

The boy finished his greasy sandwich and glanced longingly at the woman behind the counter.

'I can find you somewhere safe to stay as well,' Barnard said. 'They'll feed you.'

But the boy still hesitated. 'Where's Hamish gone?' he asked.

'Hamish is all right,' Barnard said. 'He's a tough old bugger. But you're not, are you? You shouldn't have come out of the hospital. You need looking after.'

'But you want to know stuff? You're not going to gi' me twenty quid for nowt, are you? What do you want to know?'

'For a start, where this man Les lives, the bloke who took you to this party.'

The boy glanced out of the steamy cafe window. 'Not far,' he said. 'Up by St Pancras. I can show you.'

'Do you know any other names?'

The boy shook his head. 'Nobody tells you names, do they?' he said.

'It's a deal, then?' Barnard asked, feeling a stir of excitement. A lot of his work consisted of harassing people he pitied more than he condemned, but the men who had abused this boy he badly wanted to find. 'I get you somewhere safe to stay and you help me? Starting by tracking down this Les?'

The boy nodded, running a finger round the last remnants of bacon fat and licking it.

'And the twenty quid as well?'

'Fine,' Barnard said. 'The twenty quid it is.'

The Rev David Hamilton had turned to God after his army career had pretty much ended at Dunkirk, where he was one of the troops defending the evacuating army from the rear around Calais. Wounded in the thigh, he had been picked up close to death by the advancing Germans as the last rescue ships and flotillas of small boats headed away into the Channel without him and the rest of the rearguard. In pain and bleeding heavily, he half expected to be shot out of hand but he was lucky with the unit who found him and spent time in military hospitals before being transferred to various PoW camps, and experiencing no more of the conflict. When peace was declared and he came back to the Home Counties with a pronounced limp, he resigned his commission, to his army family's consternation, and signed up for the Anglican ministry at an evangelical training college in the north of England.

He had taken over as rector of St Peter's, a gothic barn of a church on the edge of Soho, five years before, taken a single walk around the red light district after dark on his first evening, and there and then decided that he had found his mission in life. He would use what God had kindly given him in the way of real estate to rescue as many of the benighted young people who earned their livings in the clubs and brothels of the neighbourhood as he humanly could. The very next morning he set in train a military campaign to raise the money and gain the support he needed from his superiors to set up the enterprise he planned.

It was not that he neglected the handful of loyal and mainly ancient parishioners who turned up each Sunday to Matins and Evensong, and the even smaller group who staggered into early Communion once a month. He simply regarded them as a very minor part of his ministry unless they volunteered to help him, as a few of the more able-bodied did. His main objective was to use the space the vast, echoing and almost always empty church offered, both above ground in the nave, which he split in two, the smaller portion at the east end for religious worship, the larger for other purposes, and also underground in the low-vaulted but spacious crypt.

By the time Sergeant Harry Barnard had joined the Vice Squad, St Peter's had established itself as a haven for young people who were either homeless or anxious to escape from the sex trade which had sucked them in and was reluctant to spit them out again. And to the surprise of outsiders, in the police force as much as the church, while Hamilton's religious rhetoric was fiercely ridiculed in what he called the devil's square mile, his refuge worked, not always or with every one of the young people he encouraged in and counselled, but with enough of them to impress those who noticed such things. St Peter's Refuge became well-established and well-regarded and was run with military precision and efficiency and a firm eye on Biblical precepts at all times, no drink, no fags and beds to be neatly made ready for inspection before breakfast every morning.

Sergeant Barnard arrived with his charge late in the afternoon, when he knew that arrangements could be made for new arrivals. The boy followed him in through the church doors, dragging his feet and peering into the gloomy interior with deep suspicion. The Rev Dave, as he insisted on being called, marched down what had once been the central aisle with his hand held out enthusiastically to the sergeant.

'What have we got here, Harry?' he asked. 'Come into the office and tell me all about it.' He put a heavy hand on the boy's shoulder and urged him forward. 'Come on, laddie, don't be frightened. We're here help you.'

Barnard watched in admiration as the vicar sat the boy down and with surprising gentleness explained that he could give him a temporary home, and even help him find a permanent one, but insisted that in exchange he must provide some information about himself. Hamilton's combination of sympathy and firmness, as he sat across the desk from the boy with his pen poised to fill in the application form which he insisted was necessary, succeeded where Barnard's attempts to elicit personal information had failed miserably and the boy at last admitted to a name.

'Jimmy,' he said hesitantly.

'And a second name, Jimmy?' the vicar insisted.

'Earnshaw,' the boy muttered, hunching his shoulders.

'And where are you from, Jimmy Earnshaw?'

'Doncaster,' the boy said.

'Age?'

'Sixteen.' The boy sounded confident but Barnard did not believe him, aware that he probably knew enough of the law to understand that if he was under that age the police were bound to return him to where he came from. But he let it pass.

'Do you have a home address in Doncaster?' Hamilton continued.

The boy shrugged. 'I were in a home, weren't I? I don't know where my mam is now.'

By infinitesimal degrees Hamilton coaxed Jimmy's story out of him, the early neglect, the abandonment, the transfer to a children's home, and the abuse which followed.

'Why didn't you complain about what these men were doing to you?' Barnard asked, unable to keep quiet any longer.

'We did complain, but we just got a right good thrashing for telling lies,' the boy muttered. 'No one wanted to know what was going on. Still is going on, prob'ly. I ain't going back there, that's for sure.'

Barnard promised himself that he would contact the Yorkshire police about the boy's story and wondered where he did want to go with the twenty quid he had promised him as he listened to the details that Hamilton patiently dragged out of him, of his escape from the home, his train ride to London funded with money that he guessed he had stolen, and then his bewilderment as he stood at the top of the fume-wreathed platforms at King's Cross station, a tiny island of despair amongst the hustling crowds, with not a clue what to do next. A man, he said, had picked him up, a sympathetic-seeming man who had promised him a bed for the night and help in finding a job. But there had been the inevitable price and he had soon found himself on the streets, penniless and knowing only one way to earn a living. Eventually Barnard broached the subject of Jimmy Earnshaw's still-healing head injury, but the boy closed up at once.

'How did you hurt your head?' he asked. All he got was a blank look and a defensive hunching of the shoulders. But Barnard persisted. 'There's a hospital said they treated a lad like you after a road accident and they're worried because he ran away. Was that you, Jimmy?'

Again the boy shook his head and Hamilton gave Barnard a warning look. 'Perhaps it would be better if we let Jimmy get some sleep and then you come back to talk to him in the morning,' he said.

Eventually Hamilton led the boy away to settle him into the cubicles in the crypt which was where the boys were housed, leaving the girls to sleep in the nave. When he came back he did not hide his anger. 'It's becoming quite common for these perverts to pick up young lads, and girls, at the railway stations. You should do something about it.'

'I'll pass it up the line,' Barnard said mildly. 'And I'll make some inquiries about this home in Yorkshire where it all began.'

'I shouldn't think he's given us his real name,' Hamilton said. 'They seldom do. Anyway, I'll see what we can sort out for him. It's surprising what the Good Lord provides if you give him a helping hand.'

'I really need more,' Barnard said. 'I want to find out who's been exploiting him here in London. I reckon there's a new outfit using kids for queer porn magazines. The really nasty sort of stuff usually comes in from abroad, but I suspect someone's had the bright idea of launching a home-grown operation.'

'Let me talk to him,' Hamilton said. 'Come back tomorrow when he's had a good night's sleep and a couple of square meals. He'll trust both of us a bit more then and may be willing to talk.'

Barnard nodded. He was content to leave his questions about

the boy's accident and lurid nightmares to the next day as well. Before he delivered him into the less sympathetic hands of DCI Venables, he wanted to be sure that there was a good reason to give him over to the murder inquiry. As far as he was concerned, the lad was a possible lead into the increasing use of children in home-grown pornography. He didn't want him swallowed up by Venables' murder investigation just yet on the basis of nothing more than a nightmare which might or might not be linked to Jonathon Mason's death. He would talk to the boy himself, in his own time and at his own pace, he thought, and then decide what to do next.

'Meantime I'll put some pressure on the queer pubs and clubs,' he said to Hamilton. 'If someone thinks it's worthwhile to produce this stuff, someone must be buying it. What adults get up to doesn't bother me too much but when they're using kids . . .' He shrugged helplessly.

'An abomination,' Hamilton agreed, though Barnard would not have put it quite like that. 'They'll burn in hell eventually, but I've never believed that's an excuse to let sinners flourish here. So good luck with your inquiries.'

Ken Fellows was not a man ever to exhibit great enthusiasm, but he did deign to show some interest when Kate dropped prints of her pictures of Cynthia Lennon on his desk that Monday morning. There was a gleam in his hooded eyes which he quickly veiled.

'Have you seen this?' he asked, pushing a copy of that day's first edition of the *Evening Standard* towards her. The point of interest seemed to be a small grainy shot on an obscure inside page of a group of teenaged girls hanging around in an unidentified street, clutching autograph books and waving towards a group of baby-faced lads with pudding basin haircuts. 'The Mersey men come to town,' the headline announced, while the couple of paragraphs beneath the picture showed a mixture of incomprehension and contempt for the hysteria on show, and did not bother to name the band.

'That's them. That's the Beatles,' Kate said. 'That's John Lennon, who I knew at college, that's Paul and George and the drummer, Ringo Starr. He's really called Ritchie. The girls in Liverpool are going mad for them. John's new wife practically has to hide from them, they're so ferocious. That's her.' She fanned out her prints of Cynthia in front of Ken. 'No one even knows they're married but she told me they really were. If they make it, these pictures will be really valuable.'

Ken raised an eyebrow at that, and Kate wondered how much more sceptical he might become if he knew the four young men had been trying to make it for six or seven years now since they had met as schoolboys and set up a skiffle group. 'It's a good story,' she said defensively.

'So we keep the pics till they make it big?' he asked.

'I don't think you'll have to wait long. Their new record's in the Hit Parade already.'

'Well, I'll believe you, though many wouldn't,' Fellows said, leaning back in his chair and stretching his arms above his head. He looked as though he'd had a rough weekend. 'But I'm more interested in the shots you took at Ray Robertson's do at Delilah's on Friday night.' He fished out a folder and rifled through her prints until he came to several of the government minister Lord Francome and his companion in the revealing red dress. 'You sure of her name, are you? Is she on the guest list?' he asked, putting an interrogatory finger on Christine Jones's well-exposed charms.

'I'm not sure if she's on the list,' Kate said. 'But I do know her name. I bumped into her in the Ladies' and I asked her. She was quite chatty.'

'Did you now?' Fellows came back with a leer. 'There's a clever girl, then. OK, I think the *Standard* diary will be very interested in that one, and maybe a few more. Not bad for a beginner.' And that, Kate thought, was about as much praise as she was ever likely to get out of Ken Fellows. But to her surprise, he had not quite finished.

'When is this girl's baby due?' he asked, putting his finger on one of the shots of Cynthia Lennon.

'In about four weeks,' Kate said.

'Well, you'd better see if you can get us some shots when it's born. If this band is really going to be as big as you say it is, we'd better keep on top of them, hadn't we? And what about the band you snapped in London on your own account? Are they going to be big too?'

Kate thought of Dave Donovan and his friends, and shrugged slightly. 'They'd like to think they are, but they didn't have the girls in Liverpool running after them the way they're doing after the Beatles and one or two of the other groups. I reckon it's wishful thinking with them.'

'You say that even though they're mates of yours?'

Kate grinned at her boss. 'Especially because they were mates of mine,' she said.

She found the filing and office chores less frustrating that morning, thinking that at last she was making some progress towards making her job permanent. At lunchtime, she put her coat on, glanced in her bag, where she still carried the magazine that Declan Riley had given her, concealed now in a plain envelope, and set off resolutely towards Greek Street. She knew she should really hand the magazine to Sergeant Barnard, but if she did that he would want to know where she had got it, and she guessed that might put Tom at risk. Best, she thought, to check it out first, and she thought she knew exactly where to do that.

She felt slightly sick as she stood at the entrance to the alley where her brother had shared his flat with Jonathon Mason. There was no policeman on duty there any more and no one else at all in the dead-end street, but she could see a light on in the window of ABC Books, so she took a deep breath, approached slowly and pushed open the door. Pete Marelli emerged from the back room, shutting the door against his dog's menacing growls but when he saw who had come in he scowled.

'You again,' he said. 'I told you already. I know nothing about your brother.'

'I know,' Kate said. 'I wanted to ask you about something else.' She pulled out the magazine Declan had given her and flicked it open at the page where they thought they had recognized Mason in a clinch with another man. 'This looks like my brother's friend. I just wondered if you knew where these magazines come from. If Jonathon was mixed up in this sort of stuff I should think he was much more likely to get himself murdered by someone he met through this than by anyone else.' She knew it sounded lame, but given Tom's predicament she was determined to explore every faint lead which might help him, and if it came to anything at all she would pass the information on to the police, rather than leave him needing to prove his innocence to Sergeant Barnard or someone even worse.

Marelli glanced at the page in question and shrugged. 'It looks a bit like him,' he said. 'But I don't sell this stuff, men with men, men with boys. Never. This one brought boys back here sometimes. I saw him. I don't like it. Police don't like it. It cause trouble.' He glanced at the back page of the magazine. 'You need to find publisher. No name here. Give it to the police and they will find.'

'If they were using English models they must be producing this stuff somewhere in London,' Kate insisted.

Marelli shrugged again. 'You hear things,' he said. 'But it's not my people. Someone came here the other day and I told him. Women is one thing, men is another.' He pulled a face and thrust the magazine back at Kate. 'Give this to police. You can't go asking questions like this. It dangerous for you. These are bad people.'

Kate sighed, knowing Marelli was right. 'If it was your brother you'd try,' she muttered and thought she saw a flicker of sympathy in Marelli's dark eyes.

'If it was my brother I would pray to the Virgin he not involved with people like this,' he said. 'Talk to police, talk to Sergeant Barnard. For policeman, he not so bad as some.'

TWELVE

DS Harry Barnard sat at his desk smoking and drumming his fingers on a pile of paperwork which he wanted an excuse to avoid. He ignored the general hubbub in the busy office, brushing off the banter he regularly met from his uniformly scruffy colleagues, who called him Flash every time he turned up in some newly fashionable item. Since Teddy boy style had caused general outrage when he was barely out of his teens, and still in uniform as a PC, he had spent every penny he could afford on the latest trend. It was a carapace he hid behind, disguising a sharp brain and a steely ambition which he was determined would take him far.

But the problem he was wrestling with this morning was tricky. He had no objection to putting Georgie Robertson away for life. While he had some affection, and even respect, for his brother, knowing it was little more than luck which had put him on one side of the law and Ray on the other, Georgie was something else. Ray was right. Georgie had been bad and quite possibly mad since he was a boy and Barnard suspected that it was only his brother's protection that had saved him from a long prison sentence already, though there had been a couple of short ones for occasional manic violence that not even Ray had been able to hush up. Even if he had not killed Jonathon Mason, Georgie Robertson either already had, or soon would, kill someone else, Barnard thought. His only problem was the mechanics of the exercise: how was he to produce Georgie as a prime suspect, like a rabbit out of a hat, when as far as he knew his name had never crossed the radar of DCI Venables' murder investigation, and especially as Venables had not even mentioned the case to him for days now?

Still ruminating, he stubbed out his cigarette, walked down the corridor to Venables' office and put his head round the door. The DCI was at his desk, with a telephone clamped to one ear and a large glass of Scotch in the other hand. That, Barnard thought, might become a serious problem for the senior officer soon. Venables waved him in, concluding his call with a curt 'I'll get back to you.'

'Good to see you, Harry,' he said, before draining his glass and stowing it away in a drawer of his desk. 'Got something for me, have you? Seen any sign of that young lad I was looking for on your travels?'

Barnard hesitated for no more than a moment before shaking his head, still nursing the not entirely rational conviction that he needed to talk to young Jimmy Earnshaw himself again before handing him over to the murder team. ''Fraid not,' he said. 'It's something else entirely, guv. I was having a drink with one of my snouts yesterday night and he came up with something very odd. He said he'd heard a whisper about your victim.'

'Mason?' Venables said, his eyes narrowing.

'The very one,' Barnard said. 'The gist of what he said was that Mason was in the queer pub about a week ago – he wasn't told exactly when, but it could have been the night he was killed. Anyway, he started chatting up a bloke my snout's mate had never seen in there before. Whatever Mason said to him seemed to annoy the other bloke and they went out of the pub together having what seemed like a blazing row. Could be significant, don't you think? Do you want me to follow it up?' He would, he thought, play Ray's game very cautiously indeed.

'Mmm,' Venables said thoughtfully. 'May tie in with something someone else told me this morning, as it goes. You know Ray Robertson, don't you, from way back? How well do you know his brother Georgie?'

Barnard took a deep breath, trying to conceal his surprise. Ray hadn't wasted much time, he thought, and he wished he had taken the trouble to tell him exactly what he might be going to say directly to Venables. 'I knew him when I was a kid,' he said. 'I must have told you. We were all evacuated together. But I always thought he was a bit of a nutter, to be honest.'

'Is he queer as well?'

Barnard shrugged, surprised by the question. 'Not as far as

I know,' he said. 'I never saw any sign of that. He's got a rep as a bit of a ladies' man. He'd have had a tough time in Bethnal Green if he'd been bent. Nancy-boys weren't favourite in that neighbourhood. Why d'you ask?'

'Right, well, that figures,' Venables said. 'Some tom said a john refused to pay her and flew into a rage and pulled a knife when she objected. Her description might fit Georgie Robertson.'

'Could be our Georgie,' Barnard said, without a qualm on that score. 'Though I'd be surprised if he has to pay for sex. But he's always had a temper on him. I saw him coming out of the Delilah in a fury after the Robertsons' do there last week. You were there. Maybe you know what that was all about?'

Venables looked blank and shrugged. 'I didn't really speak to him that night,' he said. 'Just passed the time of day in the bog. You were there, weren't you? I don't think we need to take this tom seriously, but we are looking for a knife-man for the Greek Street job, so we'd better cover our backs, just in case. Would you like to have a word? It's your patch, after all. She's working just off Soho Square. Not out of your way, is it?' He scribbled a name and address on a piece of paper and handed it to Barnard. 'And while you're at it, get some mug shots up to the queer pub if you reckon Mason's been seen in there, rowing with someone. See if you can pin someone down, though if what you say about Georgie's right, I can't see him darkening that door.'

'Unless there's money in it,' Barnard said. 'But it does sound like Georgie's losing it, one way or another. Did the john use the knife on the tom?'

'I don't think so. The desk sergeant sent her away with a flea in her ear. If we listened to every aggrieved tom in Soho we'd never finish. You know what they're like. But he did mention it to me in passing. And he made a note of her description. See what you think. Let me know.'

'Give me the address,' Barnard said. 'I'll have a word later. I'll be out and about over there this morning.'

'And don't forget to keep an eye open for that young lad I want to talk to. He's a possible witness in another case I'm on, and I want him found,' Venables said.

'Right,' Barnard said, suddenly intensely curious about what Jimmy Earnshaw might have been a witness to if it wasn't the Mason murder.

Later that morning, Barnard went back to St Peter's, and walked into the twilit nave where an animated group of young girls were gossiping and laughing amongst the surviving pews. There was a light on in David Hamilton's cubicle of an office and he tapped on the door before going in.

Hamilton glanced up from the pile of paperwork on his desk with a look of relief. 'I'm glad you came,' he said. 'You need to talk to this lad, Earnshaw. He seems to have stumbled into something really nasty and he needs more protection than I can give him.'

'You got him to talk, then?' Barnard asked.

'A bit, late last night. I went downstairs to look at the lads late on, as I usually do before I go back to the vicarage. We just have one person on duty at night to keep an eye on the little devils. We don't want them jumping in and out of bed with each other or we'll have the newspapers leaping on us from a great height, won't we? There's a few of our neighbours don't like us, as it is. Not much Christian charity around in Soho, is there?' Hamilton gave a short, sharp bark of laughter. 'Shouldn't expect it, I suppose. Anyway, Jimmy was restless, and seemed very nervous, and I brought him up here for a chat. And eventually it all came tumbling out: how men were using him for disgusting photographs, and something else, something he says he saw, someone who invited him back to his flat but got his throat cut by the time he got there. Sounds far-fetched, I have to say, but Jimmy swears it's true and that's why he's so desperate to get out of London, why he wants your twenty quid which he says you've promised him, to get away in case the killers saw him in Greek Street.'

Barnard's mouth felt dry and his palms sweaty. 'Killers?' he asked sharply. 'No one's suggested there was more than one person involved. Do you think he'll talk to me? Or will he just clam up again?'

'You'll have to take it gently,' Hamilton said. 'He'll run again if he's frightened.'

'I can't have him on the loose if he's got information about a murder,' Barnard said flatly. 'On the other hand, I can't arrest him as a witness. I just need him kept safe, and preferably not in Soho. It's too damn close to the scene of the crime.'

Hamilton gave Barnard a long look. 'It's a real crime then, is it? He's not just inventing it?'

'A young homosexual bloke was found with his throat cut a week ago in a flat just off Greek Street. I'm surprised you haven't heard about it, though to be fair the papers didn't give it much coverage. They knew he was queer, so they didn't bother. Anyway, we've been looking for his flatmate, who's disappeared, which doesn't look good. But maybe we've got it wrong. I need Jimmy Earnshaw to tell me what and possibly who he saw. Perhaps he's closer to the truth than we are.'

'I could maybe find him somewhere safe out of town, if that would help,' Hamilton said thoughtfully. 'I've got a colleague who's vicar of a parish in Surrey who's interested in the work we do here. He might just possibly take him for a while.'

'That might be an answer,' Barnard said. 'But first I need to get a proper statement out of him. Do you think you can persuade him to do that?'

'I don't see why not,' Hamilton said. 'Let's go down and see him.'

He led the way down a narrow stone staircase to where Jimmy Earnshaw was sitting on his bed in the gloomy crypt, well apart from a group of boys smoking and laughing in a corner. He gave both men an anxious look as they approached. He looked pale and tired and had blue-black circles under his eyes as if he had not slept properly for a week which, Barnard thought, was quite likely, given that he seemed to have been at the scene of a murder and had been abused since. His sweater barely covered the bruises around his wrists and neck.

'Can I have my twenty quid now?' he asked Barnard in a low whisper as he sat down on the bed beside him. 'I don't like the other lads here.'

'Soon,' Barnard said. 'When we've had a little chat about what you told Mr Hamilton last night, and tried to sort you out with somewhere out of London to stay where you'll be safe for a while. Would that suit you?'

The boy tried to stand up but Hamilton gently pushing him back down.

'You're not going to lock me up?' Jimmy said, with the eyes of a frightened animal.

'No, of course not,' Barnard said. 'But it sounds as though you witnessed a serious crime and I need to know a bit more about what you saw that night.'

There was, in the end, little enough to tell, although all of it grim as the boy described, in a halting whisper, the pick-up in Piccadilly, the walk through Soho with his companion, lagging behind a little as they approached the flat and then going upstairs only when the coast seemed clear and a couple of men in the alleyway had hurried away down Greek Street.

'You knew what you were letting yourself in for?' Barnard asked, horrified by how matter-of-fact the transaction obviously seemed to the boy.

''Course,' Jimmy said. 'Any road, I knew the bloke. I'd been to his place before.'

'So tell me about the men in the alley. Did you get a good look at them?' Barnard asked.

The boy shrugged. 'I weren't that far behind my mark,' he said. 'But when I got to the corner these blokes were coming towards me. Looked like they were in a hurry. I stood in a doorway in Greek Street and waited till they'd gone. They didn't see me, at least I don't think they did. I can't be right sure. Any road, when they'd gone, I went upstairs and found my bloke dead.' He shuddered slightly at the memory.

'Can you describe these men for me, Jimmy?' Barnard said. 'They may have nothing to do with the murder but they could be useful witnesses if they were there at the same time Jonathon Mason got home that night. I need to know everything you can remember about them.'

Hesitantly the boy dredged his memory, his eyes flickering between the two men facing him. 'One were taller, the other shorter,' he said. 'One had a coat on, and a hat, the big bloke, but the other didn't. He were just wearing a jacket, leather, I think, even though it were right cold that night.'

'Did you see their faces? Would you recognize them again?'
Barnard asked.

'I thought I did the day I had the accident. I saw a man
who looked a bit like the big bloke, in one of them camel
coats and a brown hat, and I ran away, not looking, like, and
got hit by a car. Stupid. There were lots of blokes in coats
like that.'

Barnard produced a mugshot of Georgie Robertson which
he had pulled from the files after he had left DCI Venables,
and laid it on the table alongside the snapshot of Tom
O'Donnell.

'Could either of those two be one of the men you saw?' he
asked.

The boy studied the photographs carefully but seemed
unsure. 'Nay, I don't think so,' he said. 'I can't be right sure.
I didn't get a good look at the smaller one's face. He had dark
hair, and he were younger and skinnier than the big bloke with
the hat, but tough-looking. I don't think this is him.' He pushed
the picture of Tom O'Donnell away. 'This might be,' he said,
looking again at Georgie Robertson. 'But I'm not right sure.
I got a better look at the big bloke. I might know him again
if you've got his picture.'

Barnard smiled slightly. The boy was right. Georgie
Robertson had always seemed puny beside his brother, who
had fought as a heavyweight, a small volatile boy and a small
volatile man, always in the shadow of Ray one way or another,
and resenting every minute of it. If it was Georgie Jimmy had
seen, was it perhaps Ray he was with that night? If so, Ray's
game might be even more devious than Barnard had guessed.

'So you think you might recognize the taller man again?'

'Maybe,' the boy said.

And that, Barnard thought, was a pity. For the moment,
he'd put a formal statement from Jimmy Earnshaw on hold
until he was sure how Venables' investigation was panning
out. He glanced at Hamilton. 'I'll get some more mugshots
for him to look at in case he can identify the taller bloke,' he
said. 'In the meantime, Jimmy, I think we should get you out
of London until we catch up with these men, don't you?'

Leaving David Hamilton to make the arrangements to

transfer Jimmy to the care of his colleague in Surrey, Barnard walked slowly from St Peter's towards Soho Square. Halfway up Dean Street, he paused outside one of the many doors with peeling paint and multiple doorbells in a side alley and pressed the lowest bell, marked Evie. He waited impatiently for several minutes before it opened a crack and a blonde head and grey face peered out.

'Jesus, Harry, this is early. What the hell do you want at this time of day? I didn't stop work till three,' Evie said.

'Not what you think, sweetie,' Barnard said. 'Just a chat. Can I come in?'

Reluctantly, she opened the door wider and he followed her into a ground floor room, where it was obvious she had just got out of the rumpled double bed. She pulled her pink robe more tightly around herself and sat on the edge of the bed, waving Barnard into a corner armchair where he perched on top of her abandoned underwear. He offered her a cigarette which she took gratefully, accepting his proffered light and drawing the smoke eagerly into what sounded like congested lungs.

'I've not been well,' she said.

'The same trouble?'

'No, but I got a bad cough after that little episode. Can't seem to shake it off.'

'You should get off the street, Evie,' Barnard said. 'It's no good for you.'

'That's easy for you to say,' the girl snapped. 'Not proposing, are you? Anyway, what do you want, if it's not the obvious?'

Barnard reached inside his jacket again for the mugshot of Georgie Robertson and handed it to Evie. 'Have you ever seen him around?'

Evie studied the picture for a moment but shook her head. 'Not one of mine,' she said. 'He looks an evil bastard. What's he supposed to have done?'

'Not sure yet,' Barnard said dismissively. 'But if you do see him, can you give me a bell? Don't let him through your door, though, sweetie. We've had a complaint from one of the girls on the street which could be about him.'

Evie shrugged and rolled herself back under the blankets.

'Professional hazard,' she said. 'Violent men. I don't worry about it unless girls are getting their throats cut. And as far as I hear it, it's a nancy-boy that's happened to recently. Am I right, Harry?'

'You're right, sweetie. By the way, is this a girl you know?' He handed Evie the piece of paper Venables had given him, but again she shook her head.

'Don't think so,' she said. 'Is that her real name or the name she uses on the street?'

'Her real name, I think. It's the name she gave at the nick when she made a complaint.'

'Yeah, well, she may call herself something else, to confuse you buggers, you know how it is? Now, can you piss off and let me get some sleep? Make sure you close the front door behind you. We don't want any old sod walking in. We need to see the colour of his money first.'

Barnard grinned and stood up. 'Sweet dreams,' he said, though he doubted that was likely. He strolled further up Dean Street and then turned right to cut through towards Soho Square. Almost on the corner he stopped at a door very similar to the one he had just closed firmly enough behind him for Evie to hear the thud, and again rang a bell. This time it was opened promptly by a smartly dressed young woman in a tight-fitting dress with a skirt above the knee, and very high heels, fully made up and attractive enough to stop Barnard momentarily in his tracks.

'Are you Sue Heddon?' he asked. She nodded and Barnard pulled out his warrant card. 'You made a complaint about a punter,' he said. 'Is that right?'

'Well, you're a turn-up,' Sue Heddon said. 'I didn't think your man at the nick gave two flying hoots for my complaint.'

'If he pulled a knife on you, we'll take it seriously, whatever the desk sergeant led you to believe.'

'You'd best come in then,' she said and for the second time that morning Barnard found himself settled in a tart's boudoir, cigarette in hand and looking entirely at home while the mugshot of Georgie Robertson was being studied carefully.

'That's him,' she said. 'He seemed OK to start with. He phoned first. I've got cards out and about. I don't work on the street any more. So that was fine. He was well-dressed, obviously not short of a bob, so I let him in when he turned up. But he wanted me to do some stuff I didn't fancy, and then he turned nasty.'

'What sort of stuff?' Barnard asked.

'He wanted to tie me up. I won't do that sort of thing. I know you can charge more, but I don't like it. So I said no, and we've got a sort of alarm system here, sounds a bell in the hall if there's any trouble, so I showed him that, and that's when he pulled his knife, so I did set the alarm off and he went pretty quickly after that. Nasty bit of work, I thought he was. Vile temper on him. It's the first time I've ever had to set the alarm off. And it worked like a dream. He was out of the door like a shot. Will you charge him?

'I'll get back to you on that,' Barnard said, not sure whether arresting Georgie for a threat which ended up hurting no one would be a help or a hindrance in the larger scheme of things. But knowing he carried a knife and had threatened to use it could well be useful later, if not now. His next step would have to be very carefully considered, he thought, if Ray was to succeed in getting rid of his younger brother in a way that old Ma Robertson would accept and a jury would buy. But there was no doubt that Jimmy Earnshaw's evidence was an awkward stumbling block in Ray Robertson's way. The boy might have seen two men hurrying away from Jonathon Mason's flat, not one, but while he was definite that neither was Tom O'Donnell, which was good news for Tom's sister, he wasn't sure he was Georgie Robertson either. As far as Ray's plot to put his brother away was concerned, Jimmy Earnshaw might turn out to be a powerful witness for the defence rather than the prosecution.

One way or another, the kid had seen too much for his own safety and he had to be got out of London quickly, Barnard decided. His long-term survival might depend on him staying away for good. Barnard might go along with Ray's schemes just so far, but leaving an inconvenient witness, who was little more than a child, directly in Ray's path was not included in the deal. And it was still essential, he thought, to find Tom O'Donnell, who might turn out to be another loose cannon.

He must catch up with his pretty sister again, he thought, and he could think of more than one good reason for that.

Halfway up Greek Street, heading back to the nick, he turned into the alleyway where ABC Books was situated, with Mason's flat above, and pushed open the shop door. What he found inside hit him like a kick in the stomach. Pete Marelli was lying on the floor surrounded by tumbled heaps of his blood-soaked merchandise while beyond him his German shepherd Hector lay on his back, his tongue lolling between his teeth, his head almost severed from his neck.

'Jesus wept,' Barnard muttered, leaning over Marelli for no more than a second to confirm what was entirely obvious. Like Jonathon Mason, who had died in the flat above the shop, the Maltese had also been killed by slashing blows to his neck. Barnard glanced behind him and moved to close the shop door with his shoulder and twist the sign to Closed before he leaned against the barred glass and surveyed the carnage, breathing heavily. Moving carefully so as not to leave any traces of his own presence, Barnard took a careful look round but found nothing unusual except a couple of bloody fingerprints on the glass counter which had been smashed as the Maltese had fallen. They might be useful, he thought, if only to calm the tension which he was sure would erupt with this death. The chess game being played in the Soho underworld by Ray Robertson and the Maltese, Frankie Falzon, had been overturned and the pieces scattered all over the floor. For once in his life, Harry Barnard felt slightly afraid.

THIRTEEN

DS Barnard had found nothing unusual amongst the pornography in Pete Marelli's porn shop except for a single crumpled copy of a magazine which surprised him. He stared at the photographs for a long time before he realized that one of the young boys involved looked suspiciously like Jimmy Earnshaw and one of the men in another shot was undoubtedly Jonathon Mason. Before he had used the dead man's phone to call DCI Venables and pass on the news of the shopkeeper's violent demise, he had folded the magazine carefully and put it in his inside pocket. The fewer people who saw a photograph of Jimmy, he thought, the safer the boy would be.

'What the hell's going on?' Venables snapped in obvious disbelief.

'I wish I knew,' Barnard said. 'But I'm completely baffled by this. If the Robertsons' mob's involved, it makes no sense at all. I thought they were trying to get some sort of deal with the Maltese but this will put the kibosh on that. It's likely to start a war.'

'Get out on the bloody street, and see what you can pick up, Harry boy,' Venables said. 'This is really going to muddy the waters with the other case. I'll get over there with the murder team straight away.'

Barnard shrugged and hung up thoughtfully before leaving the shop more or less as he had found it, stepping carefully around the two bodies, human and canine, and around the pools of blood and scattered books and magazines which surrounded them. Marelli, he knew, was no more than a foot soldier in Frankie Falzon's private Maltese army, but his death would undoubtedly be avenged, unless it was a punishment by his boss for some infringement of the mob's perverse moral code, maybe even possession of the queer magazine Barnard had picked up. As he left the shop, he glanced around the immediate vicinity and spotted a newspaper seller on the corner, but the rheumy-eyed vendor claimed to have seen nothing at all, and Barnard guessed that he could ask the same question any day of the week and get the same answer.

He made his way back slowly to Frith Street where he knew the very attractive Kate O'Donnell was probably at work just a couple of blocks away. This new killing would probably let her brother off the hook, he thought, but it was far too soon to pass on that opinion to her, especially as he would not put it past DCI Venables to continue that particular manhunt for as long as it suited him. Abruptly he spun on his heel, furious to be so at a loss on what he regarded as his own personal turf. He headed west, weaving his way towards Berwick Street and a pub in the bustling market where he knew that some of the Maltese loosely attached to Falzon's mob hung out. It was still early and while the fruit and vegetable stalls which almost blocked the narrow street were doing good business the bar was almost empty. He glanced around the tables which were only just being washed down after the previous night's business and would have gone out again until he noticed Joe Inglott sitting in the far corner of the room, nursing what looked like a double Scotch. He looked up as Barnard approached and the sergeant could see the fear in his eyes.

'Not here, Mr Barnard,' Inglott said, his eyes flickering around the empty bar.

'Round the corner in the coffee bar,' Barnard said curtly, waving a hand towards D'Arblay Street. 'You know it?'

Inglott nodded and took a gulp of his Scotch. Barnard went ahead, sure Inglott would follow. The man owed him too much to disobey. And sure enough, within minutes of his ordering a cappuccino from the bored Italian boy behind the counter, Inglott sidled through the door and took a plastic chair opposite him.

'What the hell's going on, Joe?' Barnard snapped, without preamble. 'There's another corpse in Greek Street, killed the same way as the first lad. And this time your man's not going to be best pleased. What have you heard? You're obviously scared witless. Who's the knife man, Joe? And why the hell was Pete Marelli picked on?'

Inglott licked dry lips. 'I can't go on talking to you like this,' he said. 'Is too dangerous.' Barnard sighed dramatically and put a hand on Inglott's arm, gripping more tightly than was comfortable. 'Joseph, Joseph, you really don't have much choice, do you, let's be honest. You're in this up to your eyes already. What's your man's reaction to this? Is he behind it himself, or is he hopping mad someone has almost sliced the head off one of his men? That bookshop must be making him a fortune, the stuff Marelli had stashed away in his back room. I thought I'd pretty well seen it all but . . .' He shrugged as expressively as any Maltese and Inglott scowled.

'I don't know anything about what happened there,' he said. 'And I think the man is not happy. That is what I hear. I think Marelli was close to Mr Falzon, good friends, same village, you know how it is?'

'So are we looking at a turf war here?' Barnard asked, feeling queasy. 'Do you know who he's blaming?'

'I know nothing, I hear nothing,' Inglott said. 'I only a tiny sardine in this sea. You must look for much bigger fish, shark maybe.'

Barnard gazed at his informant but was forced to the conclusion that the frightened man playing nervously with his teaspoon was very probably telling him the truth. All of a sudden, out of a clear blue sea, something very like a shark had invaded the relatively calm lagoon that Soho had become recently, and it was impossible to predict just where the bloodstained ripples caused by Marelli's death would wash up. He finished his coffee and passed Inglott a couple of crumpled pound notes.

'Keep me in touch, Joe,' he said harshly. 'Absolutely anything you hear, right?'

The Maltese nodded miserably. 'OK, OK, Mr Barnard,' he agreed. 'Anything I hear.'

Barnard was walking slowly back to the nick, furiously dissatisfied with his morning's investigations, when he became aware of a sleek black car pulling into the kerb beside him. The back door opened wide and Ray Robertson beckoned him in.

'Good morning, Flash,' Robertson said as the car pulled slowly away in the direction of Regent Street. 'Come down to the club and have a drink. I'm getting some strange reports this morning, all sorts of unpleasant whispers, and I want to know what the hell's going on.'

Barnard was not used to being in the dark and Ray was the last person he was going to admit to that he was, for the moment, floundering. He kept his own counsel as the Jag glided effortlessly the half mile to the Delilah and he followed Ray into the bar where he accepted a Scotch as large as the gangster's own.

'Cheers,' he said, slugging the drink back quickly, although it did not make him feel much better. He glanced around the half-lit bar, the Delilah being a place which only came to life in the late evening as serious drinking and illicit gambling took over. He lit a cigarette. 'That was a good bash you had last week.'

But all Ray Robertson could manage was a faint smile of acknowledgement. 'Don't beat about the bush, Harry. What the hell's going on with this new killing in Greek Street?'

Barnard shrugged. 'I hoped you might be able to tell me something about that,' he said.

'You're joking,' Robertson said. 'You know that's not my style. Was he one of Falzon's mob?'

'He was Maltese, yes,' Barnard said. 'Ran the bookshop for them. But who cut his throat, I've no idea. Or why.'

'But your man Venables might just think it was down to me,' Robertson said heavily. 'And so might Falzon, though he should know better. Just between us, I'm talking to Falzon just now about some other stuff, not porn, you know I don't like that, but a big deal is on the cards. Anything which messes that up could be a serious inconvenience.'

'I'm sure,' Barnard said drily. 'But if you're sure your hands are clean . . .' He realized immediately that he had rashly let a note of doubt insinuate itself into his voice as Robertson's face darkened angrily.

'Persil-white,' Robertson snapped.

'OK, OK,' Barnard came back quickly. 'Then we have to assume it was either Falzon's mob, for some reason we can only guess at, in which case it's not a problem for you and him, or a loose cannon we know nothing about.'

'A loose cannon like Georgie, obviously,' Robertson said quickly. 'This happened in the same building, for God's sake, and maybe with the same knife.' He paused to let the implications of what he was suggesting sink in. 'Convenient all round, wouldn't you say, in the light of what we already talked about?'

Barnard groaned inwardly, wondering how far he could get Venables to go along with Robertson's ambitious scheme and how successfully he could keep the boy's evidence out of the picture. Jimmy Earnshaw was the loosest cannon of all, and the most vulnerable. 'I assume you can get Falzon to buy that,' he muttered. 'If he didn't have him eliminated himself, that is.'

'I think so,' Robertson said airily, but the more Barnard thought about it the more he became convinced that Ray Robertson was almost as dangerously out of control as his more volatile brother. Venables was simply not going to buy into this, he thought. It was just too bizarre for even Georgie's reputation to bear.

Kate O'Donnell stood in her boss Ken Fellows' office looking baffled. She had got to work slightly late after being delayed on the tube. 'Some idiot's jumped in front of a train,' the ticket inspector had said with a shrug as she and Marie had tried to join the Central Line at Notting Hill. 'Take the Circle and then the Bakerloo,' he had offered helpfully before Marie, the more experienced traveller in the tunnels and tubes Kate still found confusing and more than a little scary, had led the way. But when she had got to the office she found the big photographers' room deserted, an acrid smell in the air, and several of her colleagues and Brenda the secretary crushed into Ken Fellows' sanctum, all talking loudly at once. Kate pushed her way into the throng and found Ken at his desk rifling through a jumble of prints and contact sheets on his desk. The agency was never tidy but this morning the room looked as if a hurricane had hit it.

'What's going on?' she asked Brenda, as the men ignored her arrival.

'We had a burglar in the night,' Brenda said. 'Or maybe someone who just didn't like their pic. Ken's trying to work out what they took, if anything.'

Kate glanced back over her shoulder to the photographers' desks which were, as usual, littered with cameras and photographic equipment, some of it expensive.

'They took prints?' she asked, surprised. She had her own camera in her bag, so she was not worried on that score, but most of the photographers generally left their own heavier gear lying around on open view.

'Well, they seem to have gone through the files. The stuff was scattered all over Ken's office when I came in. I started clearing it up but he started shrieking at me when he saw the mess so I packed it in. I don't know where it all came from or where it all goes. I expect you'll have to do the filing all over again.' She gave Kate a satisfied smirk and went back to her own corner of the office to put the kettle on.

'I suppose we're insured?' Kate said to no one in particular, but Ken seemed to hear her higher voice above the hubbub and fixed her with a beady eye.

'You can't insure pics that haven't been sold yet,' he snarled. 'Or repeat the moment they were taken, you silly cow. Can you go back and get those shots of randy Lord Francome and his little tart again? Fortunately the negs should still be in the darkrooms. You'd better go and check.'

Kate felt her colour rise and she turned away from the crowd of men quickly and went to do as she was told. But as soon as she opened the first darkroom door she knew that they were not dealing with a casual thief who had wandered in off the street. In one sense, the negatives were still there, but the intruder had carefully piled them into a metal tray and set them alight. All that was left was ash and a smell of burnt film amongst the normal stink of chemicals, and on the floor the shards of glass plates, everything coated with a residue of black smoke, which explained the smell which had permeated the whole office. She put her head round each of the darkroom doors in turn but with the same result. The firm's recent negatives and plates had been destroyed and it was a miracle that the whole building had not gone up in smoke with them.

Feeling sick, she went back to Ken Fellows' office and she knew that she did not even need to give him an answer to his question. He could read it in her face. She wriggled through the crowd of photographers to face her stricken boss across the heaps of material on his desk.

'Smashed up or burnt,' she said. 'I've got some of my thirty-five millimetre negs. I kept the ones of Dave Donovan's band because I thought he might like them reprinted, and a few of the shots I took at the Delilah Club were on the same reel of film. And the film I shot in Liverpool is still in my camera. I bundled all the negs up together and locked them in my desk drawer as you didn't seem sure you were interested in the bands.'

'Well, that's great,' Fellows said. 'So it looks as though the sum total of our recent negs consists of shots of a third rate rock band from Liverpool, some second rate band leader's pregnant girlfriend and a few VIPs who took the trouble to go to Ray Robertson's boxing match at the Delilah. Plus whatever old stuff is stashed in the cellar. Jesus wept, we'll get rich pickings out of that lot. Did anyone else keep their recent plates somewhere safe?' Most of the men laughed and shook their heads ruefully. The plates from their heavy flash cameras were not so portable.

'Right,' Fellows said. 'The rest of you get on with your jobs. Kate and I are going to sort through the prints and see what can be rescued and what's been nicked.'

'Are you going to call the police?' Kate asked timidly after the photographers had left her uneasily alone with Fellows.

'No point, is there?' Fellows said dismissively. 'The negs are gone and I guess if they took any prints they'll have destroyed them as well. Though God knows why. So, let's split these prints into a set for each photographer. They've all got the names on the back. Then I'll know what should be there and what's gone. Come on, girl. Don't look so miserable. It's a bloody pain but worse things happen at sea.'

'I suppose so,' Kate said, but she could not get rid of the feeling that somehow this calamity was connected to her own troubles with Tom, her rejection of Dave Donovan or even, though she quickly dismissed the idea as too far-fetched, with the fact that, as she had been about to leave the Delilah Club the previous Friday night, she had refused a lift with an importunate and obviously drunken Georgie Robertson, who had stormed out of the club ahead of her, audibly cursing as he went. She spent the morning sifting through the tumbled heaps of photographs until they were assembled in some sort of order, at which point Fellows began to put them back into the cardboard folders from which they had been tipped.

'You know what's missing, don't you?' he asked eventually, tapping a finger meaningfully on a slim folder which she could see had her own name on it. 'It's the pics you took at the Delilah the other night. They've gone, the whole lot of them. Now why the hell would anyone want those?'

'But didn't you sell some to the *Evening Standard* diary? They've been published, haven't they?'

'The *Standard* and the *News* bought a couple of them, but in the end neither of them used them. I thought it was a bit odd, but it happens sometimes, they drop things at the last minute, something juicier turns up. But I would have thought Lord F and that tart would have made it into the diaries.'

'I told you, I've still got some of the negs from that do,' Kate said. 'We can reprint them.'

Fellows looked at Kate thoughtfully. 'Do that,' he said. 'Let's have a look at what we've still got and see what's so important that someone tried to get rid of them. I can see Francome might have been embarrassed to have them in the papers, but surely not to the extent of getting this place burgled. What's the point? They're old news now. The Robertsons' boxing do was days ago. No one's going to use anything after all this time.'

Kate spent the rest of the morning in one of the darkrooms, developing and printing the stock of negatives which she had kept in her own possession, and then scanning them carefully for any hint of a reason why anyone would want to steal them. Lord Francome, she thought, might not want his flirtation with Christine Jones put on show in the papers, and John Lennon might still be keen to keep Cynthia's pregnancy and his marriage under wraps, but the photographs she had taken were not the only means by which either secret might, and probably would, leak out sooner rather than later. It made no sense.

By lunchtime, she had put the prints in a new folder for Ken Fellows, put on her coat and dropped the folder on his desk.

'I'm off for some lunch,' she said and he nodded abstractedly. She walked slowly north towards Oxford Street where she normally had a frugal snack by herself in an ABC cafe, given that none of the men in the office ever invited her to the pubs where they had a largely liquid lunch, but before she got to Soho Square she became aware of a figure she recognized and, too late to avoid him, found herself face-to-face with DS Harry Barnard, looking almost as harassed as she felt herself.

'Come and have a drink,' he said abruptly, glancing up and down the crowded street as if worried that he might be seen.

Against her better judgement, she allowed herself to be led through the doors of the nearest pub and settled into a corner of the smoky bar. She did not trust this policeman who seemed to be able to switch from charming to alarming at a moment's notice. While Barnard went to get their drinks, she took stock. All the pubs in Soho were different, she thought, as she took in the noisy groups who surrounded her, a motley collection of long-haired men in hairy tweeds and one or two women engrossed in fierce debate or poring over books and magazines as if their lives depended on it. It reminded her slightly of Ye Cracke in Liverpool, although these were not students. They were far too old and intense for that.

Barnard came back and put a Babycham, with a cherry on a cocktail stick, in front of her and took a long gulp of his own pint before he sat down. There was not much charm in evidence today, she thought.

'I'm glad I saw you,' he said. 'There's been another murder.'

Kate felt her mouth dry. 'Where?' she asked.

'More or less the same place. The bookshop under Jonathon Mason's flat, your brother's flat, as it goes. The bookseller's been killed in much the same way as Mason. I thought you'd want to know before it appears in the *News* and the *Standard*.'

She tried to conceal the sense of relief which almost

overwhelmed her but she didn't think she succeeded very well. 'Well, Tom couldn't—' She stopped, aware that she was giving too much away.

'Couldn't he?' Barnard asked, with a hint of a smile but unfriendly eyes. 'So you do know where he is?'

Kate shook her head. 'No, I don't,' she said flatly. 'He was very careful not to tell me that when I spoke to him.'

'When you went to Liverpool?'

'That was a work trip,' she said. 'Nothing to do with Tom. I went to take some photographs. Ask my boss if you don't believe me.'

'And that's the late Dylan Thomas pickled in alcohol over there,' Barnard said, waving at a heavily built man already the worse for wear in spite of the time of day. 'And I'm Father Christmas. This really was his favourite pub when he was in London, by the way. Dylan Thomas, I mean. Anyway, I don't really think the Murder Squad have your brother down for this latest killing, but I know DCI Venables still wants to talk to him about his flatmate. It's not over yet, by any means. The only thing which will get him out of this is if he can prove he has a solid alibi for the night Mason died.'

Kate took a sip of her Babycham and wondered how long it would be before this nightmare was over. 'We had a burglary at work last night,' she said, wanting the subject changed. 'Why do you think anyone would break in and steal photographs, and take the trouble to burn a whole lot of negatives?'

Barnard looked at her curiously. 'What were the photographs of?' he asked.

'Some of them were the ones I took at the boxing match last week, the Robertsons' big do.'

'Were they likely to be embarrassing? Someone with someone they shouldn't have been with? Something like that?'

'I don't think so,' Kate said. 'They all seemed happy enough when I asked them to pose. My boss tried to sell some of them to the papers.'

'Not likely to have been much use to a blackmailer then,' Barnard said dismissively. 'Has your boss reported the robbery?'

'I don't think so,' Kate said.

Barnard drained his glass and leaned back in his seat, his eyes unexpectedly drinking her in until she flushed slightly. 'Maybe you should let me have a look at them to see if I can see anyone with someone they shouldn't be,' he said lightly.

'I might take you up on that,' she said. 'Maybe you can help me for a change.'

'When this business with your brother is settled – I mean when he's off the hook, as I'm beginning to think he will be soon – will you have dinner with me?' he asked. 'I know a little Italian place I think you'd like.'

Kate pushed her half-empty glass away and stood up abruptly. 'Italian?' she said suspiciously. 'What's that? Spaghetti and stuff? I don't think so. Anyway, I think that would be a bit difficult in the circumstances, don't you?' And she turned on her heel and walked away, leaving him smiling faintly at his empty pint glass.

Kate turned sharply after she had flounced out of the pub door and made her way to the Blue Lagoon where Marie was in sole charge of the steamy coffee machine and a handful of customers at the plastic tables. Her friend made her a frothy cappuccino and waved at the array of food.

'Anything to eat?' she asked. 'You look a bit fraught.' She brought her a sandwich and slipped into the seat opposite Kate. 'What's happened?' she asked, and between mouthfuls Kate told her about that morning's discovery of the burglary at the agency, and an edited version of her meeting with Barnard. She did not know what to make of his unexpected invitation or whether her reply had been the right one.

'But that's good news, isn't it? If they're not so interested in Tom any more? If they've got another similar crime and you know Tom's safely up north.'

'He didn't exactly say that,' Kate said. 'And anyway, I'm not sure I trust him an inch.' And that at least was true, she thought, she didn't trust him an inch either as a bizzie or as a potential friend.

FOURTEEN

Kate O'Donnell walked thoughtfully across Soho Square that evening towards the underground at Tottenham Court Road and, as she snuggled deeper into her scarf, wondered if this long, grim winter would ever end. The snow and ice which had hung about for months in grey, solid piles in the gutters and at the corners of buildings had slowly disappeared but the spring bulbs had barely struggled into life in the flowerbeds and no one had yet given up on their bulky winter coats and warm boots. As she cut through Soho Street towards the glittering lights of Oxford Street, she was suddenly overtaken by a middle-aged woman in a smart coat, with matching hat and gloves, a glimpse of pearls at the neck and a determined expression on her face, made fiercer by the lack of even a smudge of lipstick. She turned unexpectedly into Kate's path, breathing heavily. She looked like one of the women who had occasionally turned up at her school, Kate thought, to present prizes or give a talk about the good work being done by missionaries in the heart of Africa.

'Are you Miss O'Donnell?' the woman asked, effectively blocking the pavement so that Kate had to stop. Kate nodded, unable to imagine why she was being accosted like this.

'The young lady who takes photographs?' the woman demanded and again Kate admitted that she was. The woman's face softened slightly, although she had looked slightly startled when she heard Kate's accent. 'You must think me very rude, my dear,' she said. 'But I've been looking for you. My name is Veronica Lucas and I called at your agency but you'd already left. I thought if I hurried I might catch you up. They told me what you were wearing. You've made yourself quite noticeable around Soho apparently.' She glanced around. 'Would you join me for a cup of tea?' she asked.

'Am I going to be told what this is all about?' Kate asked, feeling resentful at the intrusion.

'Of course you are, my dear. Here, come on into the warm and I'll explain.' Veronica Lucas, after a careful assessment of just where she was going, preceded her into a cafe in one of the streets on the quieter north side of Oxford Street and had ordered tea for two before Kate could find any reason to object to the way she had been effectively hijacked. She was, it appeared, the answer to Mrs Lucas's prayers, and Kate could tell that she meant that literally. Veronica Lucas explained, in tones of absolute certainty, that she was one of a group of Christian women engaged in cleaning up Soho and she needed a photographer, preferably a woman, to help in that task. Having learned enough about how the square mile of Soho earned its dubious living, Kate knew the unfeasibly vast extent of such an ambition, but it was obvious that this woman would not be deterred by any objection she could make. Her eyes positively sparkled with zeal. In any case, Mrs Lucas seemed to be offering some extra employment which Kate was reluctant to turn down out of hand. It wasn't as if Ken Fellows' wage was generous.

'What is it exactly you want me to do?' she asked cautiously, sipping tea which Mrs Lucas had poured carefully from a china teapot into a china cup. This was about as far from Marie's cheap and cheerful coffee bar as you could get, she thought.

'We're preparing a report on prostitution in the area to present to Parliament when they finally get around to considering the Wolfenden Report,' Mrs Lucas said. 'You know about that?'

Kate nodded. Since she had learned about her brother's tastes she had taken more than a passing interest in one of its proposals which was to make some homosexual acts legal for the first time.

'We're especially interested in how the law should deal with the exploitation of young girls, runaways mainly. They come down from the north and from Scotland and there are evil men waiting to pick them up at the railway stations. There used to be a lot at Euston but, now they've pulled it down, King's Cross and St Pancras seem to be the favourites.'

Kate knew well enough that what the woman said was true.

She had seen girls in unseasonable clothes hanging around the
station entrance looking pinched and shivering when she had
gone back to Liverpool only a few days ago. Mrs Lucas pulled
an envelope of snapshots out of her bag and fanned them out
across the table. They were black and white pictures, most of
them blurred and slightly out-of-focus, and probably taken, Kate
thought, with someone's family Box Brownie in a bad light.
Some of Mrs Lucas's pictures showed girls sheltering under the
massive stone classical arch, itself condemned, which still stood
between the ruins of Euston and the main road.

'I'm told that these won't print very well in a leaflet,'
Veronica Lucas said, a note of irritation in her voice.

Kate smiled. 'You're right,' she said. 'You'll be lucky if
they'll print at all.' She looked at the pictures more closely.
Most of them were of young girls and women on the streets,
either looking cold and lost, or approaching men or being
approached by policemen. The nature of the trade was obvious.

'What we want is similar pictures of a better quality, suitable to print in our report. We have a lady journalist on our
committee and she says that one photograph is worth a hundred
words.'

'You only have to look at old copies of *Picture Post* to know
that's true,' Kate said. 'Do you remember *Picture Post*? I used
to buy it with my pocket money.'

'A publication produced by communists and fellow-travel-
lers, as I recall,' Veronica Lucas said tartly. 'I wouldn't have
it in the house personally. But I'm sure my colleague from
the *Daily Express* is right about pictures. What I want to know
from you is whether or not you can take some for us? You're
ideally placed working in the area yourself. We'll pay you, of
course. Unless you feel you can donate yourself to the cause,
as it were.'

Kate smiled. 'I wish you luck with your campaign, though
I think you've got a mountain to climb. But I can't afford to
work for nothing. The agency doesn't pay me much and there's
the cost of materials for developing and printing. I'll charge
you ten per cent less than the agency would charge if they
took it on, if I can persuade them to let me use a
darkroom.'

'Fine,' Mrs Lucas said without hesitation.

'So what exactly do you want and how soon?'

Mrs Lucas pushed her smudgy snapshots across the table to Kate. 'This sort of thing,' she said. 'And one more place. St Peter's Church has a refuge which we support. They take in young people at risk on the streets. It's run by a Rev Hamilton, David Hamilton, and he knows someone is coming on our behalf.'

'Right,' Kate said faintly, alarmed at how efficiently she had been ambushed into helping this woman and wondering whether or not there was catch somewhere. 'How do I get hold of you?'

Veronica Lucas handed Kate a card with her address in Surrey and phone number and *Clean Up Soho* in red letters across the top. 'A lot of people are getting to know us,' she said.

'I'm sure they are,' Kate agreed. 'You seem to know how to get what you want.'

The next morning, Kate got up early before either Marie or Tess had emerged from the tiny bedroom they shared, with its two narrow single beds and little else. She folded up the blankets from the sofa where she had slept, stowed them away and was out of the tall, dilapidated house by seven thirty, strap-hanging her way to Tottenham Court Road and then making her way through the still quiet streets of Soho to St Peter's which, she thought, might be the one place where people got up early round here. To an extent she was right. The heavy church door opened to her touch and she found herself in the area that had been separated off for the young people's refuge and amongst a dozen or more young girls, some of them still in pyjamas, and, in a separate area, a couple of middle-aged women who were assembling a breakfast of cornflakes, bread and jam and tea on trestle tables.

'Come on, girls,' one of the women said, with the voice of a schoolteacher who stood no nonsense. 'Get dressed. The boys will be upstairs in a minute.' With a few shrieks of derisive laughter, the girls retreated into their sleeping area and drew a curtain behind them, while their supervisors turned towards Kate and enquired what she wanted. She explained.

'Do you know Mrs Lucas?' she asked.

The older woman, who seemed to be in charge, nodded. 'Oh, yes,' she said. 'We know Mrs Lucas. She's not directly involved here, but she comes in occasionally when we're looking for foster homes and that sort of thing. We don't always see eye to eye with her but her heart's in the right place, I suppose.'

'Why's that?' Kate asked.

'We're Anglicans and she's a Catholic and when it comes down to it she's more interested in finding Catholic homes for Catholic children than helping the rest. And she takes a very hard line on contraception, while we have a sympathetic doctor who will help unmarried girls out with the cap. Not many will, you know. Most want proof of engagement if not marriage before they'll advise.'

Kate knew, but only vaguely. If mention of homosexuality had been taboo at home and at school, birth control had been even more unmentionable. Even now she half believed that it was something which should be left to men. That was what Dave Donovan had assured her in the back of the group's van when she finally gave in to his importuning, and although she had remained almost beside herself with fear for a long month afterwards, the precautions he claimed he had taken seemed to have worked. The idea that a woman might take charge of such things was one she was only slowly getting used to since she had read that there was a pill which might soon allow women to do just that. She was sure that would not please her mam or the Pope, or Veronica Lucas, though she thought she might soon get used to the idea herself.

'But I thought you were trying to get these kids off the streets,' she said, pulling her thoughts back to the Soho campaigners' concerns.

'We are, but it's not always easy,' the woman said, buttering bread busily. 'We try to get them out of London, into foster homes if they're under sixteen, into hostels and jobs if they're older. But there's always some backsliding.'

'I expect there is,' Kate said non-committally.

The heavy church door behind them opened noisily, letting

in a blast of cold air, and closed again with a bang, and the women turned to greet a heavily-built man in casual tweeds and a clerical collar who greeted them cheerfully and glanced at Kate with inquiry in his eyes.

'Ah, the saintly Veronica,' he said wryly when she explained why she was there. 'You're one of her acolytes, are you?'

'Not really,' Kate said sharply. 'I'm a professional photographer.' The claim still felt strange and gave her a surge of excitement. 'She asked me to do a job for her, that's all.'

'Well, you'll have to ask the youngsters if they want their pictures taken,' Hamilton said. 'I doubt you'll have much luck. There's not one of them would want their families to see where they've ended up, that's for sure. But you can ask, I suppose. Explain to them what it's for.' Hamilton went downstairs to the crypt and came back with a raggle-taggle group of boys, who took their seats for breakfast beside the girls amongst much banter and laughter, but as Kate watched them wolfing down the plentiful supply of food on the table, she could see that many of them were painfully thin and pale and the eyes, which glanced sideways at her, were wary. One boy in particular caught her eye because of the livid cut on his head, where the hair was only just beginning to grow again. She helped herself to a cup of tea from the urn at the end of the table and went to sit beside him.

'What's your name?' she asked him as he loaded his bread with jam.

He glanced at her like a trapped animal. 'What's it to you?' he muttered.

Kate explained why she was there, but he was not reassured and looked nervously around the cavernous church as if demons lurked in its shadowy corners.

'I don't want no more pictures taken,' he muttered. 'I've had enough of that.' He glanced around him wildly for a moment until David Hamilton came up behind him and put a hand on his shoulder.

'I'm sorry,' he said to Kate. 'Jimmy's not the best person to ask. He's had some bad experiences with photographers. In fact, he's had some bad experiences, full stop.'

Kate found her mind racing with wild speculations as to

what possible harm could come to a boy from an innocent tool like a camera but she supposed it had something to do with the sort of magazines in which she had seen Jonathon Mason's photograph. It had not crossed her mind that children as well as adults might be involved in that sort of photography and she felt suddenly out of her depth and slightly sick. She got to her feet and put her hand briefly on Jimmy's shoulder, feeling him flinch from her touch.

'I'm sorry,' she said. 'I'll talk to some of the others.' She glanced at Hamilton ruefully. 'I'm not sure I'm up to this job,' she said quietly.

'If it will help some of these kids, you should carry on,' he said with robust enthusiasm. 'They need all the help they can get. I actually caught a chap trying to get in here last night as I was locking up. I'm sure he was trying to get hold of someone we had staying here. They don't like to be thwarted, you know, the pimps and pornographers. They regard children they've picked up as their personal property. They want to recoup the cost of housing and feeding them, and then make a profit. It's a business for them. Sometimes good people ask me why I'm bothering with these youngsters. They seem to think they're too degraded to be rescued, that I'm wasting my time. But I know that's not true.'

Kate had cut herself off from her religion as soon as she went to college and realized that much of the rest of the world seemed to manage quite well without the embarrassing torture of confession and weekly sermons by men in long dresses for whom she had long ago lost any respect. Her mother had railed and threatened when she refused to get out of bed on Sunday mornings for Mass, but she had been stubborn, especially after Tom disappeared, and the parish priest, who had turned up to add his remonstrations to her mother's, had implied that the family might be better off without him. Kate knew now what Father Reilly had evidently known back then, that Tom was an unrepentant sinner in a way that even as a student she had not understood. But she had loved him then and missed him, and she still did, and that would never change. David Hamilton, she thought, in his cord trousers, jacket and a thick sweater which almost covered his clerical collar, was a different kind of priest and one which she thought she might be persuaded to get along with.

'Have you told the police about this intruder?' she asked. 'Sergeant Barnard would be interested in him, I think.'

Hamilton looked at her curiously. 'You know Harry Barnard, do you?'

'I've met him, yes,' Kate said. She didn't want to go into the details of how and why she had come to the Metropolitan Police's attention.

Hamilton gave her a faint smile. 'A man to watch, I think, if you're female and even remotely attractive,' he said. 'But you're right. I will tell him about the intruder. It was odd, I thought I half-recognized him. Harry might know who he was.'

'So, can I see if any of these youngsters will agree to be photographed?' she said. 'I haven't got a lot of time, but I could come back later if necessary. I don't think Mrs Lucas has any deadline to meet.'

'Carry on,' Hamilton said. 'Come back whenever you like, my dear. We're all on the same side here.'

Kate did not go back home to Notting Hill that evening. She shared a sandwich with Marie in the Blue Lagoon, packed with young people taking a break on their way from work before plunging on to crowded buses or underground trains to the suburbs. As Marie toiled behind the bar handing out cappuccinos in glass cups and saucers from the hissing machine, Kate filled her in on her unexpected commission from Veronica Lucas as best she could over the sound of the jukebox.

'You're going to do what?' Marie shouted over the sound of the Beatles' 'Please Please Me' which had hit the big time just months before. 'Take photographs of prostitutes?' A young man standing beside Kate in Mod parka gave the two of them a funny look and moved further away to wait for his order to be taken.

'I'm going to see what I can get tonight when the girls come out on to the streets. I can't waste any time because I'm not sure how good my camera will be in the artificial light. It's dark by six and I don't suppose there's much going on so

early. Later I'll have to rely on my flash and that'll be a bit
obvious.'

'Are you sure this is safe?' Marie asked, leaning close to
Kate's ear. 'Maybe people won't want their picture taken.'

'Well, I may have to take long distance shots and blow them
up later,' Kate said with more confidence than she really felt.
'I'll tell anyone who asks I'm just taking general shots of
Soho at night. It'll be fine.'

'I hope so, la,' Marie said doubtfully.

'What time do you finish? I'll come back later and we can
go home together if you're worried.'

'I won't finish till midnight,' Marie said. 'If I were you I'd
get home well before that. It's really not a place to be making
yourself conspicuous when the pubs turn out.'

'I'll be careful,' Kate said cheerfully. And as far as she
could be, she was. But although her camera was small, it was
noticed and, as darkness fell and the street lights came on,
making it essential to screw in her flashbulbs every four shots,
it was noticed more and more. A group of women in skirts
above the knee and high boots, standing outside a busy pub,
turned as one to look her over when she aimed in their
direction.

'What the hell do you think you're doing?' a busty blonde
asked, her heavily made-up face twisted aggressively.

'Just taking some pictures of Soho for a magazine,' Kate
said, suddenly realizing how impossible her commission
actually was. She could hardly ask these women if they were
prostitutes without risking a serious reaction, whether they
were or not. She was saved that time by the arrival of four
young men in suits and stringy ties, their hair slicked back
Elvis-style, who distracted the women's attention long enough
for her to slip away down a side street and make herself
scarce.

When she had got her breath back she noticed that the doors
close by were those which frequently had a number of bells
one above another, each with a woman's name on it. Suzie
nestled beneath Zsa Zsa, Marilyn above Sabrina. Perhaps, she
thought, if she hung about here for long enough, one or two
of the women, perhaps as pneumatic as the names they had

adopted implied, would come out of the tall, thin house and she could snatch a shot. Just for luck she snapped a couple of the front doors. That at least gave some indication of the trade that went on inside. She hung around for a while, stamping her feet to keep warm, and eventually saw men begin to go in and out of the houses, seldom staying longer than half an hour. She stood well back, and took a couple of shots of the visitors, taking care not to catch their faces, only their anonymous back views. But in the end even that attracted attention and one man leaving the house noticed the flash of her camera and came over to her.

'What the hell you doing, girl?' he asked in a heavy accent. He was tall and dark, with his hat brim pulled well down, and obviously angry.

'I'm just taking some shots of Soho for a magazine,' Kate said, feeling slightly breathless.

'Well, go and take them in some other bloody street, not here,' the man snapped. 'Bloody cameras are no good for trade. These are my girls and they don't need no publicity in magazines, so fuck off.' He looked her up and down in the dim light. 'Unless you want a job?' he said, and leered. Kate flinched and backed away, before turning on her heel and hurrying into the brighter lights of Dean Street with panic threatening to overwhelm her. She had, she thought, underestimated the risk of what she had agreed to do for Veronica Lucas and she wondered if the woman was as naive as she was, or whether she had known the danger Kate might run into and had chosen not to tell her.

As she turned into the main road she was suddenly aware of steps close behind her and turned round, her heart thumping, imagining the man who had warned her off had followed her. She was surprised to find Sergeant Harry Barnard with a hand outstretched to grasp her arm.

'What the hell do you think you're doing?' Barnard said angrily. 'I just caught sight of you with Jackie Zahra. Have you the faintest idea how dangerous that man is?'

Kate shook her head, feeling numb. 'I was just taking pictures,' she said faintly. 'I wasn't doing any harm.'

'Pictures?' Barnard said incredulously. 'You tried to take a picture of a Maltese pimp? Do you even know what a pimp is?'

'I think so,' Kate said.

'Jesus wept,' Barnard said. 'Come on, I'll buy you a drink and you can tell me what this is all in aid of, and I'll tell you how stupid it is. If you carry on like this you're going to get yourself killed.'

FIFTEEN

Harry Barnard sat across the table from Kate O'Donnell and sipped his double Scotch thoughtfully. She was flushed but the look on her face was defiant rather than contrite as she took a sip of Babycham. She looked about sixteen years old, he thought, and he did not know how to start telling her the extent of the risks he had seen her taking. He put his glass down and sighed. The only way forward, he thought, was to come at the girl obliquely, through her brother, and then perhaps take her out for a meal later.

'I can look after myself, you know, la,' she said, breaking the silence and glancing at him over the top of her glass, her Liverpool twang very strong. 'Liverpool's not exactly a garden of roses or anything. There's some bad things going on. I learned to look after myself when I was a kid.'

'I'm sure you did,' Barnard agreed solemnly. 'But just at the moment, right here, it looks like we've got two major gangs at each other's throats and two deaths which may or may not be connected. Believe me, they won't be too fussy about getting rid of anyone who gets in their way. We don't know whether your brother's friend was involved with one or other of the gangs, or whether his death was something entirely separate. Either way, it makes no sense for you to be out on the streets drawing attention to yourself with a bloody flash-bulb. If the do-gooders want pictures of the dark side of Soho at night they should ask someone to go out with you and tell you what's safe and what isn't. But if I were you, I'd give up on the whole idea.'

'I'll think about it,' Kate said. 'I was a bit amazed to find all these people actually trying to help the prostitutes. I don't think anyone bothers much up north. They still call them fallen women where I come from.' She gave Barnard a cheeky smile. 'At least, some do, if they've got a pulpit to stand in,' she said. 'Father Hamilton doesn't seem to be like that.'

'He's OK, is the Rev Dave,' Barnard said. 'He tries hard. But with a lot of those kids he's wasting his time. They're jail bait.'

'He wants to talk to you,' Kate said. 'I was down there earlier and he was complaining that someone's been mooching round trying to get at the kids.'

'I'll have a word,' Barnard said. 'What were you doing at St Peter's anyway?'

'I went up there to get some shots of the place for this Mrs Lucas person but the kids were very wary. I couldn't understand why some of them hated the idea of having pictures taken till Father Hamilton explained.'

'Does he know who it was, this intruder?' Barnard asked, very much the copper suddenly.

'No, I don't think so.'

'There's at least one young lad there who seems genuinely to be trying to get away from that sort of thing. I'll make sure I look in on them in the morning to find out what's going on. In the meantime, I think I should run you home to Notting Hill, don't you? Get you out of harm's way – though I'm not sure that's an area I would like my sister living in. It's a bit rough as well.'

Kate laughed. 'You've obviously not seen Scottie Road, la,' she said. 'That's where I lived when I was a little kid, before we got a corporation house, and believe me, that's rough.'

'Have it your own way,' Barnard conceded. 'You want to go then? Or will you let me buy you a meal? If you don't like Italian there's a good little Greek place round the corner.'

Kate finished her drink, shook her head and got to her feet. 'I'm not hungry,' she said. 'And I'll take the Central Line home, ta very much. It's only ten o'clock. I'll be fine.' She turned away, her face still slightly flushed, leaving Barnard to ask himself what had happened to his normal lady-killing skills. He watched her go as he finished his drink and wondered not for the first time if Kate O'Donnell had ever slept with anybody. It was obvious she had been brought up a Catholic and he knew about their unbending priests and strict moral rules, and yet she seemed like an independent girl, independent enough to come south and make her own decisions about her own life in the sinful city – and not always wise ones, at that. He was sure that she could not be nearly as innocent as she looked. In his book, nobody was.

But she had left him frustrated. The night was young, he was not tired, and he wanted to get away from the sleazy streets where he spent so much time. Suzie, or one of her colleagues, he thought, all of them willing enough to accommodate a copper, would not, on this occasion, fit the bill. He smiled faintly to himself, wondering if the stars were his way inclined tonight, went over to the bar to use the phone and dialled a north London number. The voice which answered sounded husky, although he did not think that it was likely to be sleepiness which caused it.

'Harry, you're taking a risk calling here,' Shirley Bettany said.

'Is he at home?' Harry asked.

'You're out of luck, sweetie, he went to Rome for three days on business and he's just back. He's in the shower right now.'

Barnard groaned. In his head, he had already taken the journey through Camden Town towards the Finchley Road, up Fitzjohns Avenue, through Hampstead village and on to the Heath, to the wide, tree-lined avenue where the Bettanys lived. It was a place where the large houses smelled of money and Barnard liked it very much, and liked even more the woman who occasionally came to his place and even more occasionally invited him there. The whole enterprise, he knew, was fraught with risk but he liked that too.

'Very quickly then,' he said, lowering his own voice almost as much as she did at the other end, as if Fred could overhear. 'Does Fred ever tell you what's going on between Ray and Georgie Robertson?'

'Is that the reason you rang, you bastard?' she asked.

'You know it's not,' Barnard said, telling her in no uncertain terms what more he had hoped for. 'But you know the brothers and I go way back, and it's the first time I remember that Ray has been so seriously fed up with his little brother. And Georgie seems even madder than usual at the moment. What the hell's going on?'

'I hate Georgie,' Shirley said with venom. 'Every time I
see him he has a grope. He's an animal. And yes, you're right.
He and Ray are rowing. They were at each other's throats at
the party at the Delilah. I overheard a bit of it. Ray was telling
Georgie not to do something, saying someone wouldn't wear
it. Some foreign name. I don't know who he was talking about.'

Barnard's hand tightened on the receiver. 'Foreign?' he said
sharply.

'Falcon, something like that? I have to go. I think Fred's
finished in the bathroom. I'll see you soon.' She hung up,
leaving Barnard leaning against the bar frustrated in more
ways than one. He stubbed out his cigarette but stayed where
he was for a moment thinking furiously. Falcon, Falzon, he
thought. And if Falzon disliked something Georgie was up to
while Ray was trying to get a deal with him, it explained a
lot. But what was Georgie doing to cause such a rift? he
wondered. It was undoubtedly time to find out.

Halfway through the next morning, DS Harry Barnard stormed
out of the nick in a fury. He had put his head round DCI
Venables' door with the intention of reporting on the very
limited progress he had made with his inquiries, only to be
summoned in peremptorily as the senior officer slammed his
phone down.

'Have you picked up any new leads on what the Robertsons
are up to?' Venables snapped.

'I haven't, guv,' Barnard said. 'Except that whatever it is,
the brothers seem to be at each others' throats. They're having
furious rows about something. And the only time I've seen
Georgie recently – which was at the Delilah – he was certainly
in a bit of a strop about something.'

'So I heard, though I didn't see much of either of them that
night,' Venables said. 'You know you told me that some bloke
had a row with someone who sounds very like Mason in the
queer pub in Wardour Street a couple of weeks ago? One of
my snouts is saying he thought the other bloke might be
Georgie Robertson, though I don't know how that can be right.
You told me he wasn't a nancy-boy.'

'He's not certainly not queer, as far as I know. Quite the

opposite. Women are always complaining about his unwanted attentions. And the tom who was threatened with a knife certainly thought her john could have been Georgie.' Barnard felt uneasy, wondering how far Ray Robertson's plans had advanced without his knowledge. What was Georgie's name doing cropping up alongside Mason's at this late stage if it hadn't been carefully planted in Venables' way? Things, he thought, were slipping out of his control, and he did not like that. He regarded the Robertsons as part of his own personal empire. And while they had largely confined their activities to the East End, where they had been brought up and where their mother still held court over a criminal clan which seemed to go back generations, that had certainly held true. He owed his smart flat on the edge of Highgate to the Robertsons one way or another, he thought, but now they were expanding into Soho he felt his grip on their activities was slipping. He turned his attention back to Venables, who was obviously still furious about something.

'What the hell's going on?' he snapped.

Barnard shrugged. 'I've no idea,' he said. 'Doesn't your snout know?'

'Not really,' Venables said. 'He just thought it was two queers sounding off at first, as they do. And he can't remember exactly when it happened, except that it was obviously before Mason got his throat slit. But then this week, when he saw Mason's picture in the *Evening News,* he says he realized there might be more to it than a pansies' tiff. Can you use your contacts, Harry, and find out what's going down? Find out who Mason was really having a row with, if you can. I can't imagine it was Georgie and I certainly don't want to tangle with the Robertsons if I don't have to. Round a few of the buggers in the pub up for gross indecency if you have to and see what you can shake out of them. That'll go down well with your boss too. See if you can get a more positive description.'

'I'll give it a go,' Barnard had said cautiously. 'But does this give us a new suspect then? Someone else Mason was on bad terms with. And what about Marelli? Have you got a result on the fingerprints in the shop?'

'What fingerprints?' Venables said. 'No one found anything except Marelli's own prints.' Barnard hesitated for a split second but said nothing.

'And what about O'Donnell? Have you given up on him?' he asked.

'No, I bloody haven't,' Venables snapped. 'He's by far the most likely killer. I think this is all a wild bloody goose chase, but we'd better check it out.'

Which was all very well, Barnard thought, except that Jimmy Earnshaw had seen two men close to Mason and O'Donnell's flat at the time he must have been killed, and he couldn't finger either of them as Kate O'Donnell's brother, or Georgie Robertson for that matter. But until he knew that Jimmy was safely out of London he didn't choose to share that information with anyone. The boy needed to be kept safe until his evidence was needed, he thought. He was the one person involved in this mess who had no reason not to tell the truth.

'I'll do a trawl around the gay pubs, guv. See if we can pin down who was really rowing with Mason. That might give us a new lead.'

'You do that,' the DCI agreed. 'And leave Georgie Robertson to me. You're too close to those two beggars. I'll talk to him myself if I think I need to.'

'Right,' Barnard said equably enough, relieved that if anyone was going to interview Georgie for anything at all it wouldn't be him. If he needed to talk to Georgie, he wanted to pick his moment himself and pick his words very carefully indeed. He went back to his own desk but had only begun to flick through the paperwork which was beginning to pile up on top of the battered typewriter when the internal phone rang. It was Venables, with a note of triumph in his voice.

'The Liverpool force have picked up O'Donnell,' he said. 'They'll bring him down. He'll be here in the morning. So now at last we might get somewhere.'

'Great,' Harry Barnard said, trying to inject some enthusiasm into his voice, but failing. He was surprised at how much, when it came to it, he did not want Kate O'Donnell's brother to go down for this. Even worse, he knew Kate O'Donnell would have to be told and he guessed that he might be the best person to do it. He pulled on his coat, jammed his hat on to his head and flung himself angrily down the stairs and out into the street, heading across Regent Street into Soho and towards the Blue Lagoon, constantly glancing at his watch. Lunchtime was coming up and he guessed that would be where he would find Kate. And when he had broken the unwelcome news to her, probably making sure that the girl would never speak to him again, he would deliver a bit of sound and fury to the handful of pubs frequented by queers. It sounded far-fetched, but perhaps Ray Robertson, who clearly believed he was setting his brother Georgie up, was trying to frame him for a murder he had actually been involved in, in spite of Jimmy Earnshaw's failure to identify him. And if that was so, who was the other killer? And what possible motive could any of them have for slitting Jonathon Mason's throat, and quite possibly Pete Marelli's as well? Could there be a connection between Mason and Marelli that no one knew anything about? And if there was, could he find it before Venables charged Tom O'Donnell and closed his investigation down?

Kate O'Donnell sat on the sagging sofa beside Tess and Marie with tears running down her face. Tom, Barnard had told her, was on his way to London with two Liverpool detectives, and so far she had not been able to discover how the police had found him or even where they were taking him. She supposed she should have thanked Harry Barnard for taking the trouble to come and tell her what had happened, but she had turned on him when he did and beaten her hands against his sturdy chest until he had taken her wrists and held her still.

'This is all wrong,' she said. 'You know it's all wrong. He told me he went up there long before Jonathon was killed. Dave Donovan took him back up in his van.' She had stopped then, realizing she had blurted out too much, while Barnard looked at her sideways.

'I think DCI Venables is going to want a little chat with you,' he said mildly. 'And where can I find this Dave Donovan?'

Kate looked mutinous for a moment but in the end she gave him Donovan's address. 'It's somewhere called Archway,' she said. 'He's sharing a flat with his mates.'

'Yes, I know it,' he said. 'The guv'nor will certainly want to talk to Dave Donovan too. What does he do?'

'He's in a band,' Kate said.

'Jesus wept. Is there anyone in Liverpool who's not in a band?'

'Not many,' Kate conceded. 'Though Tom's not. He did a bit of skiffle but mostly kept away from all that. He was more interested in clothes than music.' She shuddered slightly and glanced at her watch. Barnard had caught her leaving the Blue Lagoon on her way back to the office after her lunch. 'I'll have to go back to work, though I can't say I want to. Will you let me know where they take Tom?'

'They're not going to let you see him,' Barnard said. 'If DCI Venables seriously thinks he's got enough evidence, he'll charge him and take him to the magistrates' court tomorrow morning and on a charge of murder he'll be remanded in custody.'

'Jail?' Kate whispered. 'He'll find that hard.' She could see from the look in Barnard's eyes that she probably had no idea just how hard it would be.

'I'll try to keep you in touch with what's going on,' he had said. 'If he's going to appear in court I'll let you know when.'

She turned away and waved wanly to Marie who was watching the pair of them anxiously through the window, and made her way towards the agency, not wholly aware of where she was going.

'After you'd gone, I told that detective what a fool he was,' Marie said, putting an arm round Kate's shoulder and handing her a grubby handkerchief. 'He told me Tom had been arrested and I told him Tom's as likely to be a murderer as St Teresa herself. And if you want to know something else for nothing, I told him he could stop making up to you while he's doing his best to hang your brother.'

Kate smiled faintly through her tears. 'And what did he say to that?' she asked.

'He called me a little Scouse harridan,' Marie said. 'And that he'd have to keep right out of your way now, until it's all over. And that's the best bit of news I've heard for weeks.' Marie smiled to herself as she recalled how she had flapped the dishcloth she had in her hand perilously close to the police-man's silk tie before wiping down a table. 'And good riddance,' she had added for good measure, almost flinging two foam-flecked cups on to the counter, as he opened the door to leave. But the worst bit of news she kept from her tear-stained friend.

'How long will all this take if they charge him?' she had asked the departing detective before he closed the coffee-bar door.

'Could be months,' Barnard had said, slamming the door behind him.

Kate had walked slowly back to the office and slumped down at her desk as she tried to absorb Barnard's bombshell, desul-torily picking up some of the pictures which had been disturbed by the burglars and now had to be painstakingly filed all over again. In amongst the heaps, she discovered a cardboard file of her own images from the charity evening at the Delilah Club to which someone – presumably Ken – had attached captions with a note asking her to file those under the various names of the guests. He couldn't have found them of much interest, she thought, even though they were amongst the few negatives that had survived. She flicked through them idly, barely able to concentrate, wondering how far south Tom's train had got by now. Or maybe he was being brought by car down the new M1. That would be an adventure he would enjoy in any other circumstances, but what if they kept him in handcuffs?

She shook her head helplessly and tried to concentrate again, her eyes taken eventually by one image of a man she recalled from that evening, the man pointed out to her by his brother as George Robertson, one of the hosts for the evening's events and, to judge by her own experience and others she had witnessed, a serious menace to women, with wandering hands that she had pushed away herself when he got too close at the end of the evening. In this photo, he appeared only in the background of a shot of Christine Jones, posing for the camera with obvious enthusiasm. Georgie was talking animatedly to a much taller and more well-built man, and was probably not even aware that he had been photographed, she thought. She wondered idly who his companion was, and why they were toasting each other with champagne, before she labelled a file 'Robertson Brothers' and slipped it inside.

Somehow she hung on until the end of the day, glad for once that no one coming in and out of the office took much notice of her. Ken Fellows was preoccupied with the chaotic aftermath of the burglary and most of the other photographers had gone out on their assignments. Just before it was time to leave, the phone in the photographers' room rang. Brenda was closeted with Ken, so Kate picked it up and was surprised to hear a familiar voice, very Scouse and slightly crackly.

'Is that you, la? Can you hear me? It's Dave.'

'I can hear you,' Kate said. 'Where are you? Have you heard what's happened?'

'I've been rehearsing all afternoon, la, but yes, I heard. The bizzies came round to our gaff but no one knew where we were, or at least they said they didn't, said we might be in Liverpool, so they went away again. D'you know what they want?'

'They know you took Tom up to Liverpool,' Kate said.

'Oh feck,' Donovan said.

'You lied to me, Dave,' Kate said angrily. 'Why didn't you tell me you'd taken him up north?'

'I'm sorry, pet, really I am, but Tom made me promise not to tell anyone, especially his family. He didn't want his mate following him and letting on about what they'd been up to.'

'Well, if you ask me, the police will think you know where he's been hiding all this time. And they won't be very pleased about that, kidder.'

'I don't know where he was, la. I haven't a clue. He gave me some cash for the petrol and I dropped him off on Lime Street, by the Adelphi. He said he was meeting a friend in a pub down by the river, was planning to stay with him for a while because he'd split with his mate in London. He looked pretty rough, if you really want to know. But it was nothing to do with me. He has his own mates, you know what I mean? I don't like to get involved.'

'But you must talk to the police,' Kate said urgently, feeling slightly sick and trying to keep her voice from rising. 'You can give him an alibi. Don't you realize that? You know when you took him up there and it was long before his mate was killed. You can clear him, get him out of this mess.'

'There's nothing to say he didn't come back, is there?' Donovan objected.

'What? What did you say?' Kate shouted, sure she'd misheard. But she realized she hadn't. 'Dave, we need to talk. Where can I meet you? Not round here. It's too close to the police station.' Reluctantly he agreed to meet her in the refreshment room at King's Cross station, which they could both easily reach on the Northern Line, and which would be busy enough, she hoped, to cover their movements. After she had hung up she sat at her desk for a long time feeling cold and close to tears. She had relied on Dave Donovan's evidence to clear Tom if it were ever needed, but now she could see that by itself it was not enough. She did not doubt that Tom had gone to Liverpool and stayed there after abandoning Jonathon Mason, but there would have to be cast-iron proof of that from the friends he had been with that week, and she did not even know who they were. She would have to go back to Declan Riley and start again.

She met Dave Donovan in the steamy murk of the British Rail refreshment room, but as Kate expected, he offered little comfort beyond a brief squeeze of the hand as she sat down opposite him at the littered table. He bought her a cup of tea and sat facing her looking gloomy.

'The bizzies are looking for me,' he said. 'You're right. I'm going to have to talk to them.'

'What are you going to say?' she demanded. 'What did Tom say to you on the way up? He must have told you something about what happened between him and Jonathon. Did he really give you the impression he would go all the way back and kill him?'

'He didn't talk much, la. If you must know, most blokes don't want to talk about that sort of thing. It's not something we want to know about, is it? We keep well clear. He just said they'd split. That's it.'

Kate looked at him in despair. 'This is Tom you're talking about. You've known him since we were all at juniors.'

'Doesn't matter,' Donovan said. 'I don't really like queers. I didn't really want to take him with me. I did it for you, if you really want to know. I thought you'd be pleased.'

'I am pleased,' Kate snapped. 'Thank you. But now we have to try to keep him out of jail. Whatever you think about his life, there's no way he could have cut someone's throat.'

'Kate,' Donovan said. He hesitated while she waited impatiently. 'I'll do my best to help him with the bizzies,' he said. 'I promise. But I'll be doing it for you, you know what I'm saying? Now you're down here in London, I thought . . .' He trailed off and Kate put her hand briefly on his. She should, she knew, turn him down flat but some uncharacteristic caution held her back.

'Let's wait until this is all over. I'm sure the bizzies won't keep him long. They just want to ask him some questions and then it'll be finished. Give me a ring when you've been to the police, la. And then we'll see where we are.' Soon, she thought, this nightmare must surely be over, but she had a sick feeling that it might only get worse. After studying the tube map, she ventured on to the Circle Line and walked slowly back to Marie and Tess's place from Notting Hill Gate. Finding Marie waiting for her in the tiny living room, she collapsed, sobbing, into her arms.

SIXTEEN

DS Harry Barnard did not often use the police canteen but today he had wanted some information which he was unwilling to seek out officially. He pushed open the door to be met with a wall of steam reeking heavily of chip fat and acquired a mug of bright orange tea while surveying the crowded tables intently. After a couple of sips he spotted his quarry, Bill Sanderson and Derek Pratt, both DCs in Ted Venables' murder team and both tucking into heaped plates of fried food which would keep them occupied for some time. He made his way through the tables and pulled up a chair alongside them.

'I hear you got a result, lads,' he said. 'Well done. I didn't turn up much useful myself around my patch. Close as clams, these nancy-boys.'

Sanderson and Pratt sniggered over their sausages.

'Bloody thick scousers pulled their fingers out in the end,' Sanderson said. 'Dead slow and stop, they are. But old Ted rattled their tree somehow and out dropped our laddo in the end. Easy'

'Has he charged him?' Barnard asked.

'Don't think so. He came in a bit the worse for wear, apparently,' Pratt said, mouth full of food. 'Serves the little pervert right. Had to see the doc before the guv'nor could question him. He's with him now.'

'Got him sewn up then, has he?'

'You know Ted,' Sanderson said. 'If he wants someone sewn up they get sewn up.'

'And stay sewn up,' Pratt added, sprinkling more ketchup on his chips.

'Funny. I heard a whisper Robertson might be involved in both the killings. The lad from Liverpool's hardly likely to have offed Pete Marelli. And weren't there fingerprints in the shop? I thought I saw some when I found him.'

'I don't know anything about that,' Sanderson said. 'But the guv'nor doesn't buy that idea anyway. Why would a serious player like Robertson kill some little ponce pretending to be an actor? There's no motive, is there? He reckons Marelli was in on their little games and the Liverpool lad came back to see him off too.'

'Aren't you eating, Harry?' Pratt inquired. 'These bangers are good and that little blonde bird'll give you extra chips if you smile at her nicely.'

Barnard glanced at the food in distaste. 'Not hungry,' he said.

'Want to keep your figure more like,' Sanderson sneered. 'Bloody pin-up boy with your fancy suits and flowery ties. The birds don't care, you know.' He patted his belly contentedly. 'I never have any trouble.'

Barnard drained his tea without further comment and made his way back upstairs to Vice where, to his surprise, he was met by Venables himself, sweating in shirt sleeves and looking, for him, slightly flustered.

'Can you spare me half an hour, Harry?' he asked. 'Sit in on the interview with this pansy from Liverpool. You interviewed the sister, didn't you? I reckon we could get him to cough quite easily if we put a bit of pressure on with the family angle. Are you up for it?'

Barnard barely hesitated. 'Right, guv,' he said. He turned his back on his desk and followed the older man back downstairs to an interview room where they found a uniformed constable minding a figure slumped across the table in the centre of the room. Venables waved the uniformed officer out and shook the shoulder of the man at the table.

'Come on, come on, you great big girl, you're not really hurt. We need to talk to you.' The man at the table looked up and Barnard struggled to conceal his shock. Both Tom O'Donnell's eyes were blackened and half-closed, and he was clutching a bloodied handkerchief to his mouth. Yet in spite of that, the resemblance to his sister was uncanny. They could almost have been twins, he thought.

'You didn't tell me he'd been hurt,' Barnard said mildly to Venables.

'He's seen the doc,' Venables said. 'No major harm done. Happened on the way down from Liverpool, didn't it, Tommy? They stopped for a slash and he tried to scarper.'

O'Donnell looked at them with pure hatred in his eyes but he said nothing.

'Sergeant Barnard here's been talking to your sister,' Venables said, and that did attract the prisoner's attention, his bloodshot eyes swivelling in Barnard's direction with fear in them now. It was a look Barnard had seen dozens of times before when men arrested and facing a charge of gross indecency had realized the effect the trial would have on their families. Tom O'Donnell was in the same place with knobs on, he thought, and if Venables proved his case he faced an even worse fate than the poor bastards who were routinely picked up in pubs and clubs and public lavatories and locked up for months or years. For O'Donnell it would be life.

'Kate was very worried about you, Tom,' Barnard said. 'You know that? And I think the best thing you can do for her now, and for all your family, is tell us what happened the night Jonathon Mason died.'

'I wasn't there,' O'Donnell muttered. 'I told the bizzies back home. I got to Liverpool with Dave Donovan on the Monday, three days before Jon died, apparently. I was two hundred miles away. Dave'll tell you.'

'I'm sure he will, but you'd plenty of time to get back again,' Venables broke in, his voice harsh. 'So far as I know, there's still trains running between Liverpool and London.'

'But I didn't get a train,' O'Donnell said. 'It was finished with Jon, it was all over. Why would I have come back? I wanted to put as much distance between him and me as possible.'

'Even at the risk of your family finding out about what you'd been up to?' Barnard asked. 'You didn't want your mother to know, did you? A good Catholic boy like you?'

O'Donnell did not answer and Venables suddenly banged his fist on the table, making him flinch. 'So if you stayed up there you can tell us where you were and who you were with. You'll have a cast-iron alibi for the night Mason was killed, won't you? We can go and interview all your little pansy friends and you'll be in the clear? Isn't that right?' But Barnard knew from O'Donnell's face that it was not right at all. 'Take a strong line on gross indecency, do they, the Liverpool coppers?' the sergeant asked.

O'Donnell nodded imperceptibly and Barnard was suddenly certain that he would not be asking any of his queer friends to back up his alibi, in which case he would not be walking away very soon.

'A full trial could last weeks,' Venables said. 'And you'll have a long wait for it. It'd be all over the *News of the World*. Much easier to plead guilty and get it over with quick. Much better for your ma and your sister.'

'What'll happen to me?' O'Donnell whispered.

'They won't hang you, if that's what you're thinking,' Venables said airily. 'More's the pity. A life sentence is all you'll get now. You'll probably be out in ten years or so, still have a life ahead of you.' Venables was not just downplaying what would happen but grossly deceiving O'Donnell, Barnard thought, and bit his tongue. An attractive young man convicted of such a murder would be fair game in one of Her Majesty's prisons for dozens of frustrated men. His life inside would be made hell.

Venables lost patience then and slapped O'Donnell hard across the face, before putting his hand around his throat and pushing him back in his chair. 'I'm going to put you back in a cell now, Tommy, to have a little think. When you're ready to make a statement about the night you slit Jonathon Mason's throat just tell the custody sergeant and I'll be ready for you.' He marched out of the interview room without a backward glance leaving Barnard sitting opposite Tom O'Donnell waiting for the uniformed constable to return.

'I don't believe you did this but you must get your mates to back up your alibi,' Barnard said quietly. 'There's no other way.'

O'Donnell stared at him for a moment, the side of his face reddening where Venables had hit him. Then he simply shrugged and buried his battered face in his arms and Barnard realized that he had effectively given up. There was no more fight left in him.

*   *   *

DS Harry Barnard stormed across Soho in a fury. It was gone six o'clock and the lights were already coming on in the coffee bars and cafes and he guessed he was probably too late to catch Kate O'Donnell as she left work. He would have to follow her home to west London, he thought irritably. He desperately needed to catch up with her to tell her that the only chance she had of extricating her brother from Ted Venables' clutches was to go to Liverpool herself and persuade Tom's mates to take a risk and vouch for his whereabouts the night his former lover had been killed.

He turned into Frith Street, but before he got to the Ken Fellows Agency he was aware of a dark car pulling up beside him. Without much sense of surprise, he found himself facing Ray Robertson again, beckoning him through the open rear window of the Jaguar.

Reluctantly he pulled open the door. 'I'm in a hurry, Ray,' he protested.

'So am I, Flash, so am I,' Robertson snarled and hauled him into the back seat beside him. 'What the hell's going on, Harry? We don't seem to be getting anywhere with the little scheme we discussed. And Georgie's becoming a serious liability. I want him off the streets, and I wouldn't have thought that would do your career any harm either. I've given Venables a sighting of Georgie and the dead nancy-boy together having an argy-bargy. What more does he want?'

Barnard shrugged. There was no point prevaricating. If Venables charged O'Donnell tonight, he would appear in the magistrates' court tomorrow and the news would be in the evening papers when the late editions hit the streets.

'He still seems to favour the boyfriend for it,' he said. 'He's had him hauled back from Liverpool and seems to think he's got it all sewn up. And when Ted Venables thinks that, it generally turns out that way.'

Robertson flung himself back into the car's upholstery and sucked angrily on his cigarette. 'Has he got this lad down for the Pete Marelli killing as well? he asked. 'Because that'll really piss the Maltese off. He was one of their own.'

'Not that I know of,' Barnard said. 'But I wouldn't put it

past him to add it to the charge sheet just to tidy up the loose ends. You know how it is.'

Robertson took a deep breath. 'You don't know where you are with these bloody bent coppers, do you, Harry?'

Barnard could only offer a weak grin. 'Venables has his own priorities,' he said. 'Maybe someone else is pulling his strings. I wouldn't know. Or maybe he just wants to get his pension with his record looking good.'

'Stuff his pension,' Robertson said. 'See what you can do, Harry, will you? What we need is a witness who'll swear he saw Georgie come out of that flat that night all covered in blood. No one will be able to argue with that, will they?'

'I think you're more likely to be able to set that up yourself, Ray,' Barnard said. 'There's only so far I can go or I'll get some busybody from the Yard looking at what I'm up to myself.' And there is the small problem, he thought, that a witness exists who is pretty sure that neither Tom O'Donnell nor Georgie Robertson came away from the murder scene that night but someone else entirely. And the more people there were who did not want to hear what Jimmy Earnshaw had to say, the more precarious his position became. This whole affair, he thought, was turning into a nightmare. And as he slid out of Robertson's limo, right outside the Fellows Agency which was, as he suspected, shuttered and in darkness, he felt an urgent need to check up on Jimmy's safety. In these shark-infested waters, tiddlers like the homeless boy were unlikely to survive long if someone did not look out for them.

So instead of heading back to pick up his car, which was parked outside the nick, he turned north towards St Peter's. The heavy doors were unlocked and he could hear the laughter of young people even before he pushed them open. Once inside, he found the residents around the long dining table eating bread and jam and drinking mugs of tea, loosely supervised by two motherly- looking women in flowery aprons whom he had met before.

'Is the Rev Dave in?' he asked, but they both shook their heads.

'He's gone off with that new lad, Jimmy, Sergeant. Said he

wouldn't be back tonight.' Barnard nodded, feeling slightly reassured.

'That's fine,' he said. 'He told me he'd found him somewhere to stay.'

'What's so special about Jimmy?' the other woman asked. 'There's lots of these kids need somewhere to stay.'

'Oooh, he says he saw a murder, miss,' one of the boys sitting at the table said, full of contemptuous disbelief. 'He wakes up in the night shouting about blood and knives and stuff. If you ask me, he's nuts.'

Barnard struggled to keep the alarm he felt out of his face. If the kids here knew this much it was only a matter of time before the information leaked out into the wider world. It was no wonder, he thought, that David Hamilton had spirited his charge away so promptly.

'Do you know where Dave has gone?' he asked quietly, without much hope. If Jimmy's secrets had leaked out so comprehensively, Hamilton would have been extra careful not to tell anyone where he was taking him.

Both the women shook their heads in unison. 'He never said,' one of them said. 'Just went off without a word. Someone else was looking for him as well. Someone said they had a boy needed a roof over his head. I told him we were full up but then with Jimmy gone I wasn't even sure about that. I told him to come back tomorrow and there might be a place.'

'Funny bloke,' the other woman said. 'Got quite shirty. Kept looking around as if we were hiding something.'

'Had you seen him before?' Barnard asked, suddenly anxious.

'I had,' one of the boys at the table said suddenly. 'I saw him talking to Jimmy yesterday outside in the graveyard. He was asking Jimmy to do something and then he shoved him away and the bloke looked like he was going to hit him but he didn't in the end. Jimmy came back indoors then and went to see the Rev Dave.'

Barnard reached into his jacket pocket for George Robertson's mugshot. 'Was this the man?' he asked.

The two women and the boy studied the photograph for no more than a couple of seconds before they nodded.

'Little bloke,' one woman said.

'Evil-looking,' the other added.

'Do you know what he wanted Jimmy to do yesterday?' Barnard asked the boy.

'Nah,' he said. 'He was talking quiet like. But Jimmy didn't want to, whatever it was. Jimmy was really scared after. Terrified.'

The sergeant turned to the women. 'You're quite sure Dave took Jimmy away? He didn't go off with anyone else?'

"Course not. He said he was going to the station, though he didn't say which one. Very mysterious, he was.'

Barnard sighed. He wasn't going to get any further here, he thought. 'I'll just leave a note on his desk asking him to ring me in the morning when he gets back,' he said. 'I need to talk to him.'

At least partially reassured that Jimmy Earnshaw was out of London, he walked back to the nick to pick up his car. There he found an unusual amount of activity outside the station, mainly uniformed officers piling into squad cars and vans with anticipatory gleams in their eyes.

'What's going on?' he asked a grizzled sergeant well known for keeping his head down while he put in the last handful of statutory months to his pension.

'The super's been seized by one of his fits of morality,' the sergeant grumbled. 'Doesn't like perverts cutting each other's throats on his manor and threatening Christian civilization as we know it. We're going to raid the queer pub and put a few of them behind bars for a while. As if that will do any good. Still, it's good sport and a bit of overtime for the lads.'

Barnard felt a surge of anger, which he was careful to keep well hidden. The sergeant's reluctance to launch a crusade just as he would usually be retiring to the pub with his mates for an evening's boozing was down to laziness rather than any remote sympathy with queers. He would leave them to it, he thought. He needed to find Kate O'Donnell, give her the latest news about her brother and tell her in no uncertain terms what exactly she must do about it. He knew he had Jimmy in reserve, but the idea of the homeless boy being cross-examined at the Old Bailey did not fill him with confidence in his witness.

Kate undoubtedly needed to take a trip home and drum up some support there for her brother if she wanted to see him get out of DCI Venables' clutches. It was belt and braces time.

Kate herself was slumped in a corner of the Blue Lagoon, gazing sightlessly into an almost empty coffee cup. She had come back to see Marie after finishing work, rather than go home to the flat which she knew would be empty until Marie ended her shift. Tess had announced over breakfast that she had a date with another trainee teacher at her school to go to the pictures to see a new film called *From Russia with Love*, a sequel to *Dr No* which they had all enjoyed the previous year. Kate wondered idly where she might meet anyone who would ask her out to the pictures. The men at the agency were uniformly middle-aged and married, spent their lunchtimes and after-work hours together in the pub, and anyway seemed to regard her with more supercilious amusement than romantic interest. They neither expected nor wanted her to succeed as a photographer.

But the main cause of her depression was her failure to find any way to extricate Tom from the situation he found himself in. She had heard no more from Harry Barnard since the previous day and she seriously doubted that Dave Donovan would help Tom's cause as energetically as she would like him to. She glanced at Marie, who was busy serving a group of lads in Mod suits and parkas, and suddenly felt overpowered by the bright lights, the clatter and chatter and background beat of Gerry and the Pacemakers on the jukebox. On second thoughts, she decided, she would rather be on her own somewhere quiet. She would go back to the flat after all.

She set off in the direction of the Underground, weaving her way through the gathering evening crowds and dodging the cruising cars looking for parking in the narrow streets, until to her surprise found her way blocked by half a dozen police cars and vans outside what she now knew was the queer pub. Intrigued, she pulled out her precious camera and began to take shots of men being led out by officers who did not seem too bothered about how roughly they handled their prey. Trying not to draw attention to herself, she stepped back into a doorway only to find that as she stuck her head out to take a shot of a man with his head streaming with blood as he was shoved into a police van, she had been spotted by a uniformed sergeant who headed in her direction with an angry expression on his face.

'What the hell do you think you're doing, young lady?' he asked.

'Taking pictures,' she said with her sweetest smile. 'Do you always beat up people like that, la?'

'If they resist arrest,' the sergeant said.

'And is that what they really did?' she asked innocently. 'They don't look the violent type to me.'

'And you'd know all about that, would you? I think maybe you'd better let me have the film out of that camera of yours, don't you?'

Kate froze. There was no way she would hand over her precious camera but she was not sure that she would not be arrested if she did not comply, and that was the last thing she wanted with Tom in his present desperate situation.

'I don't think my friend Harry Barnard would like you bothering me like that,' she said, putting on her sweetest smile.

'Flash Harry?' the sergeant said, his voice heavy with scepticism. 'How well do you know him, then?'

'Quite well,' Kate said, crossing her fingers. 'You can check me out with Harry.'

'Oh, I will, miss,' the sergeant said. 'I will. Now I suggest you get yourself home. This is no place for a respectable girl on her own at night, especially not drawing attention to herself like you are.'

'I'm a professional photographer,' Kate said with as much dignity as she could muster as she held her offending camera behind her back.

'Well, if I were you, the next time you see Harry Barnard I should ask him where it's safe to take pictures and where it's not,' the sergeant said. 'Now be off before I change my mind.'

Kate took his advice and headed back towards Oxford Street briskly, but before she had crossed the next intersection she felt a hand on her elbow and found the flamboyant figure of

Vincent Beaufort, slightly less flamboyant without his hat, which he had scrunched up in his hand, falling into step beside her.

'I saw you back there, dear, taking snaps. What was all that about?'

'I just happened to be passing. I thought the police were being very rough.'

Beaufort laughed mirthlessly. 'You really are the innocent abroad, aren't you, dearie? They come in mob-handed every now and again just for the fun of it, as far as I can see. I expect they get bored at the nick. I was lucky tonight. I slipped out for a slash just as they burst in, and managed to get out of the back door in time. What are you taking pictures for anyway, dear? It's a funny thing for a girl to be doing round here.'

'Mainly for some people who want to get kids off the streets in Soho,' she said. She guessed that Veronica Lucas would not be too worried about the raid on the queer pub but at least her commission made her interest sound plausible.

Vinnie peered cautiously back the way they had come. 'Photographs?' he said. 'There's a lot of people wanting to take photographs at the moment. I hear the lad who got his throat cut was into that sort of thing, and not too scrupulous about how old his friends were either. Now that's something that can really get you into bother, and not just with the Old Bill either.'

'I heard something about that,' Kate said.

'And the word is that there's some kid around who knows something about that murder, a little boyfriend maybe, if that's what Mason was into. Maybe you'll come across him on your travels.'

'Does he have a name?' Kate asked, her mouth dry.

'Not that I heard,' Vinnie said. 'If he's any sense he'll have scarpered by now. He's likely not safe on the streets.'

'And if he hasn't left London where might he be?' Kate asked, wanting the idea which suddenly flashed into her mind confirmed.

'The holy roller at St Peter's might have taken him in, I

suppose,' Vinnie said. 'Why don't you ask that sweet-talking bastard of a copper who's always about the place? I know for a fact he takes kids down there sometimes to get them out of harm's way. Barnard, he's called. Harry Barnard.'

Of course, Kate thought to herself, and wasn't he some sweet-talking bastard, telling her nothing about this boy. 'I went to St Peter's to take some pictures. I think I may have met this boy you're talking about. I'll go down there again and see if I can track him down,' she said, taking the flash-bulb off her camera and stuffing the whole works in her bag. *And when I see Harry Barnard again*, she thought, *I'll find out what the hell he thinks he's playing at because as far as I can see he's been lying to me from the moment we met.*

SEVENTEEN

Kate O'Donnell caught her brother's eyes briefly across the magistrates' court, before he shook his head almost imperceptibly, glanced away and refused to look at her again. Sitting in the front row of the public seats, she had a close-up view of his bruised and battered face as he was hustled into the dock by a couple of uniformed policemen, and was almost overwhelmed with anger. How had he got into that battered state? she asked herself. In a low voice, Tom confirmed his name and his address at the flat where he had lived with Jonathon Mason. The charge of murder was read out and when he was asked to plead, he said 'Not Guilty' in a faint voice and was remanded in custody for a week. And to Kate's surprise, that was the end of the proceedings. Her brother was hustled away again, and the court resumed its processing of petty criminals.

Kate hurried out of the room and went back to the front of the building where she found a uniformed policeman who gazed down at her benignly enough until she explained that she was Tom's sister, when his face clouded over.

'Can I see him?' Kate asked, feeling frantic. 'He'll need a lawyer. How do I find out if he's got a lawyer? He'll need help. The rest of his family's in the north. I'm the only one he's got in London.'

'Whoa, whoa,' the officer said. 'You'll not get to see him here, darling. You'll be able to visit when he gets to jail. If you leave your name and address at the office, they'll tell you where he's been taken, though he won't get there till the end of the day. He'll wait here until the prison van turns up at four.'

'You mean he's got to sit here all day by himself?' Kate said, horrified. 'That's terrible. Surely you could get me in to see him for a few minutes? Come on. I'm not going to do any harm. I haven't got a file stashed away in my handbag, you know. I'm not going to help him escape. I just want to talk to him. He looks desperate. In fact, he looked suicidal when they took him out.'

The officer looked startled at that.

'He's tried to kill himself before, you know,' Kate lied, spotting a weakness she could exploit. 'I bet they don't know that. Shouldn't we tell them?'

For an instant the officer hesitated before Kate felt a firm hand on her elbow. She spun round to find herself face-to-face with DS Harry Barnard.

'You certainly believe in the direct approach,' he said. 'Come over here and I'll tell you what we'll do.' He drew her away into a relatively quiet corner of the crowded lobby. 'I reckon I can get you in to see him, but we'll have to use a bit of subterfuge. Can you pretend to be a solicitor's clerk? I'd say a solicitor but you look too young and there's not many women in that game.'

'Another unsuitable job?' Kate muttered.

Barnard ignored her. 'You'll need some sort of file to carry, a notepad, all that. But if I vouch for you I'm pretty sure I can get you in. A brief is the one person who's got a right to talk to a prisoner. Go down to the Strand and kit yourself out and I'll see you back here in fifteen minutes. All right?'

Kate nodded. 'What do you get out of this?' she asked.

'I want to sit in with you. I want to hear what he says.'

'He won't confess,' Kate said angrily. 'He didn't do it.'

'I know that,' Barnard said unexpectedly. 'I was looking for you last night to tell you to go back to Liverpool and get his mates to confirm his alibi.'

'I was out,' Kate said quickly. She would not, she thought, tell him about her late visit to St Peter's where she had been unable to find any trace of the boy or anyone willing even to confirm that he had ever been there. Someone, she had thought at the time, had very effectively silenced St Peter's. She looked at Barnard doubtfully. 'You really believe he's innocent?' she asked.

'I have some evidence,' he said. 'But it's fragile. It would still be better if you could prove he was in Liverpool at the time. Now, do you want to see him, or not?'

'Of course I do,' Kate said angrily. 'I'll see you back here in fifteen minutes.'

The holding cell beneath the magistrates' court was small and filthy and reeked of urine and cigarette smoke which made Kate catch her breath. Tom O'Donnell was sitting hunched on the bare bunk when a uniformed officer opened the door for his sister and Harry Barnard and at first he looked more startled than pleased to see Kate.

'This is a clerk from your solicitor's office,' Barnard said quickly before the PC closed the door behind them and left them crammed into the tiny cell. Barnard had warned Kate not to show any sign of affection in case the policeman outside chose to watch them through the grille in the door and Kate put a warning finger to her lips as Tom stood up and moved closer to her.

'I'm not supposed to be here,' she whispered, sitting down on the bunk and opening her completely blank file. Barnard waved Tom on to the bunk beside her and then positioned himself against the door, blocking the peephole. Kate put an arm round Tom's shoulder and kissed his cheek. 'I'm so pleased to see you,' she said, in a barely audible voice. 'This is Sergeant Harry Barnard who knows you didn't do it, and wants to help you to get out of here.'

Tom looked doubtfully at the London copper and then at his sister. 'Are you sure?' he asked.

Kate glanced at Barnard for a moment and knew that with him she would never be sure of anything. 'I'm sure,' she said. 'What I want you to do, Tom, is tell me exactly what happened between you and Jonathon Mason before you left and exactly what you did after that, once you knew he was dead. Just what you told me that day we met back home. Sergeant Barnard needs to hear it from you. And then we need to know who can vouch for you in Liverpool on the night your friend was killed. If you've got an alibi you need to prove it. Then we can get you out of here.' Tom slumped back against the graffiti-covered wall for a moment and shut his eyes.

'You really think they'll believe me?' he asked. 'I told the bizzies who came for me I was nowhere near the flat that night, and all they did was laugh and give me a good thumping.'

He touched his bruised face gingerly. 'They all hate us,' he said. 'They think we're fair game. One of the bastards who brought me back said he'd have to fumigate the car once he'd got rid of me. Why should this beggar be any different? Why's he going to believe me?'

'I'll tell you why,' Barnard said very quietly. 'I once had a brother. He was only a baby when the war started so he stayed with my mother when I was evacuated. He was much younger than me, so I can't say I ever got to know him that well, my brother Derek. But I always had this feeling he was different, a quiet lad who wasn't interested in rough games, like the rest of us. He took a lot of teasing for that. By the time I was pounding the beat as a probationer I guessed he was queer and I knew that wasn't a good thing to be in the East End. My dad worked on the docks and he'd have killed Derek if he'd guessed. In the end though, he didn't need to. Derek hanged himself when he was fifteen. He was being used by an older man who threatened to tell my family if he didn't do as he was told. It was all hushed up at the inquest but I made it my business to find out what happened and later on I got that bastard sent down for ten years for inter-fering with young boys. That's why, if your story hangs together, I'll believe you. What grown men do together is their business, what grown men do to kids is my business. Clear enough for you?'

The brother and sister sitting on the bunk stared at him for a moment in astonishment.

Tom shook his head, as if to reorder his thoughts. 'Fair play,' he said. 'Like I told Kate. This is how it was.' And he quickly ran through the months of his disillusionment with Jonathon Mason, his suspicion that he was involved with more and more unacceptable friends and the final certainty that he was picking up very young men or boys. 'And it was getting worse. I think even Jonathon was getting uncomfortable. I saw him in the street one day with some bloke I'd never seen before, having a furious row. I couldn't hear what they were saying but it looked as if the big fellow was threatening Jon. When I asked him about it, he said the bloke owed him money but wouldn't pay up, money for some work he'd done. And I didn't think the work could be anything legal, or why would they be arguing in the street about it? I had to get out. Like I told Kate, I left on the Monday that week, hitched a lift with Dave Donovan and the band, and stayed in Liverpool with a mate until the bizzies came for me the day before yesterday. I had absolutely nothing to do with Jonathon's murder.'

'If you thought your friend was getting into something criminal, why didn't you go to the police?' Barnard asked.

Tom gave him a pitying look. 'Because I knew Soho well enough by then to know I couldn't trust you bastards,' he said. 'Half the time you're in on the crime yourselves, or turning a blind eye for backhanders, according to what I hear in the pubs and clubs.'

Barnard did not comment on that in spite of the sharp look Kate gave him, and she guessed that what Tom said was true enough.

'If you can get one of your friends up in Liverpool to vouch for you when you come back to court next week, you should be able to get the charge thrown out,' Barnard said. 'I've got hold of another witness who saw someone else entirely coming out of your flat that night, but he's only a kid, and a homeless lad at that. His testimony on its own may not be strong enough to clear you. You need to establish your alibi as solidly as you can. I've already suggested to Kate that she goes up north and drums up some support for you.'

'I'll do it, Tom, I promise. We'll get you out of this,' Kate said.

For the first time since his visitors had arrived, Tom O'Donnell's face lightened slightly. 'I'll tell you who to talk to back home,' he said. 'Write these names down in your little notebook, Miss Solicitor's Clerk. If anyone can persuade them to help, I'm sure you can. You could charm the birds out of the trees if you tried.'

When she had finished, Barnard pushed himself away from the door. 'We'd better go. We're pushing our luck as it is,' he said. 'I've just one piece of advice for you, Tom. When you get to the nick, ask to be put on the segregation wing on your own. You'll be a bit lonely, but it's better than the alternative, believe me. If you think the police hate queers – and most do

– they don't often get the chance to make your life the hell
that people get in jail. So look after yourself.'

Feeling slightly sick, Kate kissed Tom and followed Barnard
out of the cell and back up the ground floor and out of the
court building, with not a word spoken. Back in the bustle of
the city, she looked at him and found him grim-faced.

'Do you really think we can get him out?' she asked.

'It should be easy if he's telling the truth, but to be honest
there are things going on around this case which I don't
understand, not least why the DCI in charge seems so convinced
Tom did it when there are good leads to follow in other
directions.'

'This witness, this boy you never bothered to tell me about,
is he the one who was at St Peter's?'

Barnard looked at her curiously. 'How do you know that?'
he asked.

'I came across him when I went there to take some photographs. Most of the kids thought having their picture taken
was a great lark, but he wouldn't let me take one. He was
very nervous, terrified in fact. I thought it was odd.'

'That lad's existence is the worst kept secret in Soho, and
it's his friends who look like landing him in trouble. Anyway,
it's all taken care of now. He's somewhere safe.'

'You mean you took care of it?' Kate asked, her perception
of Barnard taking another unexpected lurch, but the sergeant
merely shrugged.

'Maybe,' he said. 'Where are you going now? Will you be
OK?'

'Back to work,' Kate said. 'There's still masses of filing to
do after the burglary. Seems to be my role in life as far as my
boss is concerned. It looks as if that boxing do at the Delilah
Club will remain the highlight of my career. At least some of
those pictures survived. I'd kept the negatives myself so they
didn't get incinerated.'

'Do I appear in any of these pictures?' Barnard asked,
slightly amused, not wanting to let Kate go, but also intrigued
by this bizarre burglary which had been seemingly aimed only
at destruction.

'I don't think so, unless you're in the background

somewhere.' She glanced at her watch. 'Do you want to have a look? It's lunchtime and they'll all be in the pub. They never bother to invite me. The place will be empty.'

They walked back to Soho slowly and, as Kate had anticipated, found the office empty, her desk piled even higher with loose prints than she had left it.

'You have to sort all this lot?' he asked. 'I thought you were a photographer, not a filing clerk.'

'I don't think I've quite proved that to Ken Fellows yet,' she said gloomily. 'He'll probably have me back in Liverpool for good when my two months are up. In the meantime, I'll go up at the weekend to talk to Tom's mates. That won't be much fun.'

'Let's see some of the pictures you took at the Delilah then,' Barnard said. 'I'll soon tell you if you're any good or not.'

'Well, thanks,' she said drily, opening a drawer in her desk and pulling out a folder of the pictures which had survived. He flipped through them idly, looking for himself at first, but then going more slowly as a quite different face kept cropping up.

'You've got a lot of wee Georgie Robertson,' he said. 'Any particular reason?'

Kate came round the desk and stood beside him, suddenly very aware of his closeness. 'He was everywhere, that man. Ken said get the Robertsons' main guests, and Ray introduced me to them at the beginning, but it was Georgie who seemed to be sticking close to them. And I must say, I got the feeling some of them didn't like him much. Look at that one of Lord Francome, there, with Georgie. He looks furious about something.'

'What's that Georgie's got in his hand?' Barnard asked himself as much as Kate, spinning the picture round to try to see more clearly.

Kate looked more closely but in the end could only shrug. 'Can't tell,' she said. 'I could enlarge it for you if you think it's important.'

'Might be,' Barnard said. 'I'd really like to know what Georgie's up to that's annoying his brother so much. And a few more people by the look of it. Could be blackmail.' He flipped through the rest of the photographs and drew a sharp breath as he came to another close to the bottom of the pile, this one of Georgie with another man in the background, both smiling broadly this time and offering each other a mock toast with their glasses of champagne, and he wondered why DCI Ted Venables had claimed he'd barely seen Georgie Robertson that night.

'I don't know who that is,' Kate said. 'But he looks a lot happier than most of them.'

'He certainly does,' Barnard said thoughtfully. 'I wonder why.' He turned and put an arm lightly round Kate's shoulder. She flinched slightly but did not pull away.

'I know you're not very keen on the police at the moment. That's understandable, but Georgie Robertson is a nasty piece of work and I'd dearly like to get him off the streets for good. These pictures might be useful to me. I don't want to get you into trouble with your boss but could you make me copies of all the ones with Georgie in the frame?' He could see the hesitation in her face as she pulled out of his grasp. He knew he could make the request official but he did not think that would do her much good with her boss either.

'And in return?' she said. 'Will you help Tom?'

'In return, I'll do everything I can to make sure your brother is cleared when he comes back to court next week. I'll get a cast-iron statement from my witness and make sure it goes to his brief. If you can stand up his alibi in Liverpool the prosecution won't have a case.'

Kate nodded. 'All right,' she said. 'Meet me at the Blue Lagoon about five. I'll be there as soon as I finish work, la, with a set of prints. And you'd best not let me down.'

It was just before five that Kate glanced through the steamy windows of the Blue Lagoon and failed to spot Harry Barnard. She shrugged and decided that there was time for her to do one more thing before she kept her appointment. She had a brown envelope full of enlarged photographs for him and she did not doubt that if she was late he would wait for her. She knew that there was something in the pictures which had excited his interest, though she did not know what it was. She turned away and wove her way through the homeward-bound crowds to St Peter's, hoping that she might catch David Hamilton and persuade him to take her to see the boy on whose evidence the fate of her brother seemed to rest. Before she went back home to persuade Tom's friends to help, she thought, she needed to know how firm this boy's testimony was.

It was already dusk, and almost dark amongst the unkempt yews in the churchyard, and as she made her way up the pathway to the doors, she nearly screamed as a figure loomed towards her from the side of the porch.

'Dinna fash yersel', lassie,' the man said in a broad Scottish accent. 'I was just in the churchyard hoping I might see a wee laddie, if he came back here, but then I found something bad. I dinna want to be talking to the polis again, but somebody needs tae.'

'What do you mean?' Kate asked, her mouth dry. 'What did you find?'

'Ye'd best come and see, though ye'll not want to go close,' the old man said, and he took hold of her arm, pulling her round the side of the church towards a lean-to outhouse at the back where the door was ajar.

'I saw two men come out,' he said. 'And when they'd gone, I put my heed round the door. And I wished I hadnae.'

Kate looked at him doubtfully. 'Is there a light?'

'Ye'll not need a light to see what ye need to see,' Hamish said. 'Best not.'

Kate swallowed hard and pushed the door open. It was almost completely dark inside, but there was a throbbing noise from the back of the small space which she guessed must be the boiler which heated the church. Close to the door she could just make out a huddled figure which she knew instantly was human and instinctively was dead. Tentatively she touched a limp wrist but could feel no pulse. She stepped backwards out of the door and glanced round to find that the old man had vanished. Swallowing hard she made her way back round the side of the church and opened the main doors where she found David Hamilton's ragtag assembly of youngsters noisily eating their supper, with, to her relief, Hamilton himself presiding over the tea-urn. He glanced at her in surprise which turned to consternation as he took in her shocked face and wild eyes

'I wasn't expecting to see you again,' he said quietly. 'You look as if you need a cup of tea?' Kate nodded and felt her knees sag slightly.

'Please,' she said, stuttering as if words were hard to find. 'I need to talk to you.'

Hamilton quickly stirred sugar into a cup of tea, handed it to her and shepherded her to a pew much further down the nave where no one could overhear them. 'Drink first', he said.

She sipped the sweet brew, realizing that her hands were shaking almost uncontrollably.

'I've found a dead body in your boiler room,' she whispered. 'It's difficult to see very much but I think it's Mrs Lucas, the woman who asked me to take photographs for her campaign. Someone's killed her. Why in the name of God would anyone do that?'

EIGHTEEN

David Hamilton seemed to have aged ten years in ten minutes. He sat opposite Kate O'Donnell in his tidy study at the vicarage from where they had made their phone calls, he dialling 999, and she the Blue Lagoon, where she asked Marie to give a message to Harry Barnard, who she guessed would by now be waiting in the coffee bar for her with some impatience. Not surprisingly it was Barnard who turned up at the vicarage first.

'What the hell's going on?' he asked Hamilton, offering Kate the merest nod.

'I'll show you in a minute,' Hamilton said. 'It's not pretty. I've not seen anything so bad since I was at Dunkirk.'

'Do we know who it is?'

'Oh yes,' Hamilton said. 'It's a woman called Veronica Lucas.'

'I thought so,' Kate said faintly to herself.

Barnard turned towards her quickly. 'You know her?'

'She's the one who asked me to take pictures of prostitutes,' she said, her mouth dry. 'I told you. Don't you remember?'

'She works for a Catholic charity trying to get kids off the streets,' Hamilton explained. 'She's a good woman. I didn't touch the body, of course, except to feel for a pulse. There was a lot of blood. I don't know what they did to her but it looks bad.'

'You'd better show me,' Barnard said. He glanced at Kate. 'Will you stay here and show the Murder Squad where we are when they turn up? They'll want to know how you found her. And answer the phone if anyone rings? Technically I'm off duty and haven't got a radio with me.'

Kate nodded, feeling numb and grateful that she did not have to go anywhere near the huddled body again. 'You'd better take these now you're here,' she said, taking her collection of pictures out of her bag and handing them to the sergeant.

He nodded and put them in his inside pocket. Then he turned back to Hamilton. 'What have you done about the kids? We don't want them running riot round a murder scene.'

'I told my helpers to keep them inside,' Hamilton said. 'They don't know what's going on but they know something is. They're not stupid.'

'When we get some reinforcements, I'm sure DCI Venables will keep them where we want them,' Barnard said, looking grim. 'I'm glad we got young Jimmy well out of the way. Are you all right, Kate? Can you cope?'

Kate nodded and the two men left her alone, sitting close to the phone on Hamilton's desk. The silence in the old Victorian vicarage was intense and slightly unnerving and she passed the time surveying his bookshelves, and flicking through the magazines on his desk. Only then did she notice Jimmy Earnshaw's name on the notepad by the phone, together with a phone number and the address of a vicarage in Guildford. She drew a sharp breath, not in any doubt that this was where Jimmy had been taken but not sure what to do about it. Then she took her diary out of her handbag and carefully noted down the information. She was sure that when Barnard said he would obtain a statement from Jimmy Earnshaw, he meant it, but her faith in the police had been profoundly shaken and she decided to talk to the boy herself if she possibly could. She pushed the notepad under a magazine so that it could not be seen by a casual observer, just as a thunderous knocking began at the front door. She went to open it and found herself face-to-face with a well-built, florid man in camel coat and trilby standing impatiently on the doorstep, with a couple of other men hovering in the background.

'DCI Venables,' he said abruptly. 'I was told there was a dead body. Where's the bloody vicar and who are you?'

Kate told him and in return he studied her more closely.

'Haven't I see you somewhere before?' he asked.

'You might have done. I was at the Robertsons' do at the Delilah Club last week. I was taking photographs. I think I saw you there.' Better that connection, she thought, than allowing him to recall that she had been at the magistrates' court that morning where he might also quite possibly have seen her.

'Photographs,' Venables said, obviously surprised. 'I didn't think girls did that.'

'You'd be surprised what girls do these days,' Kate came back sharply. 'But if you're looking for the body it's not here. It's at the church. The vicar's gone over there with Sergeant Barnard. The boiler room's down the left side from the main door.'

'Harry Barnard? What the hell's he doing here?' Venables asked, looking even more surprised and certainly not best pleased.

'I think he just happened to be passing,' Kate said quickly. 'He'll be waiting for you.' She suddenly wanted rid of this man before he connected her with her brother. Venables spun on his heel, not thinking to ask her why she happened to be there, and Kate heaved a sigh of exhausted relief. It was time to get back to the job she really had to do, which was to get her brother out of jail. She put her coat on, turned out the light, and closed the vicarage door behind her, wondering how far away from London Guildford was. As she passed the gate to the churchyard, she could see the police milling around inside and there were several squad cars parked in the street. She walked quickly past in the direction of Oxford Street and was soon swallowed up by the home-going crowds of commuters heading for the tube.

Harry Barnard picked up his car and drove east faster than was either safe or legal. All the anxieties which had plagued him over the last week had come to a head as he had stood in the dim light of St Peter's boiler room looking down at the tormented body of Veronica Lucas. There was, as Hamilton had warned, a great deal of blood and Barnard did not think that she had died quickly, though the dirty rag stuffed into her mouth had probably guaranteed that in the end she had died quietly. But what possible motive could there have been for anyone to kill this God-fearing woman, in her smart coat and hat, court shoes flung to one side, with such psychotic ferocity?

DCI Venables had arrived quickly, in a flurry of blue lights and aggression, and Barnard took the first opportunity to get away, leaving the scene to the Murder Squad. The DCI had seemed to accept Barnard's excuse that he and Rev Dave Hamilton were old friends and that it was pure chance he had arrived when he did, although he made it perfectly obvious he did not want him involved in the investigation. But as Barnard walked slowly back to the nick to pick up his car, the more sickened he felt at what had happened and the more the one person who had always been able to produce this sort of revulsion in him intruded.

When he got to Whitechapel, he found the young men in the gym hard at work and Ray Robertson watching at the ringside where two boys were sparring.

'A word, Ray?' Barnard said quietly.

Robertson gave him a sharp glance and led the way to his office, waving Barnard into a chair. 'What can I do for you, Harry?' he asked.

'Do you know where Georgie is?'

'Have you got him pinned down then?' Robertson shot back. 'I got the impression Ted Venables wasn't biting, though I can't imagine why.'

'There's been another killing,' Barnard said. 'And this time it's got Georgie's MO all over it, if you know how to read it. And it's not some low-life Maltese pornographer, or some queer, that no one gives tuppence for this time. It's a respectable middle-aged woman who looks as though she's been deliberately tortured to death. Scotland Yard's going to take an interest in this one. They're going to pull all the stops out. So if Georgie's involved, you'll get what you wanted without anyone perjuring themselves to kingdom come. Satisfied?'

'But you're not sure?'

'Not yet, no,' Barnard said. 'And before I tackle Georgie, I need to know what the hell he's up to. Otherwise I'm floundering around in the dark.'

Robertson nodded slowly. 'All right,' he said. 'But this is for your ears only, not for the whole of the Metropolitan bloody Police. Understood?

'Understood,' Barnard agreed.

Ray steepled his hands under his chin as if considering

some business problem, which Barnard supposed in a way he was. Whatever affection there had been between the brothers when they were kids, he thought, and he didn't think there had ever been much, had long ago gone rancid.

'Right, let's put it this way,' Robertson said. 'My aim is to expand the business. I think you know that. We've done very well here in the East End, but there's richer pickings up west and I want some of them. This doesn't please a certain Maltese gentleman who's got a lot of fingers in a lot of Soho pies. You know who I mean?'

Barnard nodded.

'So there's two choices, right? We can muscle in on his territory, and there'll be a bloody war. Or we can do it more civilized, and split the trade up between us. And that's what I want to do. Saves a lot of aggravation. Basically, I want the protection business and he can have the porn and the women. But wee Georgie thinks different. He seems determined to get into the sex trade, porn magazines, women, blokes, boys, the whole bloody lot, queers and all. And Mr Falzon doesn't like that. The last straw was when I caught him blackmailing someone who'd been at some steamy party out in Essex, using my contacts in high places, guests at my parties . . . One of them came to me complaining. That was when I decided Georgie had to be stopped. Falzon won't have anything to do with queers. Georgie's putting everything I'm working for at risk. So how can I help you, Harry boy? How can we pin the little bastard to the floor?'

'Do you know where he is?' Barnard asked.

'No, but I know where he's going to be at seven. We're both going to see our ma. We always do on a Thursday night. Old family tradition. You remember Ada Street?'

'She's never moved out, then?'

'Nah, we've offered to buy her a new place a hundred times, but she won't have it. Won't hear of moving away. She was bloody lucky Hitler didn't blow the place to smithereens, but it's still standing, just about. She's getting more and more cantankerous as time goes by but she still thinks she rules the roost.' Robertson laughed. 'She doesn't know the half of it.'

'Right, I'll pick him up for a chat,' Barnard said. 'Nothing heavy at this stage. It'll all have to go back to DCI Venables in the end. It's his case. But I've got Georgie in the frame for this one. Though whether he had a motive for picking on this woman or whether it was just for kicks, I can't imagine.'

'I can,' Ray said. 'He's still the same Georgie who incinerated moggies when he was nine years old, don't forget.' He sighed heavily. 'It's time he was stopped,' he said.

'So tell your ma Georgie might be a bit late tonight,' Barnard said. 'I'll pick him up before he gets there.'

'Nice to see you, Harry,' Georgie Robertson said expansively when Barnard swung open the passenger door of the Capri as his quarry parked his car an hour or so later in Bethnal Green and walked past on the way to his mother's house. 'What can I do for you?'

'A quick word, Georgie,' Barnard said and waited patiently while Georgie pulled at the knees of his beautifully tailored dark suit so as not to crease them and settled himself into the passenger seat. 'We'll just take a quick spin round the block, shall we?'

Georgie nodded approvingly as Barnard swung away from the kerb and cut into the traffic stream on Roman Road. 'Not a bad motor,' he said. 'You doing well for yourself, then? I guess you are, working in Soho.'

Barnard merely grunted as he manoeuvred round a bus and then turned into a side street and stopped halfway along beside the bombed-out wreck of a factory which had not been touched since it had gone up in flames in 1941.

'Smoke?' Georgie asked, pulling out a pack of Balkan Sobranie and offering one.

'No, ta,' Barnard said. 'We need to talk.'

Georgie shrugged and lit up.

'There's been another killing on my manor today,' Barnard said. 'Some poor woman died very messily indeed. At St Peter's Church. You know it?'

'That place that takes in kids off the streets? Yes, I know it. Padre's wasting his time, isn't he? Like trying to empty the Thames with a bloody sieve. There's always more kids coming off the trains and plenty of people ready to snap them up for this and that.'

'Just like you snap them up, you mean?' Barnard said harshly.

'Nah, not my line of country,' Robertson said easily. 'I leave the street girls to the spics like Falzon. And the protection to my bloody stupid brother. He's got no imagination, Ray. You know that? I'm looking for bigger fish to fry these days. A much classier clientele. Ask my mate Ted Venables if you don't believe me. He knows what's going on.'

Barnard's stomach lurched suddenly. If Venables knew what was going on and was doing nothing about it, it could only mean one thing: Georgie was paying him off. That was something Ray had not mentioned when he outlined his brother's unwelcome venture into freewheeling pornography and black-mail. And it explained perfectly why Georgie and Venables had been on such good terms at the Delilah Club.

'Yeah, yeah, Ted's on the case. I know that,' he said as if his colleague's involvement was stale news. 'But this latest killing's someone from out of town, some toffee-nosed woman from the suburbs, and pretty nasty at that. Scotland Yard aren't going to like it. Coming on top of the two killings in Greek Street, Pete Marelli and the queer actor, they're going to get very twitchy. And I happen to know you've been mooching round St Peter's. You were recognized.' But if Barnard thought that accusation would throw Robertson he was soon disabused.

'I reckon Ted's got all the angles covered,' Georgie said easily. 'They're not going to bust a gut over a pervert and a porn merchant, are they? As I hear it, you've got a suspect for those two anyway. I'm sure Ted can add another victim or two to the list. If not, I can tell you for a fact that Pete Marelli got it because he crossed the big man. He'd agreed to help me out with some of my publishing plans, a nice line in stuff for the queer boys, and Falzon didn't like it. You know what the spics are like. Cut your throat as soon as look at you. But if you can't pin it on Frankie's lads, I'm sure you can pin it on this suspect for the other job. Two in the same building? Got to be connected, haven't they? And this woman? No trouble as far as Ted's concerned, I reckon.'

'Not if the suspect was securely locked up at the time,' Barnard said. 'Not even Ted can put his suspect at St Peter's torturing an old bird when he was in a remand cell in jail.'

But Georgie just shrugged. 'D'you want in, Harry? I reckon we could stretch to a cut if that's what you fancy. As you're based in Soho it could be useful. Eyes and ears and all that, now Ted's moved onwards and upwards and doesn't get out on the streets like he used to.'

Barnard took a deep breath. 'I'll think about it,' he said. He had, he thought, already been handed this partnership on a plate, and had not realized its significance, when Kate O'Donnell had shown him a photograph of Georgie Robertson and Ted Venables raising glasses of champagne to each other at the Delilah Club. Though how far the partnership stretched might be very difficult to unravel. Blackmail victims were notoriously reluctant to complain to the police and the sleazier the things they had been involved in the more reticent they would be. And there was no way Georgie or anyone else was going to give him chapter and verse on the links between the private parties young Jimmy had been taken to and the pornographic magazines and blackmail attempts which seemed to follow.

'I need to get to my ma's,' Georgie said, suddenly impatient. 'She doesn't like it if we're late.'

'We'll talk again, Georgie,' Barnard said as Robertson opened the car door and he noticed a low-slung dark car pulling in behind him. He had not realized they were being followed nor that Georgie now commanded that level of heavyweight protection.

'Okey-dokey,' Georgie said, so cheerfully that Barnard wondered for a moment if his suspicions were some sort of dark fantasy. But as he slipped the car into gear and pulled away from the kerb, closely followed by Robertson's limo, he knew that even amongst the gangs of the East End and Soho there were very few men who would kill with Georgie Robertson's expertise and enthusiasm. As he had said to his brother, and Ray had not bothered to argue, this had Georgie's fingerprints all over it, though it might be much harder to prove than he had anticipated now he knew that Georgie had heavyweight support right at the heart of the murder investigation. No wonder Venables had looked a much happier man just recently, he thought. He might be getting that boat he coveted much earlier than he had expected.

Barnard drove thoughtfully back to St Peter's and parked outside the churchyard railings, beyond which temporary lights slung from the trees now illuminated the side of the building as forensics officers and photographers waited their turn impatiently to carry out their duties in the confined space of the boiler house. A coroner's van, with a couple of men idling beside it as they waited to remove the body, was parked behind the squad cars. Barnard sat for a moment watching the bustling scene, which had attracted an audience of gawping passers-by on their way to an evening's entertainment in the nearby pubs and clubs. He wanted to talk to David Hamilton again, but very much did not want to talk to, or even see, DCI Venables. The bombshell Georgie Robertson had dropped about his relationship with Ted needed some time to assimilate, he thought. The landscape had suddenly lurched around him and he was sure that there were mantraps and unexploded bombs strewn around his manor which could catch him out any time. He no longer knew who he could trust and that made him very edgy indeed. His train of thought was disturbed by a slight tap on the window and he wound it down to find himself face-to-face with Hamish Macdonald, breathing alcohol fumes into the car.

'What the hell do you want, Hamish?' Barnard said impatiently.

'I've been here a wee while,' the Scot said. 'A man sees things if he's got his eyes open.'

Barnard felt suddenly cold. 'Get in the car,' he said, swallowing his reluctance to let the malodorous vagrant through the door. Hamish slid into the passenger seat and Barnard turned to face him. 'So what did you see?' he asked, almost afraid of the answer.

'I was waiting and watching, to see if the wee laddie was still here,' Hamish said, sounding more sober than Barnard expected. 'I saw people going in and out, the woman who's dead. She went in but I didnae see her come out again. And then two men, a big fellow in a hat and coat, and a wee chappie, wi' dark hair. They went in, and after a long while they came out again. They'd been round the side of the kirk, so when they'd gone I went to take a look, and told the young lassie who came in later.'

'You sent her off to find a body in that state, you stupid bastard?' Barnard complained. 'Why didn't you tell the vicar or call the police yourself?'

'Ach, well, I'd had enough of the polis, hadn't I?' Hamish came back. 'I didnae want to be involved. But that's not the main thing. Not at all.'

'So what is?'

'Ye'll only want tae know this if ye're an honest man, Mr Barnard. And how can I be sure of that?'

Barnard sighed and met the sharp blue eyes of the old man. 'You'll have to take it on trust, Hamish,' he said, his voice weary. 'Tell me what you saw.'

'The man who came earlier came back again,' Hamish said. 'The big man, he came back with the polis. He was one of them.'

'Could you swear to that in court? Identify him and swear he was here twice?' Barnard asked, his heart thumping.

'If I had tae,' Hamish said. 'That was a terrible thing they did.'

Barnard turned away and stared out of the windscreen in silence, watching the comings and goings in the churchyard again for a moment and then suddenly drawing a sharp breath. 'Is that him?' he asked Hamish urgently as Ted Venables came out of the churchyard gate and made towards his car.

'Aye, that's him,' Hamish said, confirming something Barnard really did not want to know.

NINETEEN

Kate O'Donnell took a train to Guildford from Waterloo, gazing sightlessly out of the window as it clattered through south London and out into the Surrey country-side. The late commuters filling the carriage thinned out past Wimbledon and only a few dozen people got off at her desti-nation, slamming the train doors behind them and hurrying out of the station like zombies towards the car-park or up the hill towards the town. She paused briefly to buy a map at the bookstall which was about to pull down its shutters for the night, and then followed the other passengers up the station approach and after studying the map carefully under-neath a street lamp she found her way to the long High Street, up the hill, past the main shops and into the darker suburban streets beyond.

The vicarage was in an ill-lit, tree-lined road alongside a Victorian church, not unlike St Peter's in Soho, as far as Kate could judge. The church was in total darkness but there were lights in the downstairs windows of the vicarage and a car was parked on the drive outside the front door. She approached cautiously, not sure what sort of reception might await her inside. She did not expect that the vicar would be particularly pleased to know that she had been able to discover Jimmy Earnshaw's whereabouts so easily, or necessarily let her talk to him, but she knew she had to try for Tom's sake.

Her knock was answered by a tall, thin, anxious-looking man in grey flannel trousers and a dark tweed sports jacket over his clerical collar and shirt who peered at her short-sightedly.

'Can I help you, my dear?' he asked.

'I think so,' Kate said, suddenly unsure of herself. 'If you have a boy called Jimmy staying with you, I think you can help my brother.'

The vicar's response was no more than a sharp intake of

breath but he opened the door wider and beckoned her in, glancing round the shadowy garden doubtfully before closing the door again. 'My colleague asked me to keep Jimmy safe. I'm not sure—'

'I'm not a threat to Jimmy,' Kate said, regaining her confidence slightly. 'I think I need him kept safe too. I've met him before at St Peter's in Soho. I think he'll remember me.'

The vicar led her into a stuffy, overcrowded living room to one side of the front door where almost every surface was covered with books and papers, and waved her into a chair.

'My name is Stephen Merryman,' he said and Kate wondered how a man's looks could so totally belie his name. 'I only took the boy in as a favour to my colleague in Soho, because he said he was in danger. I have boys the same sort of age myself. They're at a school play tonight with my wife. I should have gone but I thought I shouldn't leave Jimmy alone, so we dropped them off and came back here. I had this odd phone call from David Hamilton telling me not to let Jimmy talk to anyone, not even the police. It all sounds very odd. Do sit down, Miss . . . ?'

'O'Donnell,' Kate said. She sat down abruptly on a sagging armchair, feeling exhausted, and told the vicar the whole story of Jonathon Mason's death and her brother's arrest and remand for his murder. Merryman listened in silence – a good listener, Kate thought, as men of his profession often were. When she had finished, he gazed at her for a moment, his hands steepled underneath his chin.

'I can see why you are so concerned,' he said. 'Jimmy's in his room at the moment. Fortunately there's plenty of space in this rambling old place to take in waifs and strays occasionally. It's due to be sold off soon and something smaller built as a vicarage. I'll ask him if he'll agree to talk to you, my dear, in spite of what David Hamilton said. Though you must understand that if he doesn't want to I shall respect his wishes. He's a very frightened child, and he is only a child, although he insists he is sixteen. Stay here for a moment while I talk to him. I'll tell him about your brother and how he could possibly help.'

Kate waited impatiently downstairs for five minutes, her

stomach knotted with anxiety, close to panic. Harry Barnard had suggested that he had a witness who could help her brother's case, but a homeless runaway, effectively living as a prostitute, which is what this lad seemed to be, did not seem the ideal person to stand up in a court of law and clear Tom's name. But when Stephen Merryman eventually returned with a skinny boy with haunted eyes close behind him she put on her warmest smile in greeting.

'Hello, Jimmy,' she said. 'I'm Kate. Do you remember me? I was at St Peter's a few days ago taking photographs. I'd be very, very grateful if you would help me and my brother out.'

The boy looked at her for a long time, as if debating with himself whether or not he could trust her. Finally he gave a faint nod and sat down. But in the end, there was not that much to tell, Kate discovered, when the boy had made himself comfortable on the sofa beside her and described what he had seen on the evening Jon Mason had been killed. But what he had to say he was quite sure about. He had seen two men coming away from the flat before he had summoned up the courage to go up the stairs himself. And neither of them, he said, had looked remotely like Tom O'Donnell. Kate leaned back on the sofa and closed her eyes for a moment, almost speechless with relief.

'We need you to tell people that in court,' she said faintly. 'Otherwise my brother is going to be blamed for something he didn't do. Can you do that for me, Jimmy? It's very, very important.'

The boy shrugged bony shoulders. 'If they promise not to send me back to the home,' he muttered. 'I'll do nowt if they do that. There's a copper who said he'd see me all right. He knows all about it.'

'Was that Sergeant Barnard?' Kate asked.

'Aye, I think so. Hamish said he were all right.'

'Hamish? Who's Hamish?' Kate felt confused.

'He's a mate of mine,' the boy said, just as they all heard a thunderous knocking on the front door of the vicarage. Jimmy jumped out of his seat with a look of terror on his face, went to the window, pulled back the curtain a fraction and turned back into the room in panic.

'It's him,' he said. 'He's found me. I knew he would. You've got me here in a trap.'

'Who?' Merryman asked, suddenly galvanized in a way which amazed Kate. 'Who is it?'

'The bloke I saw. The one at the flat. It's him. I swear to God it's him.'

Merryman took hold of Kate's arm and pushed her towards the terrified boy. 'Get him out of the house at the back,' he said. 'Don't come back till I call. I'll stall whoever it is until I can call the police and get help. Go, now. Don't waste any time.'

In a daze, Kate did as she was told but as soon as she had hustled Jimmy out of the kitchen door into the dark garden behind the house he wriggled free from her grasp and ran, disappearing into the trees in seconds and leaving her standing alone, horrified. For a moment she hesitated before deciding that if she could not find him no one else would. She turned and went slowly back into the house where she found Stephen Merryman in the hallway with a heavily built, red-faced man breathing heavily.

'What do you mean, he's not here?' he said, his voice so threatening that Kate was afraid he was about to hit the vicar. She stepped forward, her heart thumping.

'If you're looking for Jimmy Earnshaw, so am I,' she said firmly. 'Mr Merryman asked me to wait until he came back from the school play with his wife and the other boys.' The more people became involved in this drama, she thought, the safer Jimmy Earnshaw might remain.

The man looming over Merryman turned towards her angrily. 'You again!' Venables said. 'What the hell are you doing here?'

'Looking out for my brother,' Kate said, and she knew from the sudden flash of anger in the DCI's eyes that he understood how exactly she was proposing to do that.

'You could go to the school to meet Jimmy,' Merryman suggested faintly.

'What time are they due back?' Venables asked.

'About nine thirty. I took them down there but they're getting a lift back with a friend.'

'We'll wait,' Venables said, glancing at his watch.

*   *   *

Sergeant Harry Barnard had driven down the A3 towards Guildford with his foot hard down and scant regard for his own safety or that of anyone else on the notorious stretch of road where racing driver Mike Hawthorn had died a few years before. What David Hamilton had told him when he had eventually tracked him down to his study in the vicarage, sitting deflated at his desk doing nothing more constructive than staring out of his window at the police activity in the graveyard, had galvanized Barnard into action. DCI Venables, Rev Dave had said dully, had demanded to know where Jimmy Earnshaw was, insisting that he needed to interview him in connection not just with the death of Veronica Lucas, but other cases as well.

'You told him?' Barnard had said, his mouth dry.

'Of course I told him,' Hamilton said, looking surprised. 'He's investigating a murder. In my churchyard.'

'You'd better tell me then,' Barnard snapped. 'There are things he needs to know before he starts on Jimmy.'

So Hamilton had written down the address of St Luke's vicarage in Guildford where his friend Stephen Merryman had agreed to look after Jimmy Earnshaw for the duration. 'I think that young woman photographer has got hold of the address too,' he said wearily when he'd finished. 'I left her here by herself earlier and it was on a piece of paper by the phone. She could easily have seen it.'

'Jesus,' Barnard said, his stomach in a tight knot. 'Sorry, vicar. Can we phone this Mr Merryman? I'll go down there, but I need a word now, if possible.'

Hamilton nodded and dialled a number on the phone on his desk, but he listened for a long time before putting the receiver down again. 'No reply,' he said. 'Which is odd. He's got a couple of boys of his own, so I shouldn't have thought he'd be out at this time of day.'

'I'll catch up with DCI Venables,' Barnard snapped, getting to his feet and glancing at his watch. 'Can you keep trying Mr Merryman and tell him I'm on my way to see him? Tell him to keep that boy away from anyone who turns up before I arrive, absolutely anyone, even the DCI himself. It's very important.'

It was fifteen minutes since he and Hamish had watched the DCI getting into his car and Barnard had persuaded Hamish Macdonald to stay out of sight in the Farringdon encampment until he came to fetch him. He had raced back to his own car and set off, weaving his way impatiently through the early evening traffic, over Westminster Bridge and through Wandsworth and Roehampton until he could let the new, more powerful engine of the latest Capri rip on the Kingston bypass. Guildford was at least an hour away from Soho and he had no hope that he could catch up with Venables. His only chance, he thought, was that his warning to Merryman would get through and delay Venables long enough to prevent him picking the boy up on some pretext, in which case he doubted that anyone would ever see Jimmy Earnshaw again. And if Kate O'Donnell blundered into that situation he did not give much for her chances either. He was surprised at how afraid any threat to Kate made him.

He had stopped briefly in Guildford High Street to ask directions, his much-thumbed *A-Z* of no use this far out of London, and drove more slowly up a hill leading out of town again and into a tree-lined road with a church at the far end and beside it another Victorian vicarage, not unlike the one he had just left in Soho. To his relief, he saw Venables' car parked outside and lights on in the tall downstairs windows of the house. As far as he knew, Venables had come alone, just as he had left St Peter's, but he wanted to take no chances. Very cautious now, he tried the front door but found it locked, so skirted around the side of the house to the back where the rear door opened to his pressure and he slipped inside. Apart from the slight rattle from an ancient-looking refrigerator in one corner of the kitchen, the house seemed to be completely silent and completely normal, washing up neatly stacked in the sink and the savoury smell of what must have been the family's evening meal still in the air.

Barnard moved silently across the room, opening the door to the rest of the house as gently as he could, freezing as the latch clicked slightly, but to no obvious effect. For a home with two sons and an extra boy in his teens as a visitor, the place was uncannily quiet, he thought. He stood looking into the hallway, listening, and from there eventually picked up a faint rumble of voices not far away. He inched along the hall until he located the door behind which a conversation was going on, one voice faint and apparently calm, the other – and as Barnard got closer he recognized DCI Ted Venables' unmistakable growl – growing louder and more impatient. Putting his ear against the solid wood panelling, Barnard listened.

'This is nonsense. I need a statement from that boy and I need it now, Reverend,' Venables said, his voice rising. 'I'll go down to the school and find him.'

'And I have told you, Chief Inspector, you only have to wait until my wife brings the three lads back. Surely another half hour's wait won't do any harm?' The vicar's voice remained low but even through an inch of solid oak Barnard could hear the determination in it and he guessed that David Hamilton had succeeded in warning his friend to keep Jimmy away from anyone who came calling, even the police. Then to his surprise he heard a third voice which he also recognized.

'I'll come with you,' Kate O'Donnell said. 'I need to talk to Jimmy Earnshaw too. I know he can clear Tom.'

It was, Barnard thought, probably the worst intervention she could have made and he suddenly stiffened as he realized Venables' patience had snapped and he heard a sound he recognized only too well. He flung open the door in time to see the DCI aiming a second violent blow at the man sitting cowering in a chair by the fire.

'I don't believe either of you, you're playing for time,' Venables yelled before realizing that Barnard was behind him. The sergeant was in time to catch his arm and spin him away from the horrified vicar before his fist connected with Merryman's bruised face for a second time. Venables' own face contorted with rage as he faced Barnard. He pulled his arm out of his grasp with a curse and backed towards the door.

'Are you all right, sir?' Barnard asked the vicar, who nodded slightly, obviously in complete shock as Kate put a protective arm round his thin shoulders. Barnard turned to Venables. 'I think you and I need a word, guv. In private.' He led the way out of the room into the hall. 'It's over, Ted,' he said as he

stood face-to-face with Venables, who was now red in the face
and panting heavily, as if he had run a distance. 'Georgie
Robertson told me most of it when I spoke to him a while
back, and there's another eye witness who saw the two of you
at the church before the murder of that harmless old biddy. I
assume you thought she knew where the boy was, but she
didn't have a clue. You were wasting your time with her and
she died for it.'

'What's this rubbish?' Venables snarled. 'I killed no one.
I'll have you out of the force on your ear for this—'

'You were seen, Ted,' Barnard interrupted sharply. 'You and
Georgie were seen, not just at Mason's flat, but today, in the
churchyard. And I guess there'll be more from Pete Marelli's
place. Someone left fingerprints there. I saw them myself. I
certainly didn't imagine it. And maybe there's more from the
little cover-up you tried to do at the picture agency when you
realized there was evidence of how cosy the two of you were
together at the Delilah. Georgie even offered to cut me in with
the two of you. It's finished, Ted. I've already filled the super
in with the gist of it on the phone. There'll be warrants out
for the pair of you as soon as I've made a full report, and
added this little episode in as well. I don't imagine Mr
Merryman will be reticent about giving evidence against you.'

'You don't need to do that, Harry,' Venables said hoarsely.
'There's enough in this to see all of us in clover. It's a little
gold-mine Georgie's dug. You get these well-heeled beggars
Ray Robertson's sucking up to, get them to a party where
anything goes – women, girls, boys, a bit of rough stuff, and
take a few snaps and how's your father. They'll pay up like
lambs to keep it quiet. We'll cut you in. Keep you in fancy
clothes and fast cars for years, it will.'

'I told you. Georgie made me the same offer and I turned
him down,' Barnard said, feeling weary. 'You've blown it. You
might be able to thump suspects who won't tell you what you
want to know at the nick, but not a bloody vicar in suburban
Guildford. It's probably the least of your crimes, but it's the
one that'll sink you. And remember, I've seen one of the kids
you lured to your parties. He wasn't a pretty sight.'

'And since when were you so bloody pure?' Venables

snarled. 'Everyone knows what Vice gets up to. I bloody invented half the scams.'

Barnard shrugged. 'Backhanders are one thing, we're talking murder here, and not just one, either, and illegal sex with children,' he said. 'Was it Georgie with the knife or has he been giving you lessons?'

'I had nothing to do with any killings,' Venables blustered, edging closer to the front door.

'I don't believe you, Ted,' Barnard said. 'Why else would you be so keen to lay hands on this boy if you didn't think he'd seen you at Mason's flat? Why else would you be so keen to pin that killing on Tom O'Donnell when it's perfectly obvious he had nothing to do with it? And at St Peter's you were seen going in, and coming out, and then coming back to lead the bloody investigation. You're on a hiding to nothing, Ted, and what you don't know is that Ray wants Georgie to go down. Even he's fed up with that nutter, getting in the way of his business deals and his social climbing. And if Georgie goes down, and Ray will make sure he does, one way or another, you'll go down with him. Make no mistake about that.'

Barnard thought for a moment that Venables was going to take a swing at him too, as he was wondering how to arrest him, but he seemed to think better of it at the last moment, spinning on his heel and hurling himself out of the front door before Barnard could get a grip on him. Within seconds, as he ran after him out of the front door, Barnard heard his car start up and roar away. Wearily he turned back into the house and the vicar's study to find Merryman still hunched in his chair looking white and strained. He would have a serious black eye by the morning, Barnard thought, and Venables would not get far once he reported what had happened. There was no point trying to chase him halfway across southern England personally. He was finished.

'Who are you?' the vicar asked, nodding faintly as Barnard explained and showed him his warrant card.

'I seem to be one of the good guys,' he said, with an attempt at a smile.

'And was Mr Venables really an officer too?'

'I'm afraid so,' Barnard said. He glanced at Kate with an ambivalent expression. 'Are you OK?' he asked.

She nodded, beyond words.

'To be honest, I thought David was exaggerating. I couldn't believe a senior policeman could be a danger . . .' Merryman shook his head in astonishment and glanced at Kate. 'Can you find our young friend?' he asked her.

'I'll go and see,' she said.

'We really do need a statement from Jimmy,' Barnard said to Merryman. 'But then I'll leave him safely here with you for the time being. And before I leave, I'll tell the local police that you need some protection.'

'Thank you,' Merryman said. 'I take it they'll be on the side of the angels too?'

'I think you can bank on that,' Barnard said.

Harry Barnard drove Kate O'Donnell back to London more sedately than he had driven out, pushing his own anxieties to the back of his mind and concentrating on her obvious happiness at the outcome of the evening's dramas.

'How long before they let Tom out?' she asked as the road swooped around the dark expanse of Wimbledon Common and into the bright lights of the south-western suburbs.

'It'll take a couple of days to collate the evidence we've got now and charge the real culprits, but they should drop the charges against Tom after that,' Barnard said. 'Jimmy's evidence really was crucial and he'll be kept safe now.' He glanced at his companion, who seemed remarkably untroubled by her brush with danger.

'Can I buy you dinner before I take you home?' he asked.

She brushed her hair out of her eyes and smiled. 'I'm bloody famished,' she said. 'Let's do it, la.'

'We're relying on a bunch of vagrants and queers for evidence,' DCI Keith Jackson complained when Harry Barnard faced him and other stony-faced senior colleagues the next morning.

'This investigation will be conducted from the Yard from

now on, Sergeant,' one of them said eventually. 'Have you spoken to DCI Venables since last night?'

'No, sir,' Barnard said. 'I looked into his office when I came in but he doesn't seem to be there.'

'Right, we'll deal with him. You are to hold yourself ready to make a witness statement when we are ready to hear from you in more detail. Understood?'

'Sir,' Barnard said gloomily, getting to his feet. This, he thought, might be the end of his career too before it was over.

'And next time you get even the slightest hint that something like this is going on, can I be assured that you will report it very much sooner?'

Barnard nodded, wondering how many other murderers the men from the Yard thought might be lurking in the ranks of CID.

As soon as he could get away, he left the nick quickly and drove out of town to the south west where he knew Ted Venables and his wife Vera lived in a substantial semi in Purley. He knocked tentatively on the door and it was opened quickly by Mrs Venables herself, a well-built woman in a smart beige blouse tucked into a dark skirt. She looked tired and strained, no doubt regretting her return home.

'He's not here,' she said sharply. 'I told the uniformed officers who came at breakfast-time. He didn't come back last night and I don't know where he is. What on earth is going on, Harry? What's he supposed to have done? He's going to retire in six months, for goodness' sake. What's gone wrong?'

'Have you no idea where he might have gone?' Barnard asked.

'You've always been a good friend of Ted's, haven't you, Harry? If he's in trouble, can you help him?'

Barnard shrugged but Vera Venables didn't seem to notice.

'He's got a boat down at Chichester,' she said. 'The *Vera V*, it's called. Got it a couple of months ago. Said he's had a good win on the horses. I reckon he's probably gone down there.'

'Would it get across the Channel, this boat?'

Mrs Venables looked blank. 'He uses it for fishing. I don't know how far it would go.'

It took Barnard another hour to drive down to Chichester and find the moorings where Mrs Venables had told him her husband kept the boat which Ted had always claimed he would buy after he took his pension. Obviously his finances had taken a sufficiently dramatic upward turn to enable him to get his pride and joy much sooner than he had hoped. Walking along a jetty, slightly bemused by the ranks of dinghies and cruisers on display, Barnard noticed a group of men talking animatedly at the end of the pier.

'I'm looking for a boat called the *Vera V*,' he said as he approached. 'Any idea where I'll find her?'

One of the men spun round with a look of surprise. 'We were just talking about her,' he said. 'My mate here's just come in from a fishing trip and says he saw her adrift about a mile out. No one on-board that he could see. Do you know the owner? We should report it. It's a hazard to shipping.'

Barnard gazed out over the choppy grey sea beyond the harbour for a moment.

'Yes,' he said. 'I did know the owner.'

Kate O'Donnell was late for work the next morning, after a night spent tossing and turning as she tried to process the events of the previous day, and before she could take her coat off, Ken Fellows called her into the office. Expecting nothing less than a rocket, she was surprised to see him still clutching his phone with a smile on his face.

'Get yourself down to Oxford Circus,' he said. 'Apparently there's a couple of hundred screaming teenaged girls down there chasing after four young men called the Beatles. We need some pics and we need them quickly.'

Kate gave him a flashing smile. 'I did tell you what to expect,' she said, realizing that at last the Mersey Sound had really come to London.

'You did,' Ken said. 'And I'll want all those pics of these boys you've already got. And for that, I suppose you'll expect to still be here next Christmas.'

'That would be good,' Kate said with a grin as she re-buttoned her coat. 'That would be really good.'